D1715241

1

Table of contents.

Prologue

Chapter 1

Chapter2

Chapter3

Chapter4

Chapter5

Chapter 6

Chapter 7

Chapter 8

Chapter 9

Chapter 10

Chapter 11

Chapter 12

Chapter 13

Chapter 14

Epilogue

Until Nico sneak peek

Acknowledgements

Something else you may enjoy.

This book is dedicated to little brothers
everywhere

I love you

TJ

Until Lilly

Prologue

Too bad you can't outrun destiny

About Four Years earlier

<u>Lilly</u>

The first time I met Cash, I was in my sophomore year of college, attending Alabama State University. I was pursuing a degree in Early Childhood Development. I had pulled an all-nighter, trying to prepare for an exam. I looked at the clock and realized it was after ten in the morning, and I still had a few things to go over. I was in major need of coffee if I was going to be able to process any more information. I was still in pajamas, my newly-dyed bright red hair in a crazy mess, so I took off my nightclothes and dragged a dress over my head. I grabbed my dad's old sweater off my desk chair, pulled it on, and shoved ten dollars, my key, and my phone into my pocket.

The weather was warm, so the streets were busy with college kids and young families who lived in the area out enjoying the beautiful day. When I arrived at the small café, there was a woman with a stroller trying to maneuver through the door. I jogged up to the door, pulling it open and letting her enter before me. Suddenly, I felt a chill slide down my spine. That's when I heard the loud rumble.

I looked over my shoulder as a large black truck was pulling into a parking spot in front of the shop. I watched as two men jumped down from the truck; the driver was good looking, but it was the passenger who gave me pause. He was tall, and his skin was golden brown, as if he spent hours in the sun. I could make out the definition of the muscles of his torso under his tight white t-shirt. His hair was dark brown and sticking out along the edge of his red baseball cap. When I realized I had been staring, and that he was watching me, I felt my cheeks get red, so I turned quickly and walked into the coffee shop without even holding the door for them. The coolness of the air conditioning and the smell of coffee helped to ease some of the tension that had coiled around me from seeing the guy. I wasn't someone who was used to those feelings. Lust was something my friends talked about, but I had never experienced it firsthand until that moment.

"What can I get you?" the pretty blonde behind the counter asked, pulling me out of my thoughts. I looked at the menu board behind her. I didn't even know why I bothered; I never changed my drink.

"Can I get a large iced coffee, dark, skim milk, with three Splenda?" I gave her my order, watching her eyes get large. I felt heat hit my side. I didn't have to turn my head to know who was standing next to me; I could tell by the look on the girl's face that it was the guy from outside.

"I would like a large iced coffee, black," he interjected. The girl's eyes glazed over at the sound of his voice. I turned my head to look at him, wondering how pompous someone could be. "Here, sugar, we're together, so just take hers out of that as well." He slid a twenty across the counter towards the girl, who hadn't taken her eyes off of him.

"We are *not* together." I clenched my fist; who the hell did this guy think he was?

"We are; I'm paying."

I was so flustered by this guy that I could feel my always-calm temper start to slip. I didn't know if it was the lack of sleep or what, but when the coffee girl handed us our drinks, I turned on the guy. "Here," I said, shoving the ten in my hand into his chest, making him stumble back into the person behind him. The lid on his coffee popped off when he squeezed it in his hand, making it go down the front of his shirt. "Crap, I'm so sorry. I didn't mean for that to happen." Just my luck that something like that would happen. I felt so bad that I turned around, grabbed a few napkins from the dispenser behind me, and began patting his chest down, trying to sop up the coffee. It had

7

made his T-shirt tighter, the wetness showing off his ab-muscles. I could feel my face growing redder by the second. "Why couldn't you just let me pay for my own coffee?" I asked. He started to laugh, making my head come up to hit his chin so hard that I heard his teeth crack together. My eyes watered in pain. "This is so humiliating," I whispered, feeling the tears as they began to fill my eyes. My hand went to the top of my head, where a large bump was forming.

"Let me see your head, babe," Mr. Hot Guy said quietly, pulling me towards him. He took my coffee out of my hand, and handed it to the guy I had pushed him into. He held my wrist, pulling me over to the side. "You know, now I need your name and number for insurance purposes, right?" It took a second for me to realize what he said, and once I got it, I started to laugh.

"I hope that's not a pick-up line." Looking around, I noticed a lot of people were watching us.

"Do you live around here?" He pulled my chin in his direction, forcing my eyes back to him.

"Yeah, I go to school here." He nodded, biting his lip.

"What's your name?"

"Um...Lilly. Yours?"

"You look like a Lilly."

"Do I?"

"Yeah." He chuckled, taking a piece of my hair and tucking it behind my ear. "I'm Cash."

My eyebrows drew together. "Is that a nickname?"

"Nah, Ma named me Cash, after Johnny Cash." His hand came up again, this time to run along my jaw. I thought it was odd that he kept touching me, but I couldn't find it in myself to tell him to stop. "So, I'm going to need your number."

"For what?"

"Well, I need to call you to make sure that you haven't got a concussion."

"I think I'm okay." I laughed, looking over at the guy he came in with. He was looking down at his phone, smiling.

"Here, come meet my brother." He didn't give me a chance to say no; he grabbed my hand, dragging me with him to where his brother was standing.

"What's that smile for?" Cash asked his brother, who finally looked up from his phone. I had no idea what these guys' parents looked like, but good Lord, they were seriously hot.

"Nothing, Liz messaged me."

"This is Lilly. Lilly, this is one of my brothers, Trevor."

"Nice to meet you," his brother said with a slight smile, but I couldn't think of anything except the way Cash's hand felt against my lower back.

"Hi," I took a breath, trying to get a grip. "Um, I need to go. It was nice meeting you both. Again, I'm really sorry about the coffee and the head-butt." They both laughed at the same time.

Cash's fingers grabbed onto the back of my sweater, holding me in place. "It's fine. I'll walk you out." Trevor handed me back my coffee. I gave him a small nod, leaving the shop with Cash. Once we were outside, he let go of my sweater, grabbing my hand. I didn't know how to react to this kind of attention. It felt like a hive-full of honeybees had taken flight inside my stomach.

"Do you have a phone?" he asked, his body so close I could smell the light scent of his cologne. He smelled like the outdoors and sunshine, the warmth of his body absorbing into mine. I felt inside my sweater pocket, pulling out my phone. I couldn't find my words because he was standing so close. His fingers slid my phone from my hand, his touch tingling through my system like a hot-wired fence. He started dialing a few numbers before his phone started ringing from his pocket. "Now I can make sure you aint got a concussion." He smiled, showing off two dimples. I couldn't help but smile back.

Shaking my head, I cleared my throat. "It was nice meeting you, Cash." I took a step back, seeing his brother stepping out of the coffee shop and holding two coffees.

"Talk to you soon." He looked like he wanted to say something else, but he stopped himself. I turned and walked back to my apartment. A few seconds later, my phone buzzed in my pocket.

Unknown: Let me know that you got home, okay? Don't want to worry about you having a concussion.

I looked over my shoulder, smiling and shaking my head before I turned around, heading to my apartment. After saving his number with his name, I messaged him back.

Me: Don't worry. I'm hard-headed.

When I got home, I tossed my sweater onto the back of the couch, plopped down, and leaned my head back. I thought about the last thirty minutes until my phone beeped again. My pulse sped up when I saw the name.

Cash: Are you home?

I looked around my small apartment before replying: **Yeah, just got in.**

Cash: Call you tonight when I get home.

Me: Where do you call home?

Cash: A small town in Tennessee, a little over two hours away from you.

My stomach dropped. That was really far, way too far to have any kind of relationship. Not that that's what he wanted, or even what *I* wanted for that matter. I didn't even own a car. I was in college on a full scholarship; I couldn't even afford to eat anything that wasn't microwavable.

Cash: Well, talk soon.

I looked at the phone in my hand for a second before replying: **Sure, talk to you then.**

I turned my phone on silent; I needed to get back to studying. The last thing I needed was to spend my day daydreaming about a blue-eyed, brown-haired guy with dimples.

Three weeks later

Lilly

I was ready. I looked myself over in the mirror; my cream-colored skin had darkened with the Alabama sun, making my hazel eyes look more green than brown. I had applied a thick coat of mascara, along with some blush. My red hair was curled into waves, the sides pulled back into a clip. I had on my favorite pair of dark skinny jeans, black sandals, and a black tube top. "You can do this," I told my reflection. It had been three weeks since I last saw Cash in person. Three weeks of phone calls and texting, and now he would be here any minute.

I was nervous and excited about seeing him again. I had learned a lot about him over the last few weeks. He came from a close family. He had three brothers. His mom and dad were still married, and they were still very much in love, according to him. He also had a niece who he adored, and another one on the way. His brothers and he owned their own business. He owned his own home, and he was working on fixing it up. The doorbell went off, making me jump. I looked in the mirror one last time before shutting off the bathroom light. The doorbell went off again just as I pulled the door open. I was unsure why I was caught off-guard. He wore a gray t-shirt, jeans, and boots. His hair, like the last time I saw him, was a little long and sticking out around the baseball cap he wore. His eyes darkened slightly as they roamed over me before landing on my face. I swallowed and took a deep breath, my fingers digging into the wood of the door. "Hi." At the sound of my voice, he stepped into my apartment, his arms wrapping around my waist. His face went to my neck, and my arms hung at my sides for a second before going around his back, holding onto him.

"You smell so fucking good." His voice was a soft rumble against my skin, making my pulse speed up and causing the place between my legs to tingle.

"Thanks." I smiled, enjoying the feeling of being in his arms. I had forgotten the way he smelled, and how big he was compared to me. His head came up, his hands running up my arms to my shoulders and under my jaw.

"You ready to go?"

I nodded; my mouth had gone dry with him standing so close. I felt overwhelmed. He had to be one of the most attractive men I had ever seen. He looked like a hot baseball player because of his hat, just more bulky. "So, what are we doing?"

"I figured we could go to dinner and catch a movie."

"Sounds good. Just let me get my bag." I stepped out of his embrace and walked down the short hall to my kitchen, grabbing my bag off the counter. I checked to make sure I had my phone. Cash was still standing near the door; he was looking over the photos hanging on the wall.

"Are those your parents?" He pointed to a picture of my mom and dad standing in front of Childs Glacier in Alaska. My dad was holding my mom close, her head laying against his chest, looking at the camera. I took that picture right before I left for college.

"Yeah, that's my mom and dad." I smiled. He looked at me, then back to the photo.

"You look like your mom. Just the hair is different." I reached up, automatically touching my hair.

"Since I was old enough to go to the drug store on my own, I have been changing it." I smiled at the memory of the first time I got my hands on a box of hair color. "The first time I colored it, my parents came home to find me with black hair. It wouldn't have been so bad if the towels, my hands, and the bathroom weren't also black." I laughed. "My dad says he can tell what kind of mood I am in based on my hair color."

"So what does the red say about your mood?" He reached out, running his fingers through it.

"I don't know."

"Aren't redheads known to be wild?" He smirked.

"Um...I..." I could feel my cheeks heat up.

"Or was it that they have fiery tempers?"

I shook my head. "I don't think the color of your hair has anything to do with your temper."

"So the day in the café—your temper then?"

"You were annoying."

He chuckled, taking a step back. "I was letting you know I was interested."

My eyebrows drew together. "By pushing your way into buying coffee for me?"

"I was being nice."

"Well, the gesture was nice, I agree, but your execution was horrible."

"I guess I was off my game."

"Is that what you do? I mean, do you often try to hit on women in coffee shops by buying coffee for them?"

"I can tell you with one-hundred percent truthfulness that I had never done that before."

"Never?" I asked. He shook his head. A look passed over his face. I don't know what it meant, but I didn't like it.

"Do you date a lot?" I asked quietly, wondering if he thought I would just be some kind of conquest.

"I haven't dated."

"You haven't dated?" I looked him over again. He must have thought I was stupid. Guys who looked like him must date a lot.

"I have never had to date."

"What does that mean?"

"If I want to sleep with someone, I don't need to date them."

"What?" I breathed; that is not at all what I expected him to say. "You're the guy who can get any girl he wants without ever putting any kind

16

of effort into it." He shrugs; the gesture made me feel sick, and at the same time, I wanted to kick him in the nuts. Maybe the red hair *did* make me have a temper.

"I never lead anyone on, or tell them things they want to hear."

"So that makes it okay?"

"I don't know if it makes it okay, but it's who I am."

"Well, I am glad that this is coming to light now, rather than later."

"Oh no," he shook his head, "this thing with you is something completely different."

"Yeah, I know," I told him, crossing my arms over my chest. "It's different because I will *not* be sleeping with you." I leaned forward. "EVER."

"Well, I guess we answered the question about redheads and their tempers, didn't we?" He smiled, showing off both dimples. "But trust me when I tell you, I would not have driven almost three hours just to sleep with you; that's not what I am looking for."

My pulse sped up when he repeated what he said earlier, "This thing with you is something different, something I'm looking forward to exploring."

"We can be friends, but that's it. I will never be some guy's passing conquest, or a notch on a bed post."

"Did I ask you to sleep with me?" He smirked again. He didn't, but I saw guys like him all the time around campus, and I had avoided each and every one of them. "When we do sleep together, it will mean something to the both of us."

"Did you not hear what I said earlier?"

"I heard you. I also know you should never say never." He looked at me like he knew something I didn't, making me feel uneasy. "You ready to go?"

I was *not* ready. In fact, I was sure I'd made a huge mistake. My brain was going a million miles an hour, trying to figure out what the hell was going on. He held out his hand to me, and I looked down at it. He had nice hands; they were large and masculine, and his fingers were long. But I felt like this was some kind of test, one that I hadn't prepared for.

"Hey," his fingers went to my chin, lifting my eyes to his, "we can take this slowly."

"What is this?" I asked. His eyes went warm, making my pulse speed up.

"This...is the beginning of us."

"Are you a vampire or something?" I half-joked. He looked at me possessively, making me feel warm. He started to laugh, his head thrown back, showing off his square jaw. When he lowered his head to look at me, he shook his head.

"No, not a vampire. I just know what I want."

"You're kinda freaking me out."

"Join the club," he said under his breath, as he turned to open the door to my apartment. He held it open for me to step out. Once I was in the hall, I turned to lock the door behind me. He took my hand into his; his palm was slightly callused, and I wondered what they would feel like running over my body. The thought caught me off-guard. I grew up in a very small town in Alaska—my graduating class was thirty-five people. I had one boyfriend when I was sixteen, and all we ever did was kiss. For me, the only reason we even did that was because it was what you did when you had a boyfriend. I had no idea what to do with the feelings of lust Cash brought out in me.

I took a few deep breaths, trying to calm my nerves. The feelings of nervousness completely disappeared when we got out into the parking lot and stopped at the side of a large red truck. He opened the door, and when I went to get in, I realized there was no step-thingy and no handle to grab onto in order to swing myself inside. I turned to look at Cash, who was smiling.

"How am I going to get up there?" I hitched my thumb in the direction of the cab of the truck. His smile grew bigger; he took a step towards me, his hands going to my waist. He gave a slight squeeze before I was lifted up. My hands shot out, grabbing onto his shoulders; the position reminded me of *Dirty Dancing* when Patrick Swayze picked up Jennifer Grey when they were practicing on the log in the rain. Our eyes were locked, and I had never in my life wanted to kiss someone more than I did in that moment. He sat me down in the seat; his eyes dropped to my mouth, and then came back to mine.

He tilted his head towards his shoulder. "You can let go now." His voice was slightly rough; I moved my hands quickly and turned my legs into the cab of the truck, placing my hands in my lap and noticing they were shaking.

Three months later

"I hate leaving you here. I hate I have to be without you," Cash said quietly. We were lying in bed. Cash had just made love to me, and it was more beautiful than I ever thought it would be. He was so gentle with me. Well, I guess he was always gentle with me. It was something else—it was like in that moment, we were one, and not just in a sexual way. It was something different. I knew we loved each other—he told me he loved me all the time—but now feeling it, knowing he was my first, and that I had given him a piece of myself that I could never get back...it connected me to him in a way that made it even more perfect. I cuddled closer to him, his hand running lazily down my side to my hip. My hand pressed to his chest.

"I hate it too," I told him, lifting my head, my chin going to his chest, and our eyes meeting. I searched his face, wondering what he'd think about me moving to Tennessee and going to college closer to him. I wanted to be with him all the time. I wouldn't have moved in with him or anything crazy like that, but if I could be a thirty-minute drive instead of a three-hour drive, I would have loved that. I hated that I could only see him on the weekends. And I didn't like that he had to travel so far to come see me. I was just about to say it when I realized that it would be stupid. It was too soon. I just gave him my virginity; we weren't getting married or anything. Maybe if things kept on like they were, then I would see what he'd say about me moving closer. I came back to myself when his hands touched my face.

"What's going on?" His fingers trailed from my temple to my bottom lip.

"Nothing, just thinking that my *never* didn't really work out, did it?" I smiled and laughed, thinking about the fact that on our first date I'd told him that I would never ever sleep with him.

"No, but I will cherish what you gave me for the rest of my life," he told me, making my tummy flip. The look in his eyes was so sincere that I held my breath. He leaned forward, his mouth opening over mine.

Cash

I pulled up in front of my house and shut off my car. I hopped out, opened the trunk, and pulled out my overnight bag. When I got inside, I tossed my bag into the laundry room, went into the kitchen, pulled a beer out of the fridge, and popped the tab, taking a deep drink. I pulled off my baseball cap, tossing it on the counter and ran my hand through my hair. I wanted to call Lilly and hear her voice again; we talked my whole drive home, but it wasn't enough. I needed more. I looked around, seeing my space, wondering what she'd think of it. I wanted her here with me. I hated knowing I couldn't see her whenever I wanted. I wanted to ask her to move closer, or just move in with me, but I knew it would be way too soon, so I held my tongue. I used to give Asher and Trevor a hard time about the way they acted when they both met their one...now I knew. I would die for Lilly; she was amazing, beautiful, and kind, and made me want to be a better person.

My phone rang from my pocket, bringing me out of my thoughts. I pulled it out, expecting it to be Lilly. The number was unknown. I answered, and just like that, with one phone call, my life changed.

Lilly

"I love you, but I can't see you anymore." The words played over and over in my head. I could feel his pain, but didn't understand it. I felt like my own chest was cracking open. He told me he loved me. He told me I was the one. *Oh, God,* I was going to be sick. I ran into the bathroom, the contents of my lunch coming up. Once I finished, I flushed the toilet, resting my cheek on the bathroom floor, not caring that it was probably dirty. I didn't care about anything; I just wanted to sleep. I didn't want to feel anything. I shut my eyes, trying to forget the pain that was consuming me.

I opened my eyes, feeling disoriented. The room was completely dark, and when I sat up, I realized I had fallen asleep on the bathroom floor. I turned on the light and stripped off my clothes. I turned on the shower and climbed in before the water had a chance to heat up; the cold water jolted my system. My movements were automatic; I couldn't feel anything. I got out, wrapping a towel around myself before going to my room, climbing under the covers, and falling back to sleep.

Over the next few weeks, I had a routine: class, eat, and sleep. I didn't do anything outside of my routine. I couldn't watch TV, and I couldn't spend too much time on campus—any time I saw a couple, I would break down into tears, making me feel like a bigger loser than I already felt like. I was exhausted and sick; no matter how much I slept or what I ate, nothing changed. That was when I decided to go to the doctor, and for the second time in a few weeks, my life was turned upside-down.

"I am pregnant?" I asked for confirmation. The doctor looked at me over the top of his glasses, his eyes making me squirm.

"Yes, Ms. Donovan, that is what the urine test, blood test, and ultrasound all confirmed.

"Okay." So I wanted to be sure that they were not getting false results and may have gone a little overboard, but what the fuck? I never thought I would be pregnant, especially when I had only had sex one time, and used a condom when I'd done it.

"I am going to give you a number to a clinic where you can get this taken care of," the doctor said, making me feel somewhat better.

"That would be good." I knew I would need to see someone about getting vitamins and talk to someone about how sick I had been. And I would need to call Cash and let him know what was going on, even if we weren't together. I would never keep this from him.

"The procedure takes a couple hours; you will need to have someone go with you."

"Procedure?" I knew my face scrunched up in confusion.

"The abortion." My hands covered my stomach quickly. I never even thought about that; I shook my head.

"No, no way. I'm not getting an abortion." I didn't see anything wrong with that choice for others, but for me, it wasn't an option.

"I'm sorry, Mrs. Donovan, I thought we were talking about the same thing." I shook my head, tears pooling in my eyes. "I will get you a number for an OB/GYN then.

"Thank you." I swiped at my eyes, and the first bit of warmth came into the doctor's face.

"You will be okay."

"Yeah," I agreed. I had my parents; they never let me down. I could go home...and do what? Live with my parents? Have them support my baby and me? That wasn't an option. I would have to find a way to make it here. I would find a way to finish school, even if I had to do it online, and there were lots of single mothers in the world. I would just be one more. I would find a way to make it. Once the doctor finished and gave me the number for the OB/GYN, I left the office, making my way to the bus. I pulled out my phone, and for the first time in three weeks, I sent Cash a text.

Me: We need to talk.

Cash: We have nothing to talk about.

My stomach dropped at his response. He was never short or mean to me. I couldn't understand what I had done.

Me: We do have something to talk about.

I felt my gut twist.

Cash: Get over it. We're done. Don't text me again.

My temper started to flare; I couldn't believe that he would do this to me.

Me: I am having your baby, you dick.

Cash: Get rid of it. I am having a baby with my soon-to-be wife.

I read the words, ran to the trashcan on the corner of the street, and lost it. I couldn't believe him! Who was this guy? A lady came over, offering me water and a napkin. I used it to wipe my mouth and thanked her for it. I looked down at the text, reading it again and again. I didn't even know how I got home; I just remembered climbing into bed, my hands going to my stomach. I looked up at the ceiling in my room, not really seeing anything, just replaying all the good times I had with Cash...all the firsts I had with him. I knew that no matter what, the child growing inside of me was made out of love. Even though his or her father didn't love me, I had loved him enough for the both of us.

Chapter 1

Present Day

<u>Cash</u>

"Daddy, are we there yet?" Jax moans from the backseat, making me smile. If we're in the car for more than fifteen minutes, he is ready to bust out of his car seat. He has more energy than ten kids combined.

"About fifteen more minutes, dude, then you can go wild." We are on our way to Jumping Bean, a giant warehouse full of trampolines. Hopefully by the time we leave, he will be worn out, and I can get some rest. I love my son, but damn if he doesn't wear me out.

"Are you gonna jump wiff me?"

"Yeah, dude."

"Yay!" he yells, his little arms shooting straight up in the air. I turn up the volume to the show he's watching on the back of the passenger seat's headrest, hoping it will keep him occupied until we get to the warehouse. When I found out Jules was pregnant, I was pissed off at the world. I was in love with Lilly. I hated saying goodbye to her. I knew that in order to have a relationship with my child, to have him in my life, I had to cut her out and focus on Jules. After a year, I realized it would never happen. I was killing myself. I was miserable. Almost three years ago, we divorced, and she moved into an apartment in town. My son stays with me unless I'm at work, then my mother, November, or Liz has him. His mother sees him if the mood strikes, which is rare and perfectly fine with me, but difficult for him.

"Are we there yet?" I chuckle, shifting lanes as I exit the highway.

"Two minutes."

"This is taking forebbbeerrr," he whines and sighs. I look at him through the rearview mirror. His head is resting on his fist, looking completely disgruntled.

"Look." I point out the front window to the building ahead of us.

"We should moob here."

"Wouldn't you miss grandma?" I pull into the parking lot and find a space to park.

"Well, she could come, too."

"I don't think grandpa would like that, little guy."

"Eberyone could moob here." I shake my head, getting out of the truck. By the time I have his door open, he's unbuckled himself and launches his little body at me.

"You ready to go have some fun?" I hold him upside-down, his giggling making me laugh.

"Yes-s-s-s-s," he screeches as I bounce him. I turn him upright, putting his baseball cap on his head —like me, he always wears one. I grab his hand as we walk into the building. *This place is insane!* There are kids everywhere, running and screaming, chasing each other as we stop at the front counter to pay. "I wanna go in there, Daddy." I look to see he's pointing at a giant pit full of foam blocks. I am sure it looks like a good time to a kid, but to me, as a parent, it looks like a petri dish. I am going to have to wash him down with Purell by the time this day is over.

"We will." He nods in agreement. I pull off his hat, and we both take off our shoes before putting them in one of the cubbies that take up a long wall. When his shoes are off, my little dare devil takes a running start, jumping in full-speed head-first into the pit. I laugh, watching as he tries to right himself.

"Come in, Daddy." He tries to wave, but he looks like a fish out of water flopping all over the place. I step into the pit and once I reach him, I lift him above my head and I toss him, making him laugh harder. He somehow manages to get his feet underneath himself and wades towards me, looking like he is fighting a hard current. "Let's go ober there." He points to a large trampoline that is built into the floor before taking my hand, leading the way out of the pit. I don't know who is going to be more exhausted by the time this day is over. Actually I do, and I know it won't be him.

As soon as we're out of the pit, he takes off on a run before bouncing onto the trampoline. I stand off to the side, watching him with my arms crossed over my chest. I look to the left when I see a flash of red hair in my peripheral vision. It wouldn't be the first time my mind has played a trick on me, making me think I see Lilly when I don't. The woman has fuller hips then Lilly did, and her ass is round, making me want to slap it. *Shit, I need to get laid*. The thought leaves just as quickly as it comes. My focus is my son. My bachelor days are a long forgotten memory. Now, if I need to get off, I use Miss Right or Miss Left. I'm just about to look away when the woman turns towards me, and I stop breathing. I swear to God, time stops. All I can do is stare at her. Her skin is still the color of cream; her red hair is long and hangs over her breasts that seem to be larger than when I last had them in my hands. She looks even more beautiful, if that's possible. When her eyes meet mine, she blinks then pales, her hand covering her mouth. *What the fuck?*

"Mommy! Mommy!" She looks down, and my stomach drops, seeing a little girl with dark hair pulled into two pigtails and skin the same color as her mom's. Lilly gets down to the little girl's level, pulling her close as she whispers something to her. "I don't wanna weeb," she cries, her face turning towards me. For the second time in as many minutes, my world comes to a halt. She looks so much like Jax that they could be twins. I look up, my eyes meeting Lilly's again.

"Daddy, come play with me." Jax grabs onto my pants leg. I look down at him, then back at Lilly as tears pool in her eyes. She picks up her daughter—our daughter—and starts to take a step away. Automatically, my hand reaches out to grab onto her elbow. I look down at Jax and give him a smile. "You go play, dude. I will be there in a second."

"Fine," he grumbles before running off again. I look at the little girl in Lilly's arms; her eyes are on me as she leans in to whisper something into her mother's ear. Lilly closes her eyes, hugging her tighter before saying something back to her and setting her on the ground.

"Go play for a minute, love bug," Lilly tells her. The little girl doesn't take her eyes off me. I want to pick her up and hold her so badly that my fists clench, fighting it. Lilly kisses her forehead before turning her towards the trampoline. I watch her walk away then start to bounce. It takes a second for my brain to start functioning.

"That's my daughter." My blood starts to boil. She kept her from me.

"No, that's **my** daughter." She takes a step to the side, away from the other adults around us. I follow, standing at an angle so I can watch my kids.

"I can't believe that you would keep my kid from me." I look her over, the feeling of hate consuming me.

"You're a piece of work, you know that? Your words were "get rid of it", that you were getting married and having a baby with someone else."

"What?"

"I read those words over and over a hundred fucking times, so don't tell me that she's yours." She pokes my chest, getting in my space. "She is *mine*! I suffered from morning sickness *alone*. I went to my doctor's appointments *alone*. I was in labor for forty-seven hours. *Alone.* And I have raised her *alone*." She growls the last words. I have no idea what the fuck she is talking about.

"I never told you to get rid of my child, so don't even try that shit with me."

"Oh, yeah, you did, buddy. I even have a print out of the text messages. I kept them as a reminder to myself to never trust a man again."

"I don't know what the fuck you're talking about," I say, a sinking feeling taking over my body.

"The day I found out I was pregnant, I messaged you telling you we needed to talk. You said we had nothing to talk about. I told you I was having your child, and you told me to get rid of it."

"Oh, fuck." I rub my face, knowing this is all Jules. She did this; somehow, she did this. "It wasn't me." My voice is gruff to my own ears. For the first time in years, I want to cry like a little bitch. She's watching me closely, her arms wrapped around her waist, her expression changing from anger to confusion and sadness. "What's her name?" I ask, looking at my daughter, who is now talking to Jax. He grabs her hands, bouncing with her.

"Ashlyn Alexandra." This is killing me. She gave her a version of my middle name—Alexander. I swallow the lump that is building in my throat. I look at Lilly.

"I want it back." I don't even realize that I say the words out loud. Lilly is my one, and I lost her and I'm going to get her back. I had wanted to search for Lilly a million times. I was so afraid she wouldn't want me back, accept Jax, or that she's moved on that I talked myself out of it every time. Now I wish I would have looked for her.

"What?" Her eyebrows draw together in confusion, the same way they used to when we were together, making her look adorable.

"We are going to have to figure out a way for me to be in her life, and for her to know her brother." I take a step towards Lilly. "Where are you living?"

Her eyes get big, and her breathing picks up. *Fuck yeah! I still affect her.* "Um, we just moved to Springhill because I got a teaching job," she says quietly, looking at Ashlyn and then back at me.

"Good, you're not far from me." She starts shaking her head. I bring my hand up, cupping her cheek. "We will figure out a time to meet. We have a lot to talk about, but right now, let's just have a good time. I don't want the kids to get freaked."

"Ashlyn is already freaked. She knows who you are."

"What?'

"The pictures we took with my cell phone, she has them, and she knows who you are."

"Jesus." I rub the back of my head. "Where did you say I was?"

"Here."

"Here?"

"Yes, well," she pauses, clearing her throat, "we lived in Alaska near my parents up until a few months ago when I got the teaching job."

"So you told her I lived in Tennessee?" I look to where Jax and Ashlyn are laughing with their little legs moving rapidly as they bounce in place.

"My dad wanted me to tell her that you were dead, but I couldn't do it," she whispers, and my head swings back in her direction.

"Why didn't you try harder to get ahold of me?" I rip my hand through my hair. This situation is completely fucked up.

"Why the hell would I do that when you told me to have an abortion?"

"That wasn't me," I growl.

"It was your phone." She shakes her head. "So you never got married?" She rolls her eyes. "Obviously, you had a son." She points at Jax.

I did not want to answer that question. I knew the minute I told her I had been married that she wouldn't believe that I never told her to have an abortion. She must have read the look on my face. When she answers, her words are so soft and full of pain that I swear I can feel them cutting into my skin.

"I already know you got married, so even without you answering that question, I still know." I see pain flash across her face. "I didn't want to believe that what we had could be so

36

easily replaced. I thought I had done something wrong, and you were upset. I thought you loved me. I was depressed and lonely, so I did a search of your name online, planning to come find you, and came across your wedding announcement."

"What the fuck?"

"Yeah, that is kinda how I felt." She gives a slight laugh, the kind that isn't humorous.

"I am so sorry; you will never be on your own again," I tell her, taking a step towards her because I want to hold her. She takes a step back, shaking her head.

"We can figure out a way for you to be in Ashlyn's life, but only if you plan on sticking around. I will not let her become attached to you, only to have you walk away without an explanation."

"I would never do that." I narrow my eyes and she raises her eyebrows, crossing her arms over her chest.

"You are the one who taught me the meaning of never say never, remember?" she reminds me. I told her that when we first got together. She told me she wouldn't sleep with me ever, and I told her never say never. We only slept together one time. That one time had made me fall more in love with her than I already was. The day after, I had to come back home and go to work. I never knew that it would be the last time I would see Lilly. I knew then that she was the one for me, even as young as I was. I knew, and in the end I tossed her away, thinking I was doing the right thing, not knowing how sharp the double-edged sword was that I held in my hand.

We both stand there staring at each other. I don't know what she's thinking, but I'm thinking I want to kiss the fuck out of her, hold her, love her, and remind her of how good we were together. She looks away, then waves for Ashlyn to come to her. I watch my daughter bounce all the way over to where we're standing. She is so beautiful that my chest hurts just looking at her. I have loved every second of raising my son, and I hate that I have missed so much time with her. Jax comes along with Ashlyn. When she reaches where we're standing, her head goes way back, with her cute little face scrunching up.

"Are you my daddy?"

"No, he's my daddy." Jax launches himself at me. Ashlyn looks at Jax, and then me. I drop to my knees in front of her, putting my arm around Jax's waist. I have no idea how to handle this right now, and my stomach starts to turn as my palms begin to sweat.

"Come here, love bug." Lilly pulls Ashlyn into her arms.

"Daddy." Jax puts his palm on my cheek, forcing my head to turn. "Why did that girl ask if you're her daddy?" Leave it to my kid to get right to the point.

"Well…um." *Fuck, why couldn't I think of what to say?*

"What's your name, honey?" Lilly asks. I look up to see Ashlyn in her arms looking down at us.

"Jax." Lilly smiles so brightly her whole face lights up. I forgot that smile. *How the fuck did I forget that smile?*

"Very cool name." Jax's chest puffs out under her praise.

"I'm going to be big like my daddy," he informs her randomly.

"I'm sure you are, honey." Lilly smiles again. "How would you feel about having a playdate with Ashlyn sometime?" Jax shrugs. I look at Ashlyn who smiles. "Sure, she could come to my house. I have a ferret and a tree house!"

"I'm sure she would like that. Though, I'm not sure what a ferret is." Jax laughs and so does Ashlyn. I can't believe how much they look alike. "I'm going to get your dad's number, and we can set up a time."

"Yay!" Jax yells, jumping up and down.

"Will you do me a favor, Jax?" He nods. "Take Ashlyn over to get her shoes while I get your dad's number, okay?"

"Okay," he agrees right away. Lilly sets Ashlyn down. She hasn't taken her eyes off me. Jax takes her hand, pulling her along. I watch as she shows

39

him where her shoes are. They are too high for her to reach, so he gets them for her, and then runs and grabs his before sitting next to her on the ground.

"I think it's best if we talk to them separately about what's going on. Jax is going to be very confused about this, and Ashlyn isn't going to be much better. She knows *of* you, but doesn't *know* you. I think we should set up a time for you to come alone and spend some time with her. Then bring Jax along later so they can get to know each other."

"Why are you acting so cool about all of this?"

"I don't know. I guess I will save my breakdown for tonight when Ashlyn is in bed, and I can have a glass of wine." She pulls out her cell phone from her back pocket, sliding a finger across the screen. "So what's your number?" I rattle it off, watching as she types in the numbers. My phone starts ringing from my pocket. I pull it out and save her number quickly. She turns her back on me, walking to where the kids are sitting. She runs her hand over Jax's hair before grabbing her shoes. She bends over, putting them on with her round ass in the air. I look around when I feel a sting against my skin, my eyes landing on a guy who is looking at her ass with his wife or girlfriend standing right next to him. I walk up to where Lilly is bent over, not taking my eyes off the guy who is watching her. When I get there, the guy's eyes come to me, and I give him a chin lift. He looks away quickly, making me feel somewhat better. I still have the urge to shove a foam block down his throat. When Lilly finally stands, I grab my hat after pulling on my sneakers. I put my hat on, shoving my hand in my pocket so I can grab my keys. I turn around to see Lilly looking at me funny, Jax holding one of her hands and Ashlyn holding the other. My heart squeezes at the sight of them together. She blinks, shaking her head. "You ready?" I ask.

"Yeah." Lilly nods. Jax lets go of her hand and runs to me, grabbing mine. We wait and hold open the door for the girls.

"Your hair is really red," Jax says, looking at Lilly. She laughs, shaking her head. The sun is out, beaming down on her, making her red hair shine more brightly and giving her a glow.

"She just colored it. It was brown before," Ashlyn informs us, making me laugh as I think about the last time I saw her; her hair was the same color it is now, only a lot shorter. We walk out to the parking lot, and Lilly stops at a small, piece-of-shit car. It was probably silver at one time, but is now grey and dull, with rust spots and dents. She opens the back door, and Ashlyn crawls inside. I don't like this. My body is fighting itself, not wanting them out of my sight.

"So I will call and set up a time with you," she says, watching Ashlyn buckle her seatbelt.

"Call me when you get home," I tell her, my voice rough with anger, not at her, but myself.

She shakes her head. "No, I'll call you in a couple days after you have had some time to think about this." I take a step towards her, getting in her space.

"I am not going to change my mind," I growl the words, making her eyes widen slightly.

Then she takes a breath. "Well, then call when you're ready," she says quietly before squatting down to Jax's level.

"It was very nice to meet you, Jax." She holds out her hand for a shake.

"You're pretty, like my mom." Jax is wrong. Jules is pretty, but so rotten on the inside that it started seeping out, making a once pretty girl ugly. Now, Lilly—Lilly is more than beautiful, and if the situation between us hadn't made her bitter, then nothing ever would. And I could see her light shine through every time she looked at our daughter.

"Well, thank you, honey." She gives a small smile before standing back up and opening her door. I lean in the back door so I can talk to Ashlyn.

"I will see you soon, okay?" She nods. Her eyes are big and the same color as mine.

"So are you my daddy?" she asks more quietly this time.

"Yes," I whisper, running my hand over her hair.

"Why didn't you come see me?" Oh God, this is killing me. I have no idea how to explain this to her. I don't even know how to explain this to myself.

"I am so sorry, baby." The words choke out. "I promise you that I will come see you now, every chance I get."

"Grandpa says that you hab to keep your promises."

"He is right." I smile at the way she pronounces her v's the same way as Jax. "You do have to keep your promises." She nods in agreement. "I'll call your mommy later and say goodnight to you."

"Okay." She reaches over, grabbing a small doll and holds it in her lap. I lean in a little, kissing the top of her head. I get out of the car and see that Lilly and Jax are talking.

"You ready, little dude?" I look down at Jax, who is watching Ashlyn curiously.

"I'm hungry."

"You're always hungry." I laugh, watching Lilly get in the car. She shuts the door, turning her car on before rolling down the window.

"Grandma says I'm growing."

"You are. Soon you're going to be taller than me."

"Wow!" His face lights up.

"But you have to eat your vegetables."

"I don't want to be as tall as you then," he grumbles, and I pick him up, tossing him over my shoulder chuckling.

"Sure you do." I look at Lilly, who is watching me with a small smile. "We'll talk soon." She nods. "Call me when you get home," I tell her.

"Cash—"

"Lilly, call me when you get home," I say it a little more slowly so she knows I am not fucking around. She shakes her head.

"I will message you," she sighs.

"No, no more messages. Call me." Her eyes flash like they used to when we were a couple and her temper would flare. I used to love when it happened. I would kiss her until she melted into me and couldn't remember why she was mad.

"Fine, I will call you." She rolls her eyes, making me want to fist her hair and put my mouth on hers.

"Say bye, love bug." Ashlyn waves from the backseat and Lilly from the front as I set Jax down next to me. We watch Lilly and Ashlyn pull out of the parking lot. I don't like the feelings coursing through me. I don't like them driving away, and I don't like the amount of hate I am feeling towards Jules. I didn't think I could hate her more than I did, but she's proven me wrong. I need to call my brothers. I need to talk to them and have a beer.

"How about we stop at Grandma's?"

"Okay." Jax shrugs. I can tell he's getting tired and will most likely be asleep by the time we hit the highway. After I get Jax in the car and buckled in, I hop behind the wheel and send a text to each of my brothers, telling them to meet me at the barn in an hour. I can't believe Jules told Lilly to get an abortion. The whole time she was pregnant, she'd threatened to have one if I didn't do exactly what she wanted. I shake my head and put my truck in reverse, stare at myself in the mirror, and notice my hat. It's the same hat Lilly gave me when we were dating; I haven't stopped wearing it since then. I head out of the parking lot wondering if this is my time, if I'm finally going to have a chance to be happy again.

Chapter 2

<u>Lilly</u>

What the hell just happened? I look in the rearview mirror to see Ashlyn trying to see out the back window. I never in a million years thought I would see Cash again, let alone see him when I have Ashlyn with me and he has his son. I want to puke. He had asked why I was being so cool about this; honestly, I might have been cool on the outside, but on the inside, I was freaking right the fuck out. All I'd wanted to do was pick Ashlyn up, run out of there, and get as far away from him as I could.

"Mommy, was that really my daddy?" Oh, God, I never thought I would be having this conversation. I considered that maybe when she got older she might look for him, but I never thought that I would have to find a way to explain to my almost-three-year-old something that I didn't even understand.

"Yeah, love, that was your daddy." I silently pray that she falls asleep and doesn't have any more questions. Hell, this would be so much easier if she was still a baby. She doesn't say anything else the whole way home. My mind is going over millions of scenarios, some of them involving packing up and taking off back to Alaska to the comfort of my parents, but I know I can't do that. The look on Cash's face when he saw Ashlyn and realized who she is was , just broke my heart. And then, when I looked in his eyes when he told me that he didn't send those messages, all I saw was honesty. *He didn't want to admit he was married*, I remind myself.

When I pull up in front of our apartment building, I look back and see Ashlyn asleep. I grab our bags and unhook her, pulling her out of the car. I slam the door and make my way up the two sets of outside stairs, and once I reach the door, I juggle her and our bags so that we can get inside. The first thing I do is drop our bags to the floor and go lay her down in her bed, pulling off her shoes and making sure her doll is where she can see it when she wakes up. I pull a blanket over her and make my way to the kitchen, where I pull out a bottle of moscato from my fridge, pop the cork, and fill my wine glass half-full. I down the contents, then refill the glass.

I walk to the living room and sit down on my secondhand couch, looking around our small two-bedroom apartment. It's not much, but it's what I could afford from the money I saved working over the past few summers in a fish processing plant. Most of our furniture is used, but in good condition; the only things that I bought new were our beds. When we moved from Alaska, I didn't want to pay for shipping everything, so we came with our clothes and what could fit in suitcases. I wonder what Cash will say about our home. My stomach starts to turn when thoughts of him trying to take Ashlyn from me fill my head. My phone starts ringing from my bag on the floor. I unfold myself from the couch, pick up my bag and digging to the bottom for my phone, but by the time I find it, it has stopped ringing. I flip it over in my hand, seeing Cash's name along with the words Missed Call.

"Shit," I whisper, fumbling with the phone when it starts ringing again. I drop it to the floor, forgetting I have a glass of wine in my hand, so when I bend over to pick it up, I dump the glass of wine all over it. I shake as much of the wine off as I can, then start franticly wiping it on my jeans. The phone goes silent for a second before ringing again, and I slide my finger across the screen, hoping that it will work.

"Hello?"

"Are you home?" Cash growls down the line. I look around for a second before answering him.

"Yes."

"I called and you didn't answer, and I told you to call me when you got home." I roll my eyes and take a breath.

"Well, I had to put Ashlyn to bed because she fell asleep in the car. Then I had to have a glass of wine. Then you called and I spilt said wine all

48

over my phone, so I am *so* sorry if I didn't call or answer you fast enough."

"You had to have a glass of wine? And you spilt it all over your phone?" he asks.

"Um…yes. I definitely had to have a glass of wine," I tell him truthfully, ignoring the part about spilling my wine. I have always been clumsy. "There is only so much stress a girl can take. And it's either wine or shopping, and since I am a single mother and can't afford to shop my stress away, I had to have a glass of wine." I realize I'm rambling and squeeze my eyes closed, my head falling back and hitting the wall. I hear him laughing; my eyes fly open and I remember that he used to always laugh at everything I said. In Alaska, I'd hated that I still loved the memory of the sound of his laughter; part of me still wants to hate him, but I just can't.

"You still there?"

"What?"

"I thought the call dropped."

"Oh no, it didn't," I say like an idiot; obviously, he knows the call didn't drop.

"So I…" He pauses, and I can picture him running his hand through his hair the way he always used to when he wanted to say something but didn't know how to say it. "I talked to my mom, and she will watch Jax tomorrow so I can come up and see you and Ashlyn."

"Oh."

"Oh?"

"I have the weekend off, so we will be home."

"Okay, good," he says, and I can hear the nervousness in his voice. "Did you talk to her?"

"No, I will. It's just she fell asleep in the car."

"Yeah, Jax fell asleep too," he sighs.

"This is really awkward," I laugh.

"Tell me about it." I have the urge to ask him about his wife, but can't spit the words out. The thought of him married makes me ill. Why did he still have to be so gorgeous? With his overgrown dark hair, crystal-clear blue eyes, tan skin, strong jaw, his height and body—geez, his body is as perfect as I remember—wearing dark jeans that fit just right, and a red t-shirt that was so tight I could see everything. "So I was thinking that I would come up around ten; does that work for you?"

"What?" I hear the words, but they don't register for a second because I am stuck in a daydream about his body. Maybe it's time to start dating.

"Ten in the morning...does that work for you?" I can hear the smile in his voice, and I shake myself out of my daydream.

"Yeah, sure. Ten is fine."

"Good, I told Ashlyn I would talk to her tonight before she goes to bed. Can you have her call me when she wakes up from her nap?"

"Yeah, no problem." I close my eyes.

"I am glad you don't hate me," he whispers, the words sounding pained. My eyes open.

"I want to." I really do. I want to rage and scream and cry, but I just can't. I feel like this isn't really happening.

"I have a lot to explain. I just...*damn*, this situation is completely fucked up."

"Look, we will just talk tomorrow or whenever. I will have Ashlyn call you tonight. I just...I just need to know that you plan on sticking around; otherwise, I won't put her through this."

"I told you already I won't change my mind. I have already missed out on way too much."

"All right, so let me give you my address." I rattle it off to him quickly. "See you tomorrow," I say, and before he can say anything more, I hang up. I pull the phone from my ear and it starts ringing again right away; this time my mom's number is flashing across the screen.

"Hey, Mom." I try to sound cheerful.

"What's wrong?" Dammit, I didn't want to have to tell her this. I moved home shortly after I had Ashlyn. I tried to make it on my own, but with a new baby, school, a job, and an apartment, it was just too difficult. My dad was ready to fly down and kill Cash, and my mom wasn't much better.

"IranintoAshlyn'sdadtoday,andshewaswithme," I say as quickly as verbally possible.

"You what?" she screeches.

"Oh, God, Mom, I don't know. I took Ashlyn to the place she likes with all the trampolines and he was there with his son. I tried to leave and he stopped me. He knew right away that Ashlyn was his, and I swear, Mom, I swear he acted like he had no idea what I was talking about when I told him about the messages."

"You need to come home."

"Mom," I sigh, sitting down on the couch.

"Honey, that prick told you to get rid of my granddaughter. He doesn't get to come in now, filling your head with a bunch of bull-hocky, making you believe that he never told you those things."

"I know, Mom, but what if he didn't do it? I can't keep Ashlyn away from him; she knew right away who he was. If he really does want to be in her life, I can't keep him out."

"I have a 12-gauge that says different."

"I think that's illegal, and I kinda love you, so I would hate to see you in jail."

"Honey, just," she pauses, "just promise me that you know what you're doing." I had not a clue what I was doing.

"I am thinking of Ashlyn, Mom. That's my one thought."

"How is my grandbaby taking this?"

"I haven't really talked to her about it yet. She fell asleep in the car on the way home. I have no idea how to explain this to her."

"Well," she lets out a long breath, "don't start off by saying that her dad is a good for nothing asshole." I laugh. I can't help it; my mom is funny.

"That's sound advice."

"Just tell her that he is ready to get to know her—that he missed her and is glad that you moved close so that they can see each other."

"That's even better advice."

"Well, kiddo, you know I love you, and you know if you need anything—even an alibi—me and your dad will be here for you."

"Thanks, Mom. I love you," I whisper, laying down on the couch. "Tell Daddy I love him."

"I will, honey. If you need us, you call."

"I will, Mom. Don't worry about me; everything will be all right." I hang up, staring at the ceiling, knowing I need to get up, but I don't move until I see Ashlyn standing in the hall rubbing her eyes.

I call her over, pulling her into my lap. I explain as best as I can about Cash and why he wasn't around before, and how that was now going to change. Then I tell her about him coming over the next day, and she is very excited about that. My dad was the only man who she's had in her life, so having her dad would be huge for her. After Cash, I only dated one guy. He was sweet and good friends with my dad. We didn't get serious—I wasn't ready for that. When I got the job here in Tennessee, he was a little upset I was leaving, but understood why. Plus I never wanted to feel the loss of someone that I loved again like I felt when Cash left me. So it was easier to get out before we got too involved.

Ashlyn jumped off my lap and ran to her room, yelling over her shoulder that she wanted it to be perfect for when her daddy came to play tomorrow. I snorted to myself; maybe there was a bright side to this after all.

<u>Cash</u>

"What's going on?" I turn, looking at Asher as he walks through the door. The last time I called a meeting at the barn was the day I broke up with Lilly and my life changed forever. I can't help thinking that this time the meeting is no less serious but I am praying that the outcome will lead me to my own happiness.

"No clue," Nico says, frowning down at his phone.

"Is everything okay?" Trevor asks Nico, who puts his cell phone away before sitting back in his chair.

"Work stuff." He shrugs before looking at me. "So why are we here?" he asks. Since he started working for Kenton, his whole persona has changed. There is an edge to him that wasn't there before. Now, he doesn't just *look* like a bad ass with tattoos; he *is* a badass with tattoos.

"I saw Lilly today," I say.

"That's good, right?" Trevor says, looking slightly confused.

"Well, she has a daughter." I clear my throat, running my hand down the back of my neck. "I...have a daughter," I say the words that I still can't believe myself.

"What do you mean you have a daughter?" Asher asks.

"Seems that when we were together, she got pregnant. I didn't know this, and she says that she tried to tell me, but someone sent her messages from my phone telling her to get an abortion."

"What?" Trevor asks loudly.

"I really don't know what the fuck happened." I scrub my hands down my face. The image of Lilly and the look of pain in her eyes feels like a weight against my chest. "All I can think is that Jules somehow got my phone and told her. She also told her that we were getting married, and this was long before I had even agreed to marry her."

"Dude, what the fuck?" Nico growls, and I look at him. "So why didn't Lilly try harder to contact you?"

"She Googled me at some point and saw my wedding announcement. That, coupled with the fact that I had supposedly told her to have an abortion was the final straw."

"So you have a daughter with Lilly, and what, she finally called you after all these years asking you for support or something?" Nico asks.

I shake my head. "No, I took Jax to Jumping Bean in Nashville and saw her there. When she saw me, she looked surprised, then a little girl came up to her calling her Mommy. The little girl knew exactly who I was when she saw me, and asked me if I was her daddy."

"Holy shit."

"Yeah, her name is Ashlyn Alexandra."

"Fuck *me*," Asher whispers.

"She is beautiful, and could be Jax's twin," I continue.

"So what are you going to do?"

"Get to know my daughter…and get my girl back."

"Dude, the last time that you came to us with a problem, you ended up married to Jules, who, by the way, is a fucking bitch to end all bitches," Nico says, standing.

"Look, I am going to bring her to Mom and Dad's this weekend. You will all see for yourselves the kind of person she is." Nico shakes his head, walking to the door. He has seen all the damage that Jules as has caused, and how much I've had to do in order to protect my son from her insanity.

"You know, I get that you want to get to know your daughter, but dude, no way should you try to get back with your ex. You have enough problems already," Nico says. I look at Trevor; he is the only one who knows that Lilly was mine. She is my one, and I gave her up thinking I was doing the right thing, Not that I regret for one second what I went through. If I didn't do what I did, Jax more than likely wouldn't be here, and I cannot imagine life without him.

"Lilly was my one—*is* my one," I state firmly, watching Nico's face fall. He rubs his forehead.

"Fuck me. I guess I will see you guys this weekend then." With that, he lifts his chin and is out the door.

"Have you explained what's going on to Jax?" Trevor asks.

"Yeah, I talked to him about it. Well, I tried; he doesn't quite understand what's going on, but he knows that Ashlyn is his sister."

"This is like a bad soap opera," Asher says, standing. "But I gotta say that if things work out, I will be happy for you, brother."

"Thanks," I say, and he pats me on the back before walking out the door. I look over at Trevor, who is still sitting with his elbows on his knees.

"So...when is she moving in?" He smiles, and I can't help but smile back.

"Not sure. I hope it will be soon, but it's a little harder than your or Asher's situations. We have to think about Jax and Ashlyn."

"You want some advice?"

"What's that?"

"It's something Asher told me when I was starting out with Liz." My eyebrows draw together.

"Push her," he says, nodding his head like he just told me where to find a million dollars.

"Push her? That's your advice?" I ask, shaking my head.

"Yep, if she's yours, it will work out. Push her into a corner so she doesn't have a chance to retreat."

"And Asher gave you this advice?" I do not doubt this, but seriously, what the fuck does that even mean?

"He did. And it worked, so there you go." He pats my back shaking his head, leaving me standing in the middle of the barn wondering how the fuck he and Asher ended up married.

~~*

My GPS tells me I have reached my destination, and I look around the apartment complex. I come to realize that they live in an area known as 'High Row'; the whole areas is infamous for its easy access to drugs...and my daughter and woman are living here. I shake my head when Trevor's advice comes to mind. After parking, I get out of my truck and slam the door. The doll I got for Ashlyn is in my hand as I walk up the two flights of stairs and knock on their door. I can hear laughter coming from the other side. When the door opens, Lilly takes a step back.

"Sorry, we just got up so were making pancakes," she says as I close the door behind me. She's wearing a black tank top that is completely form fitting, and her legs are covered in tight, black spandex. I growl when she turns away from me; her perfect ass is on full display. She might as well be wearing nothing with how much her pants show off. She looks over her shoulder and my eyes fly up; I can't help but smile at the look on her face.

"It's no problem." I shrug, and her eyes narrow slightly. We walk around the corner into the living room/kitchen; the space is small, and most of the items in it have seen better days. Ashlyn is sitting on a barstool stirring a bowl of pancake batter. She is still in her pajamas, her hair is all over the place, and when she sees me she smiles, showing off one little dimple in her right cheek.

"You came!" she says happily, looking at me, then her mom.

"I told you I would." I smile.

"I know, but..." She pauses, looking back at her mom.

"I told you he would be here," Lilly reassures her, and Ashlyn shrugs, going back to mixing.

"Is it time to add eggs?" Lilly asks her.

"Yes, can I crack them?"

"How about if Cash helps you crack them while I start the bacon?"

"Okay." She smiles, and all I can think is how much I love her already. "Is that for me?" she asks, pointing to the doll that's still in my hand.

"It is," I tell her, sitting the doll on the counter. "How about if she watches while we make breakfast?"

"Okay," she says, looking at the doll as I place it on the counter in front of her.

"Here you go." Lilly hands me three eggs and a bowl. "We don't want to eat egg shells, so this is easier," she says quietly before walking back to the fridge, bending over. I have to bite the inside of my cheek to keep from groaning. I haven't been with anyone since my divorce; I learned a hard lesson when that shit went down. It wouldn't matter though; even if I had been fucking everything that walked, Lilly had always done it for me. She is the perfect package of sweet and sexy. Watching her with our daughter is completely different than watching Jules with Jax. When we lived together, I may as well have been a single father. The only time Jules had anything to do with Jax was when it was time to show him off like a new handbag, but the minute he served his purpose, she would hand him back to me. I shake my head and turn, just as I see Lilly's head come up.

"You ready to do this?" I set down the bowl, hand Ashlyn one egg, watch as she taps it lightly to the countertop, and when she gets it to crack, she lifts it over the bowl. Both of her small hands wrap around the egg and her hands squeeze, crushing it. I laugh, looking at the bowl that is now full of shells and egg.

"I did it!" She smiles, and it's just like her mom's, bright and blinding.

"You did." I nod, handing her another egg. She follows the same steps two more times; I take the bowl away from her, along with one of the egg shells so that I can fish all the broken pieces out of the bowl. I feel the weight hit my chest and look up to see Lilly watching us. She's smiling, but she also looks sad. I reach over, running my finger down her arm; she shakes her head, looks away and puts more bacon into the pan.

"Now we hab to mix it." I finish removing the shells and hand her the eggs so she can dump them into the mixing bowl.

"Here." Lilly hands me a measuring cup full of milk, and I dump it in while Ashlyn stirs.

"Where are the pans?" I ask Lilly, my hand at her waist. I feel her shiver as my fingers flex against her.

"What?" She looks over her shoulder at me and I spread my fingers out, putting slight pressure on her waist. "What are you doing?" she asks.

"Asking where the pans are." I smile when she gives a slight growl, stepping out of my grasp.

"Does your wife know you're here?" She covers her mouth, looking over at Ashlyn who is not paying any attention to what we're doing; she is still happily stirring the batter.

"My wife?" My fists clench. She clears her throat.

"Never mind. The pans are next to the sink." I grab her hand, forcing her to follow me. We're going to get this shit settled right now. "Now what are you doing?"

"We're going to get a few things straight." I turn her so her back is against the wall, and she presses against my chest, trying to shove me away. Her size compared to mine makes it impossible.

"What the hell is wrong with you?" she asks, and I press into her. We're just around the corner from where Ashlyn is sitting. If I lean back, I can see her.

I put my mouth near her ear so I don't have to talk too loudly. "I am not fucking married." I press my hips into hers. "I was married. It didn't last long. I hated my wife. I hated the reasons why I had to marry her. I missed you every day, but I do not regret marrying her because I have my son now." Her eyes search mine; she crosses her arms over her chest. I pull her arms apart, putting them up above her head.

"Stop," she cries, wiggling and trying to get free. Her breathing speeds up, her eyes drop to my mouth, and just like that, it's on. My body presses the length of hers, and keeping her hands above her head, I attack her mouth. I lick her bottom lip and her mouth opens under mine. My tongue touches hers and I coax hers into my mouth then suck hard, making her moan. She pulls back, biting my lip. I drop her hands and fist her hair, forcing her head one way and tilt mine the other. I missed this; I forgot how much I loved kissing her, and she could fucking kiss like no other. I pull back, laying my forehead on hers, trying to catch my breath and calm the hard-on that is making my jeans way too tight.

"I'm going to make you fall in love with me again," I tell her without thinking.

"What?" she asks as I press my mouth to hers one more time, not answering her question. I step away, walking back into the kitchen to finish making breakfast.

I look over at Lilly, who is standing on the other side of the counter. "This weekend we will be going to my mom and dad's for a bar-b-que." I run my hand down Ashlyn's hair then look at Lilly. "I will come pick you up with Jax, and we can head over there together."

"Um," she mumbles, looking confused. Her lips are swollen and her cheeks are a light pink. Trevor's words come back to me again. I don't know if he is right, but I guess we will find out.

"You should pack a bag and we should have a sleepover this weekend," I say, making Lilly's eyes grow wide.

"Yay, sleep over!" Ashlyn claps, making me smile and bend over to kiss the top of her head.

"I don't think that's a good idea," Lilly states, crossing her arms over her chest, showing off the curves of her breasts.

"Well, if we're going to go to the zoo Saturday morning, it will be easier if we all sleep in the same place. I mean, Jax and I could stay here, but you don't have as many rooms as I do." I shrug like it's no big deal either way.

"Were going to the zoo?" Ashlyn whispers, looking at her mom. Lilly's eyes fly to hers, and her face completely changes. "Can we, really?" Ashlyn asks.

"Sure, we can go." Lilly takes a step over towards Ashlyn, looking into the bowl. "Is that all ready?"

"Yep." Ashlyn smiles, and Lilly kisses her forehead before taking the bowl away from her and setting it close to the stove. She goes about pulling out a pan and heating it up, while I talk to Ashlyn about the zoo and what she would like to see. Every chance I get, I touch Lilly, making sure she knows I haven't forgotten about her. She doesn't say anything, and I can see the wheels in her head turning. When breakfast is done, we sit down around the small table to eat.

"Where is Jax?" Ashlyn asks, taking a bite of her pancakes.

"He's with my mom—your grandma."

"Will I see him tomorrow?"

"No, you won't see him until the weekend." I look between Ashlyn and Lilly, coming to a decision. "Unless we come over tomorrow and take you ladies out for pizza?"

"Yay, pizza!" Ashlyn yells, and I laugh. I look up at Lilly, who doesn't look very happy.

"Go get dressed, love bug," Lilly says. Ashlyn scoots off the chair, and then heads down the hall to her room. Once she is out of sight, Lilly turns on me. "Look, I am happy you want to be a part of Ashlyn's life, but that doesn't include me, okay? I mean, we haven't been a *we* for a long time." She stands, picking up her plate.

"That's going to change." She turns to face me; the pain in her eyes is so raw that my gut clenches.

"I trusted you. I loved you. You destroyed me. If I hadn't had Ashlyn, who knows what would have happened."

"I know. I destroyed myself when I left you. I didn't know what else to do. Jax's mom was threatening to have an abortion. I always wanted you. I missed you every day, but I did what I had to do to protect my son. Wouldn't you do whatever is necessary to protect Ashlyn?"

"Yes." I could see tears spring to her eyes.

"You have been the only woman besides my family who I have ever loved. I never wanted to hurt you, Lilly, and I will find a way to prove to you that things are different this time. But we will work this out. You are my one. I gave you up once, but that will never happen again." I pull her into me, holding her close. She is stiff for a second before her body relaxes.

"Why can't I hate you?" Her words are quiet, and I can hardly make them out.

I whisper into her ear before kissing her under it, "Because I am your one, too."

Chapter 3

Lilly

"Mommy, why do you keep talking to yourself?" I look down at Ashlyn, who is sitting on the floor playing with the doll that Cash brought her the first time he came to visit. Since then, he has been here three times with Jax so we could all have dinner together. I have been so afraid to trust what's going on between us, but it feels so right. He hasn't kissed me since he had me pinned against the wall, but he never lets me get too far away from him, and if we're out in public, he is always touching me. I feel safe and cared for. I feel exactly how I felt the last time we were together, and I think that's what scares me the most.

"I'm not talking to myself," I say, even though I know I have been. I am so nervous I feel like I'm going to jump out of my skin. I have spent the day baking cookies, a cake, and two pies, trying to rid myself of the nervous energy that is coursing through me. I hear the knock at the door, so I run and unlock it before even checking to make sure who it is.

"You didn't check the peephole," Cash says quietly.

"Hi, honey," I say, running my hand down Jax's hair as he hugs my legs before heading inside.

"I knew it was you," I say, taking a step back.

"You didn't know it was me. You didn't call out my name, or check the peephole. Don't do that shit when you and Ashlyn are here alone. This is a bad area, and if something happens to you, I'm going to be pissed."

"You always say that. 'I'm going to be pissed.' When was the last time you were pissed?" I ask. His head tilts, studying me.

"I don't know. A while, why? You trying to piss me off?"

"What? No!" I squeal as he leans in, pressing me to the wall behind me.

"You have a perfect ass, babe."

"What?" I breathe, feeling goose bumps form across my skin.

"I can't wait to get my hands on it and turn it red, so please, try to piss me off. It will just get me what I want faster." I feel moisture flood between my thighs at his comment. I have never been spanked, and I don't understand why that turns me on, but it does.

"You did not just say that."

"You smell good." He runs him nose from my ear to my shoulder.

"Daddy, what are you doing?" Jax asks. I jump and look at Ashlyn and Jax, who are both staring at us. Cash slides his arm around my waist, pulling me closer to him.

"Are you guys ready to go?" Jax looks between us before shrugging, and Ashlyn smiles.

"I have to grab my bag." I step away.

"I forgot to tell you that we are now having the Bar-b-que at Asher's because they have a pool, so you should pack a suit.

"Yay! Swimming!" Ashlyn jumps up and down.

"We don't have swim suits," I say, looking at Cash.

"Okay, so we can stop on the way and pick something up."

"Are you sure? I don't want to be late."

"It's no big deal. Grab your bag and we can head out."

"I'm not wearing that." I roll my eyes at Cash, who keeps trying to hand me bikinis.

"Why not? What's wrong with this one?" He holds it out, looking at the front then the back.

"It's missing a huge chunk…like, the whole middle section," I tell him, picking up another one-piece and checking the size. Cash is pushing the cart, with both of the kids sitting in the large basket.

"You're kidding, right?"

"Nope." I put the suit over my arm. I already found Ashlyn one, so we could go to check out.

"You have a beautiful body."

"I had a child and not everything went back to the way it was before. And please, don't start. I'm not one of those girls who's all like, 'I'm fat blah, blah, blah'. It's not that. It's just, I jiggle now, and I don't really want to jiggle in front of anyone but myself."

"Buy both and let me be the judge."

"Um, no," I say, walking in front of the cart and heading to check out. Once there, I notice that I'm at the end and Cash is near the cashier. "Hey, I can pay." I walk up to the checker and look at Cash. "Those are mine; I'm paying."

"No, you have done enough. I'm paying."

"Cash." I try to give him a warning.

"Lilly." He puts his hand to the back of my neck, pulling me close.

"I have missed out on this. Don't argue with me about it, okay?"

"Fine." I roll my eyes just to say I don't agree. He kisses me on the forehead, drops his hand, and turns back to the cashier. Once he pays, we head out to his truck. We both get the kids buckled in before getting into the front of the cab. I can't keep still; my leg keeps bouncing up and down. I am so nervous about meeting his family. I know they probably hate me for keeping Ashlyn from them. I wonder what he has told them. We have spoken a few times over the past week about his marriage and how much his family hates his ex. I don't want them to hate me. My biggest fear is them thinking that I kept Ashlyn away from Cash out of spite, and not out of my need to protect her. I hate that he was married, and knowing that if I would have swallowed my own pride, he would have been there for Ashlyn. But I have to believe that everything happens the way it should. When I called my mom yesterday, she wasn't happy about the way things were going between Cash and me. She thought I was letting him off the hook. I know she's right; I also know that I can't be that woman who would hold it over his head. Even if we weren't together, I couldn't do that. It isn't in me to act like that. I know if I held onto the pain of our past, it would eat away at me.

"Babe, calm down," Cash says, bringing me back to the moment.

"Sorry, I'm just nervous."

"My family will love you." He grabs my hand, the warmth from his touch settling my nerves.

"I doubt that," I say quietly, looking into the backseat, noticing the kids are quiet. They both have headphones on and are watching a show on the small screen hanging from the roof of the truck.

"I know they will." He squeezes my hand.

"Do they hate me?"

"What? No, they don't hate you."

"But I—" I start but he interrupts me.

"You did what you thought you had to do." I look at him when he takes his hand away from mine to hold onto the steering wheel. I watch, as his knuckles turn white with his grip. "I fucking hate this." His words are so harsh that I can feel pain in them. "I hate that if I had chosen you, I wouldn't have Jax. I hate what I did, and that I lost you and Ashlyn."

"Hey," I say quietly, running my hand down his arm. "Please, don't do that. We both could have done a lot of things differently."

"You know, I think I would feel better if you would flip out."

I start laughing. I can't help it; he doesn't know what he's asking for. "No, you don't," I say, looking out the front window of the truck.

"I used to love it when you would get pissed." I look at him, seeing him smile. "Sometimes I would egg you on just so I would have a reason to settle you down." I clench my thighs together at the memory his words provoke.

"You used to make me so mad." I smile.

"I think you liked getting mad at me as much as I liked making you mad." I laugh at the stupidity of it, even though he is so right. I used to love when he ended a fight between us. "We were good together." I bite my lip against the pain those words cause. I feel him reach over and grab my knee.

"Give us a chance to get back there." I want to, more than anything I have ever wanted, but I don't know if it's possible. We're not the same people we were back then. We both have responsibilities that go way beyond just the two of us. I look over at him when I feel his fingers flex around my thigh. "I know that we have a lot to work on, and I know that it's going to take time for us to rebuild what was broken, but I also know that if we do, we will have something that is beyond anything that either of us thought possible."

"I just," I pause, clearing my throat, "I just need time."

"Time I can give you, as long as I know that when the time's up, we're in the same place." Tears start to fill my eyes.

"I don't know if I can get lost in you again," I whisper, looking down at his hand.

"We're going to be lost together; you won't be alone." I look at him; he takes his eyes off the road for a second and all I see is honesty.

"Okay," I say, and look back out the window. As we turn, there is an old barn and a long dirt road that looks like it leads to nowhere. Then we come over a small hill and the most amazing house appears in front of us. It's a large log home with a wraparound porch that's lifted off the ground with cars parked underneath it.

"Wow, this is beautiful."

"Yeah, Asher built it. We all helped, but most of the interior he did alone." We park on the side of the driveway. There are two cars, a couple of Jeeps, and a large truck parked there as well. I look around, seeing that everyone is here before us, and just like that, my nerves are back and I feel like I might vomit. I hop out of the truck. Opening the back door, Jax is already out of his seat and is helping Ashlyn with her buckles.

"You ready?" Cash says, opening his arms so he can carry both of them. I reached in, starting to grab bags and everything else. "Baby, don't worry. I'll come back out." When he gives me 'the look', I reluctantly set a couple of the bags back down and grab the pie. Before we even make it to the stairs, the front door swings open and a beautiful older woman with chin-length brown hair steps out onto the porch. She is slim and tall, and has on a pair of khaki shorts and a white button up shirt, with simple sandals on her feet.

"You're here!" she cries, running out to greet us. She doesn't stop at Cash, who is in front of me; she runs right to me, her hands going to my shoulder. "I'm Susan. Oh my, you're so pretty, and I love your hair." She pulls me forward, making me stumble into her. My arms try to go around her, but the bags in my hand, along with the pie I'm trying not to drop to the ground, are making it difficult.

"Ma, you wanna *not* freak my girl out?" I hear Cash say.

"I'm not freaking her out." She pulls me away from her to look into my eyes. "I'm not freaking you out, am I?" I laugh slightly; she doesn't look like she would care if I told her that she *is* freaking me out. "Oh, my goodness gracious." She lets go of me and covers her mouth, looking at Ashlyn. "Look at this beautiful angel." Ashlyn looks over at me, then back at Susan.

"Mom, this is Ashlyn." Cash says, turning his body so that Ashlyn is closer to his mom.

"Hi! I'm your grandma."

"Hi," Ashlyn says in her shy voice, laying her head on Cash's shoulder. Tears start forming in my eyes at the sight.

"You ready to go meet your cousins?" Susan asks as Cash sets the kids on the ground. Ashlyn shrugs, looking at me.

"It's okay, love bug." Jax grabs Ashlyn's hand, starts walking her up the stairs and into the house, with Susan following close behind them. I stand there and watch as Cash goes back to the truck and starts getting the rest of the stuff that I didn't grab.

"You ready?" he asks, coming to stand next to me. I take a deep breath and let it out. I'm not ready.

"Sure, let's go," I lie. The minute we walk into the house, I'm blown away. It is beautiful, with a huge open floor plan, a sunken living room, and a large kitchen with all up-to-date appliances. We step down into the living room just as the back sliding door opens. A guy who looks a lot like Cash steps inside shirtless, his arms covered in tattoos, all bright and colorful against his tan skin. His hair is long on the top and short on the sides, giving the appearance of a not-so-gothic Mohawk.

"Nico, this is Lilly. Lilly, this is my brother Nico." I look over at Cash who, yes, has the same facial features, but where Cash looks like all-American baseball player, Nico looks like the only reason he would have a baseball bat is to beat you with it.

"Hi," I say, trying to wave, and just like that, the pie I was carrying went falling to the floor, the chocolate pudding landing upright, but the force of the impact making most of the contents splash out all over my legs. "No," I whisper, looking down at the mess I made.

"Well, I can see not much has changed." I look up, seeing Cash's brother Trevor, the one I met at the coffee shop all those years ago. He still looks the same, if not a little bit more handsome. Then another guy walks in, looking like he could be Cash's twin, but upon closer inspection I can tell he's just a little older, and his hair is a few shades lighter than Cash's and cut low. I can feel my face heating up when they all surround me. I look back down at my feet, praying to disappear.

"Let me help clean this up."

"No, I think it's best if you stay where you are," Nico says with a smirk that I have the urge to wipe off his face.

"This is my other brother Asher. I don't know if you remember Trevor. Cash talks softly; my eyes go to him, and he looks like he wants to laugh. I feel a wet cloth on my leg, and I look down to see Nico wiping me off, making me jump back. I start to fall when my foot catches on something—okay, my foot caught on my other one, but whatever—then arms and a lot of bags wrap around me. "I got you."

"Thanks." I look around to see all the guys with full smiles on their faces. "This is really embarrassing." I don't even realize I say the words out loud until they all start laughing.

"What are you guys doing to her?" I hear a woman ask. I look up to see a beautiful woman with long brown hair coming in to stand next to Asher; his arm goes around her and he kisses the top of her head.

"Hey, baby. This is Lilly. Lilly, this is November, my wife."

"Hi, I'm so sorry about this mess," I say, pointing down at the pie that is being scooped up off the floor by Nico.

"It's nice to finally meet you, Lilly." She smiles, making me feel better about being here. "Let me show you the bathroom and you can wash your legs off."

"Nice to meet you too. And that would be good." I look down at my legs; one has smeared chocolate all over it from where Nico tried to wipe me off.

"I'll take her; I just need to set this stuff down," Cash says, and Asher takes the bags from him.

"Let me take those," Trevor says, grabbing the ones out of my hand as well.

"Thanks." I look up to see everyone watching me closely, then another beautiful woman comes in with long blonde hair, and she has a very obvious baby bump. I feel like I stepped into the world of beautiful people.

"Liz, this is Lilly. Lilly, this is Liz, Trevor's wife." Now my hands are free, I reach forward and shake her hand.

"Nice to meet you."

"You too. I was just coming in to see where everyone disappeared to," Liz says, and Trevor comes back over, wrapping his arms around her waist, setting his chin on the top of her head.

"Well, baby, you see, Lilly here is a bit of a klutz."

"No, I'm not." My eyes narrow on Trevor and I hear him laugh.

"I think Trevor is right. Who waves while holding a pie?" Nico points out my stupidity.

"It's polite to wave."

"When you're passing someone on the street," he says.

"I didn't think about it," I mumble, looking at the ground and feeling like an idiot.

"These guys are all big bullies," Liz says, tilting her head back to look at her husband.

"I think when they pick on you it means they like you," November points out.

"Can you watch the kids for a second? I'm gonna take Lil to the bathroom and help her get washed up," Cash asks the room of siblings.

"Is that what we're calling it today?" Asher asks, and my already red face burns hotter. I feel someone watching me, and my eyes go to the kitchen to see Nico dumping out the pie, his eyes on me. I don't know why, but I feel like he is judging every move I make.

"Mommy, they hab a puppy!" I hear Ashlyn yell as she runs into the house right to me. Her hair is a mess, with grass and twigs sticking out of it, and dirt is covering her clothes. There is another little girl following close behind, but she has blonde hair. When Ashlyn reaches me, her arms go out for me to pick her up. "Mommy, they hab a puppy and he's so cute!"

"They do?"

"Yes, and his name is Beast."

"Beast?" I wonder why they would name their 'cute puppy' that.

"Can we get one?" she asks, giving me her best pleading face.

"I, um...we can't get one now."

"Oh." Her bottom lip pops out, and I know what's coming.

"No pouting, what did we talk about?"

"But he's so cute," she says, that pouty lip trembling.

"I know, baby." I laugh, pulling her head to my chest and kissing the top of her head.

"You know, you can come visit Beast whenever you want." Ashlyn lifts her head to look at November. "Plus, I'm sure July, June, and May would like you to come over and visit." I looked at Cash, wondering if this was some kind of strange test. Who would have the name November, and then name their children after the other months of the year?"

"Yes, those are their girls' names," Trevor says reading my face. "I think they're trying to make a calendar." He shrugs, making Asher hit him upside his head while November and Liz roll their eyes at the same time. Ashlyn wiggles, wanting down.

"I will be out in a few minutes. You be good until then, all right?" I tell her, not yet releasing her to run off.

"I know," she says, completely annoyed with me. So just to annoy her more, I kiss her all over her face, making her scream with laughter.

"See you in a few minutes." I kiss her one last time then release her. When I stand back up, everyone is staring at me, but Cash's eyes are so warm that my pulse starts to race.

"Um..." I look around.

"Let's get you washed up," Cash says, grabbing a bag from the couch. I would have gone anywhere with him at that point, just to get away from the strange vibe I was getting from everyone.

"Is everything okay?" I ask as soon as the bathroom door closes.

"More than."

"Oh, it just that I felt like everyone was waiting for something to happen."

"My ex wasn't the easiest person," he mumbles, closing and locking the door behind us.

"What do you mean?" I slip off my sandals.

"She would start fights over everything under the sun. She always made it seem like everyone was out to get her."

"Were they?" I mean, I don't know this woman, but I do know women, and we have a tendency to band together.

"Nah, my family's not like that; even if they didn't like her, she would never know it.

"Oh." That didn't make me feel good.

"Let's get this off." He starts pulling my dress up.

"I don't need to take my dress off to wash my legs." I slap at his hands away.

"You're also going to try this on while we're in here." He pulls out a black bikini from the bag he brought into the bathroom with him. The same bikini he was trying to get me to buy when we were in the store.

"I'm not!" I shake my head, pulling down the showerhead and stepping into the tub. Wrapping the bottom of my dress higher around my waist, I start to rinse off my legs.

"Will you please try it on for me?"

"No." I don't even look at him when I answer.

"Please?" I finish washing the pudding off my legs, turn off the shower, dry off, and reach out, grabbing the suit from him and pulling the shower curtain closed. I forgot this about him. I forgot that when he wanted something, he would not stop until I did whatever he wanted.

"You're annoying," I grumble, pulling my dress up over my head and hanging it over the shower rod along with my bra, but I leave on my thong. Once I have the suit on, I adjust everything, making sure nothing is popping out.

"See?" I slide the curtain open, placing my hands on my hips.

"Fuck me." He brings his fist up to his mouth, biting down on it. "Yeah, you're right; you're not wearing that shit out there if Kenton or Sven come today." He starts shaking his head in the negative.

"I told you so." My stomach drops. I'm not gross to look at, but I don't look like I did before when we were together. My waist and hips expanded, along with my breasts. And I have stretch marks from when I was pregnant. I pull the shower closed, take off the top and the bottom, and reach for my dress. Just as it slides over the rod and into my hands, the shower curtain opens. "What are you doing?" I ask, covering my breasts in a slight panic. His eyes are dark and hungry, making me take a step back.

"You were beautiful when we first met." Great, I don't need him to tell me how different I am now. I know.

"But now, that beauty has become something straight out of a fucking pin-up calendar."

"What?"

"Look at you." His eyes roam my body from my hair to my toes. "I need to touch you so that I know you're real—that you're really here." He steps into the shower and pulls the curtain closed. I can't talk; I feel like I'm being cornered by a large predator. He takes another step towards me, making me retreat a step back, causing my back to hit the cold tile behind me. One of his hands goes to the wall above my head, the other to my waist, pulling my lower body against him.

"What are you doing?" I breathe.

"Gonna kiss you." His eyes drop to my mouth and my tongue wets my bottom lip. "Jesus," he groans right before his mouth touches mine; he nips and pulls my bottom lip making me gasp. "Open your mouth."

"Cash," I whimper, unsure. His fingers on my skin pull me closer and his mouth opens over mine. His tongue touches mine and one of my hands goes to his hair. He growls, his other hand tugging my head to the side as he takes over the kiss and devours my mouth. My other hand goes to his bicep to hold on. I can feel my nipples scrape against the cotton of his t-shirt as his hand at my waist moves down to my ass. He is rock hard, and I can feel the length of him against my stomach. His mouth leaves mine and travels to my ear, biting down before kissing it, then down my neck. His hand in my hair tugs to the side, giving him more access. He licks over my pulse, then down to my breast. His mouth latches onto my nipple. "Oh, my God." My head falls back against the tile. His mouth travels to my other nipple, giving it the same treatment. "Cash," I moan, my head tilting forward to watch him.

"Can I taste you, baby?"

"What?" My body is on fire. He stops what he is doing, his head coming up and his hands holding my face.

"I want to eat your pussy. Will you let me?"

"We never did that," I tell him, something he should know since he was there the night we had sex. We only did it once and it was perfect, until two days later when he called to tell me we couldn't see each other anymore. "I mean, I have never done that." His eyes went wide, then darkened.

"That makes me very happy." His mouth comes back down to mine; it feels like he is trying to brand me with his mouth, completely controlling mine. His hand on my face skims slowly down the side of my breast, along my side, and stops at the edge of my panties. I can feel the wetness between my thighs. My clit starts pulsing, needing attention. Teasingly, his fingers travel on the inside edge of my panties, then just below my belly button; my stomach muscles contract. My pulse speeds up, and finally his fingers slide in and over my clit, my body jumping at the contact. "Is all this for me?" he whispers. My answer is a whimper. "You're gonna have to be quiet, baby; my family is out there," he says softly. My body freezes—how could I have forgotten where we were? Before I can protest, he slides two fingers inside me, his mouth covering mine, and all thoughts leave my head as I moan down his throat. "That was close. Now, if you want me to eat your pussy, you're going to have to make sure that you're quiet, can you do that?" I shake my head, making him chuckle. "If you're not quiet, then you will be spanked when I take you to my house and the kids go to sleep."

"Cash." I feel my inner walls clench.

"You like that, huh?" His fingers move faster inside me and I can feel an orgasm building.

"You're not allowed to come until my mouth is on you." I want to yell at him to get to it, but he just stands there, his eyes on mine. "Jesus, you should see yourself right now." I think he's going to kiss me again, but instead, he nips my chin then drops to his knees, lifting my thigh to his shoulder. His fingers tug my thong to the side and his mouth is on me in an instant. I start grinding down against his tongue. I can feel my orgasm building—it's going to be huge, life-altering. And I know I'm not going to be quiet when I come.

"You have to stop." I push on his head, trying to get away. "Cash, I can't be quiet," I whimper. He doesn't stop; if anything, his pace increases, his tongue and fingers moving faster. "I'm going to come," I cry as I feel myself begin to contract around his fingers. My skin lights from the inside, and a million colors explode behind my eyes. I feel like I'm going to pass out. "Cash," I moan loudly before I catch myself and bite down on my arm. My head is back, eyes closed, and I feel my foot touch the floor as he lets my leg down from his shoulder. My legs feel wobbly, but he holds my hips until he stands so he can pull me to his chest. I don't know how long we stand like that, but it feels like forever. All I want to do is curl up with him and go to sleep.

"I love the way you taste, and I love the way you let go the minute my mouth is on you," he says quietly. I can feel his hard length against my stomach, and my hand starts to move towards the button of his jeans. His hand grabs mine, stopping me. "There isn't enough time for that. When I finally get inside you, I'm going to want to take my time and have you in my bed, not here in my brother's shower. Though I do plan on having you in the shower…just not this one," he says, and I can hear the smile in his voice. "We need to go out to the party; everyone is going to be wondering where we are."

"Oh no," I groan, rubbing my face. Everyone is going to know what we have been up to while we've been in the bathroom.

"Everyone's outside." He tilts my head back with both his hands at my jaw. "You're so beautiful." He kisses me softly on my lips then my forehead before opening the shower curtain. "You should just put the suit back on under your dress."

"I'm not wearing a bikini."

"Lil, your body is perfect, and it looks good on you. Wear the suit."

"I thought you said—"

"No, I said that I didn't want Kenton or Sven to see you in it, not that it doesn't look good, because it does."

"I don't know." I pick my dress up from where it fell into the tub when he surprised me.

"Baby, look at me." My eyes go to his. "You look perfect; wear that suit."

"Cash."

"Our daughter grew inside of you. I loved your body before, and I love it even more now."

"Fine, I'll wear it." I can't help but smile. I put the bikini bottoms back on, then the top before pulling my dress over my head. Once I'm dressed again, we head outside. Cash was right; everyone is out around the pool, and all the kids are playing out in the large grassy area where a large kids' playhouse is set up. Then I see it—a large dog the size of a horse. One of the little girls is laying over its back while it walks around the playhouse sniffing the grass.

"Is that Beast?" I stop, looking at Cash.

"Yep, and the little girl on his back is July." He laughs as we watch her try to stay on the dog's back; he acts like he doesn't even notice her. Cash points out each of the girls; three of them are Asher and November's July, May, and June, and one is Hanna, who is Trevor and Liz's Daughter.

"So Jax is the only boy?"

"Right now, yeah, but Liz is pregnant, and they found out a few days ago that they are having a boy."

"Wow." I look around the backyard filled with people and all the kids running around. We walk around while Cash introduces me to everyone, then wander over to the grill where an older gentleman—obviously, Cash and his brothers' dad—is standing with Asher.

"Dad, I want you to meet Lilly. Lilly, this is my dad, James."

"Nice to meet you, sir."

"Oh no, now I gotta train another one." He points the spatula in his hand towards me. "You call me James or Dad—preferably Dad—none of this 'sir' business."

"Okay." I smile and laugh.

"I feel old enough with all my grandkids running around calling me papa or grandpa. I don't need all my pretty daughters-in-laws callin' me sir."

"I'm no—"

"Oh, how sweet!" A woman's voice cuts me off. "You want Cash's new pussy to call you daddy." I look up and see a beautiful woman with short shorts, a halter-top, and shoulder-length dark brown hair. She's tall and wearing wedge heels, making her even more towering.

"What are you doing here, Jules?" Cash asks next to me, and I realize that this woman is his ex-wife.

"I came to see my son."

"You know you're supposed to call."

"Why, so you can hide this bitch away? Like I don't know that you have been sleeping around since before we got divorced."

"Seriously?" Cash growls, then I feel a hand on my elbow and I'm being tugged back.

"Mommy." I hear Jax's voice and look over to see Ashlyn standing with him off to the side of his mother. "This is my sister, Ashlyn."

"Oh no," I whisper just as Jules's eyes go to Jax, who is now holding Ashlyn's hand.

"You don't have a sister," Jules growls.

"I do!" He stomps his foot. "Daddy said she's my sister. He even said we have the same eyes, look," he says, opening his eyes up wide.

I take a step towards them, wanting to grab both of the kids and get them out of this situation. A hand holds me back at my elbow. I look over my shoulder and am surprised to see it's actually Nico. I glare, and then look back at the kids. "Ashlyn, Jax, let's go inside so Daddy can talk to Jules," I say as Cash walks over to where the kids are, picking them both up.

"My son isn't going anywhere with you, you fucking bitch," Jules says to me, and Ashlyn starts to cry. Then Susan and November are there, taking them both from Cash and heading inside. I look towards the yard and see Liz and Trevor taking the other kids into the house.

"Jules, you know that I'm Jax's granddad, and I would hate to put his mom in jail," James says; his eyes are cold, and I don't think he would hesitate to do what he says.

"Oh, like you would really give a fuck," she says leaning forward, and then looks at me. "Who the fuck are you?"

"You need to leave, Jules. Now," Cash says, taking a step in front of me. "Bro, take Lil inside for me." He looks past me to Nico.

"Sure thing." Nico puts his arm around my shoulder and starts to lead us inside.

"You should stay with him," I say quietly, looking up at Nico. I don't think he is a fan of mine, but I can tell he loves his brother, and I love—

Wait...love him? I shake my head. No, I don't. I care about Cash. Yes, as the father of my child. And want him to be safe, and I can tell that woman is all kinds of crazy. "Please." I fist my hand into his shirt.

His eyes flash something, but it's gone before I can catch it. "All right, go on inside," he says quietly. My stomach is in knots as I pull the door closed behind me. It's not jealousy; it's something else. I don't like the way that woman spoke to her son, and I also didn't like how she spoke to Cash and his family.

"She is never going to change."

"What?" I look over at Liz.

93

"When she first came forward saying she was pregnant, Cash was devastated about losing you."

"What?" I repeat like an idiot.

"I mean, he didn't say anything, but you could see it. You know?" she asks, her eyes coming to mine. I nod in understanding. I was devastated too. "But then I thought, I mean, I guess we all thought that maybe they could end up happy. Crazier things have happened, right?" She shrugs.

"I guess," I say, feeling like a horrible person for being ecstatic that he wasn't happily married to her right now.

"She was never happy, and did everything in her power to make him unhappy too."

"But why?"

"I don't know." She shrugs again. "All I know is that the day Cash told us that he was getting a divorce, I popped a bottle of champagne."

"Was she really that bad?"

"You don't even know the half of it," she says, looking out the window, watching as Cash, his dad, and Nico all stand watching as Jules flings her arms around. I can tell Cash says something to her when she looks at the glass door, her eyes on me.

"If looks could kill," Liz says.

"Yeah. I agree."

"Don't worry; she's a lot of bark, and no bite."

"Okay," I say, not believing it for a second. I could tell from the look on her face that this is just the beginning. I watch out the glass door as she stomps off through the yard. Cash's head hangs low. Then Nico is there, putting his arm around his shoulders and telling him something. Then his dad is in front of him, doing the same. I watch for a while, but once Jules doesn't come back, I go to check on the kids.

~~*

"Hey, baby. What are you doing?" My eyes open and Cash is standing above me wearing nothing but a pair of swim trunks. I guard my eyes against the sun, trying to get a better view of his chest and abs. The minute I move, Jax wiggles, and I remember that I have one kid napping on each side of me.

"We were reading a story." I look down at both kids. I put sunblock lotion on them earlier, but it may be time for more. "What time is it?" I ask as Cash lays down on the other side of Ashlyn.

"A little after two." His fingers run along the side of my face, then down and over my bottom lip. "You're getting a little pink," he says, running his finger over the bridge of my nose.

"Yeah, I should probably put some more lotion on, and put more on these two," I say, running my hands over each of the kids' heads. Cash's face goes soft and he leans forward, kissing me softly.

"You ready to talk about my ex?" he asks, and it surprises me that he's the one bringing it up. After she left and I found the kids, he came in to make sure that we were okay. Then he took Jax aside and talked to him. I don't know what he said, but Jax looked so sad that I hated Jules in that moment. I don't think any parent should talk to their child the way she spoke to Jax, or the way she talked in front of him. Her and Cash's problems were their problems and should be discussed between the two of them, not in front of an audience, including six small children.

"I don't know." I shrug; I don't know if I want to talk about his ex. The thought of him with her makes me feel sick.

"I would like to get it all out, if that's okay with you."

"Sure," I say, taking a deep breath trying to prepare myself.

"I was hooking up with her before I met you." He moves, laying on his side and propping his head in his hand. "We would hook up, but that's all it ever was."

"Okay." I swallow the lump in my throat.

"The minute I met you, I stopped seeing her and any anyone else." I nod, my eyes closing in relief. "About three months later, she calls me to tell me that she's pregnant, and that unless I want her to get an abortion, I needed to go with her to the doctor." I look down to make sure that both the kids are still asleep. I don't think that this is something they should ever know. "I met her at the appointment and the doctor did an ultrasound. I saw Jax for the first time and heard his heartbeat, and I fell so deeply in love in that moment." He takes a deep breath. "After the appointment, Jules told me that if I wanted her to keep the baby, I needed to cut everyone else off and focus on her." He looks past me, running his hand over his mouth before his eyes come back to me. "I hated doing it, but I wanted my son. I knew that Jules wasn't going to make it easy, but at the end of the day, if my child was healthy and happy, everything else would pale in comparison."

"I can understand that," I whisper, running my fingers through Cash's hair that had fallen forward into his eyes.

"Well, you know I called you and told you I couldn't see you anymore." I nod, that same pain from a few years ago shooting through my chest. "She moved in with me. I wanted to keep her close; I didn't want her to have a chance to get an abortion. I was afraid if I turned my back for a second, that's exactly what she would do. At first, our relationship was nothing but her living in my house, and then things changed. I didn't love her, but I cared about her, and I looked at Asher and Trevor's relationships and they were both so happy...and I wanted that for myself. At the time, Jules was so easy to get along with. So I tried to build a relationship with her." I bite my lip trying not to cry; I don't want to know this. "It never worked. Right after we got married, things changed. She changed. She turned into someone who was mean and manipulative. Or maybe she was like that before, but I was wanting what my brothers had so badly that I looked past it," he says quietly, reaching towards me and wiping away a single tear that has made its way down my cheek. "You know, she was bad, but I'm also to blame." He runs his thumb across my bottom lip. "I was still stuck on you, and kept comparing everything about her to you." Oh, God, I couldn't take anymore. I was going to start sobbing if he didn't stop. "I will do everything in my power to keep us together and to make you fall in love with me again." I don't think that it'll be that hard for him to do. My mom and dad are going to kick my ass, but I just can't help feeling like I'm meant to be with him.

"Cash?"

"Yeah?" He leans forward, kissing me lightly.

"What did she say to you before she left?"

"That she was going to try and get custody of Jax."

"No," I gasp as I run my hand over Jax's head at my waist.

"Don't worry; this isn't the first time she's tried. She won't take him from me. He doesn't even really know her. Yes, he knows she's his mom, but that's all. They don't have a relationship."

"That's really sad." I look down at Ashlyn. I can't imagine not having her.

"She's not like normal moms, babe. Even when Jax was a baby, she would get mad if he cried or if he needed attention. My mom has been more of a mom to him than she has."

"Maybe she needs help."

"I don't know; I tried to help her. I also tried to talk her into seeing someone after Jax was born, but she wouldn't. The last straw for me was when Jax was learning to walk and he stumbled into her. She was holding a glass of juice, and when he bumped her, the juice went all over her outfit. She pushed Jax back, and then started yelling about her ruined clothes. After that, I kicked her out of the house and told her I was getting a lawyer and filing for full custody."

"Poor Jax," I whisper, closing my eyes.

"She's not around often, and if she is, the visitations are supervised." Just then, I feel movement at my left and look down to see Jax opening his eyes.

"Hey, dude, did you have a good nap?" Cash asks him, and Jax climbs over me onto Cash's chest, kicking Ashlyn accidently in the process, waking her up.

"Hey, love bug."

"Are we going to the zoo?" She smiles sleepily up at me, then Cash.

"Tomorrow," I tell her as she cuddles into me. Cash pulls me over so my head is on his chest with Ashlyn between us, and Jax laying on top of him. We all lay there, the warmth of the sun beating down on us. Cash's fingers run up and down my arm. I feel loved, safe, and whole for the first time in years. I know it's too soon, but it feels so right that I don't care.

Chapter 4

Cash

"Hey, man, are you okay?" Asher asks. I look around the now-quiet jobsite realizing I must have been daydreaming. It's been two months since the bar-b-que at Asher's house—two months of getting to know my daughter, and two months of reconnecting with Lilly. All of it has been perfect, except I want more. I want Ashlyn and Lilly in my house with Jax and me. I want to be able to kiss them both before bed at night, and wake up and see them and my son every morning. I hate when I have to say goodbye to them, and I know Jax doesn't like it much either.

"Yeah." I smile as Asher sits, opening a bottle of water.

"How are things with you and Lilly?"

"Really good." I look at Asher, who seems to want to say something. "What is it?" I sigh. I know everyone likes Lilly. My mom loves her, but there are times I can see them waiting for her to flip out like Jules would.

"Why doesn't she live with you?"

"What? That's what you want to say?"

"Yeah, I mean, I can't imagine not having my girls there when I get up in the morning."

"I don't like it, if that's what you're thinking. But I have been trying to take things slow. I fucked up big time with her, so right now, I'm just trying to prove to her that I'm in for the long haul."

"Can you prove it by this weekend?"

"What?" I feel my eyebrows draw together in confusion.

"You know, this weekend. Can you have her move in with you by this weekend?"

"Were you listening to what I just said?" I mean, I want her to live with me; shit, there are a lot of things I want, but taking it slow includes waiting on moving in and sleeping together. Since that time in the shower at Asher's house, I haven't had my mouth on anything but her mouth. Just thinking about the way she looked—the way she fucking tasted—makes me hard.

"Come on, I can help you move her in," Asher says, dragging me out of my dirty thoughts.

"Dude, don't you think that if it was that easy, I would have had her moved in already?" I shake my head and go to stand.

"I know, but maybe you need to try harder."

"What the hell is going on?" I cross my arms over my chest, narrowing my eyes.

"Nothing, just looking out for you," he says looking away, and I know he's up to something.

"What the fuck is going on?" I repeat.

"Nothing," he mumbles before standing and walking off. I shake my head and look around the jobsite before gathering my stuff and heading over to where I was working before my break. Once I get there, Trevor comes around the corner.

"Hey, man, how's it going?" he asks, shoving his hands into his pockets.

"Good, what's up?" I look at him for a second before using the nail gun to tack up another piece of drywall.

"Good, good." He looks around before taking a step towards me. "I just wanted to see how things are going with you and Lilly."

"Things are good," I say through my teeth. "Why the fuck are you and Asher so interested all a sudden?"

"What do you mean Asher and me?" His eyes narrow; now, I know something is going on.

"Dude, what the fuck?"

"Lilly's not moving in with you, is she?" he asks, looking nervous.

"I'm going to shoot you in the ass with the nail gun unless you start talking."

"All right, we may have had a bet." He holds up his hands in front of him.

"You may have had a bet?" I repeat, my finger on the trigger starting to tighten.

"Okay, okay…we had a bet. Asher said Lilly would move in this weekend and I said no way, that it would take at least another couple more weeks."

"How the fuck are we related?" I shake my head. "Never mind. Shouldn't you be working?"

"Yeah, well, I took a break to call Liz to check on her; this pregnancy is a lot harder on her than the last one."

"She'll be fine."

"I know. I just hate when she isn't well." He hands me another sheet of drywall. "I know Jules was never sick, but was Lilly sick with Ashlyn?" he asks, holding the drywall in place.

"Yeah, she said she was nauseous up until six months," I tell him, feeling my chest squeeze. I hate that she went through that alone. I hate that I missed her body changing.

"You know, you never told me if you confronted Jules about the messages she sent to Lilly." One night, I asked Lilly to show me the messages that she had printed out. At first, I was going to burn them, but the minute I got them in my hand, I wanted to kill Jules. I read the words over and over again. I hate that Lilly had gotten that kind of response; even though I didn't send the messages, the fact that they came from my phone, at a time when she needed me, fucked with my head big time.

"I don't want to give Jules the power if she knows that she hurt Lilly, even just for a second. She would get off on that shit."

"You're right about that. I don't know how the fuck you still deal with her ass."

"It's not by choice. If I could cut her out of my life completely, I would, but I have to think about Jax."

"True. So how is it being a dad to a little girl?" he asks, making me smile.

"Fucking terrifying. I have always been worried about Jax and his safety, but with Ashlyn, it's something completely different. You know she called me Daddy for the first time a week ago?" I shake my head at the memory. "We had all gone out to dinner, and then to see the new kid's movie with the little yellow guys, and we were walking into the theater. I had my hand on Lilly's ass—where it normally ended up—and Ashlyn and Jax were walking in front of us carrying popcorn when Ashlyn turned to Jax and asked him, 'Can I sit next to Daddy?' I wanted to fucking cry, and Jax, my little man, shrugged like, 'I don't give a fuck who sits where, as long as we're watching the movie'."

"Damn, bet that felt good," Trevor said, slapping me on the back.

"Yeah, it did. It also hurt that it took her so long to say it. Knowing the reasons why she didn't."

"So what is your plan?"

"What do you mean?" I look at him, my eyebrows coming together in confusion.

"You know, moving in, getting married?"

"I don't know. I'm just taking it one day at a time. I'm just thankful as fuck that Jax has fallen in love with Lilly and Ashlyn."

"What about you?" he asks with a smirk.

"What about me?"

"Are you in love with Lilly?"

"Fuck yeah." I nod and can't help the shit-eating grin that splits my face.

"I knew it, and I can see when she looks at you and Jax that she feels the same."

"You think?"

"What, you haven't told her?" I shake my head no. "Why the fuck not?"

"Who are you, Dr. Phil?"

"No, but I do know that when I discovered that I loved Liz and held it back, it ate me alive until I cornered her and forced her to tell me she loved me too."

"Why doesn't that surprise me?" I chuckle.

"Laugh all you want, asshole, but I know what I'm talking about."

"How about you let me worry about that?"

"Sure, but when you flip the fuck out on her about it, don't come crying to me."

"You—" I start to tell him that he needs help when my phone rings, showing that it's my mom's number. I answer right away; she has been keeping Jax and Ashlyn for Lilly and me while we're at work. "Hey, Ma, what's going on?"

"I just got a call from Lilly," she says, sounding concerned. My stomach drops. I can hear the kids in the background laughing.

"Ma?"

"Oh, honey, she says she got picked up by the police," she whispers into the phone, and I know I must have heard her wrong. "She's didn't want to call you in case you couldn't pick up." Oh, God, I was going to be sick.

"What happened?" I ask, starting to wrap up my tools. I feel Trevor at my side, and I know he's waiting to find out what's going on.

"I don't know; she only had a couple minutes, so she told me where they were holding her and who to contact," she says, sounding more nervous than before.

"Ma, I need you to talk to me so I can help Lilly." It takes her a second to pull it together. She tells me where Lilly is and who to contact at the station, and the second I hang up, I'm on the phone with my dad, hoping that he knows someone who can help me out when I get there.

"What's going on?" Trevor asks as I head out to my truck.

"Lilly's being held by the police," I tell him without thinking.

"What do you mean she's being held by the police?" I hold up my hand when Dad picks up. I explain to him what Mom said, and he says he will meet me at the station where Lilly is.

"You gonna tell me what's going on?" Trevor asks. I hadn't even realized he got into my truck with me.

"I don't know. Ma couldn't tell me much; all she knows is that Lilly is being held, and the officer I need to speak to is Dan Pike."

"Did she say what she was picked up for?"

"Nope." I pull my hat off to run a shaky hand through my hair.

"It will be okay. Dad will meet us there and get everything straightened out."

"Yeah," I mumble, trying to calm down enough so I can drive the speed limit and get to the station in once piece. Trevor and I don't talk during the drive; my mind is racing with question after question and coming up with nothing. When we finally pull up to the precinct, my dad is already there waiting for us outside the building. I shut off the truck, pulling my hat back on before hopping out.

"All right, son, I just talked to an officer and he was able to explain to me that she is being held for questioning. Now, I want you to be calm when I tell you what's going on."

"Is she okay?"

"I haven't seen her, but I'm sure she will be fine. Now, she wasn't arrested, but brought in for suspicion of check fraud, and they say they have evidence against her, but he couldn't tell me what it was."

"Check fraud?"

"That's what they're saying."

"That's bullshit."

"I don't know, son. They usually don't bring people in without having a reason to."

"Dad, you've been around her; she can't even lie without fessing-up right after. I have a hard time believing that she would do what they're accusing her of."

"We'll just have to wait and see," he says, rubbing the back of his neck, looking away from me. I understand that my family is worried about me, but fuck, they needed to get over it already.

"She's not Jules."

"Son, I never—"

"Dad," I cut him off, "Jules has made my life a living hell since the day she told me she was pregnant with Jax. During that time, Lilly was alone. Yes, she had her parents, but she raised our daughter by herself, and even believing what she thought I told her, she still told Ashlyn about me. She's a good woman and a good mother; she's also honest and kind. She wouldn't do this, and if you're not going to be on my side—which is her side—then I don't want you here right now," I say through clenched teeth.

"You would choose her?"

"Fuck yes, without a second thought. I love you all, but I *love* her. She has had enough things happen over the last few years, and I don't know what's going on right now inside that building, but I do know the woman I love wouldn't do what they are accusing her of doing."

"Your mom loves her; so does your grandmother." His eyes light up.

"That's good, 'cause she's not going anywhere."

"All right, son, let's go get your girl." He pats my back before we turn to go into the building. Once inside, we're ushered into a small waiting area. There is a man there around my age; his pressed, white button-down shirt and khakis make him stand out. When he sees my dad, who is in uniform, he goes right to him.

"Do you have any information about Lilly Donovan?" the guy asks, pushing his glasses up the bridge of his nose. My hackles rise at the name of my woman coming out of this guy's mouth.

"Who are you?" I ask without thinking. His head swings in my direction, his eyes meeting mine.

"David. Who are you?" he asks, looking me over.

"Her boyfriend," I tell him, wishing that I could say fiancé or husband.

"Oh." He shrugs like it's all the same to him before turning to face my dad again. "So is she going to be okay? I mean, should I call a lawyer?" he asks, shoving his hands into the front pockets of his pants.

"Don't worry; my son will take it from here," my dad says, nodding in my direction. "He will have her call you when she's out and settled."

"Oh yeah, sure, of course," David says before turning and leaving the room without another look.

"Not fucking likely," I say under my breath and happen to look at Trevor, who is wearing a smug grin on his cocky face. If we weren't surrounded by officers, I would punch him. We all take a seat, and it's not long before someone comes to get us. We get to a section of the station that is a long hall with a few chairs spaced out. I see Lilly sitting in a metal chair; her face is tilted towards her lap, and even from a few feet away I can see the tears running down her cheeks. "Baby," I whisper when I get close enough to touch her.

"I didn't do it," she cries softly as I pull her into my arms.

"I know you didn't," I tell her, pulling her closer to me.

"They said that I stole checks from an old woman and wrote them to myself and cashed them," she cries harder, her body convulsing.

"Baby, you need to calm down before you make yourself sick," I whisper into her ear while rubbing her back.

"I-I can't ca-calm d-down. They told me that the wo-woman that this happened to d-didn't even have m-money for f-food be-because of what they th-think I d-did."

"It's okay. We're going to get this figured out; I promise," I say, trying to calm her down while the rage inside me starts to burn hotter and hotter. The minute I find out who really did this, I'm going to rip off their fucking head and shove it up their ass.

"I feel so bad," she whispers into my chest. My dad stands close by with a look of worry and understanding on his face, and Trevor looks like he is ready to help me hide the body.

"Did they say you could leave?" I ask her, pulling her small body tighter against mine.

"Yes, but I can't leave the country."

"You weren't going to anyways; so that's okay."

"I know; I told them that." She nods, sniffling.

"Good, let's get out of here. We'll stop by your house and get you and Ashlyn some clothes. Then we can head to my house for the night."

"I don't—"

"Hey." I tilt her face towards mine with a finger under her chin. "If you think for one fucking second that I'm letting you out of my sight tonight, you have lost your damn mind."

"Okay." She sighs, looking down.

"You okay, darlin?" my dad asks. Her body stiffens and she looks over her shoulder; seeing both my dad and Trevor, her face pales, and I feel her body start to shake.

"Oh no," she whispers, looking back at me.

"Hey, it's okay. My dad came when I called him. Both he and Trevor wanted to make sure you were okay," I tell her quietly.

"They already hate me," she says under her breath as new tears begin to fall from her eyes. "I think I'm going to be sick," she says before covering her mouth with her hand and running down the hall towards the sign marked restrooms.

"I think I need to apologize." My dad lets out a heavy sigh. "I didn't think that she noticed."

"She's sensitive. The day after the bar-b-que she was excited to get to know you guys. She thought you were all welcoming her into the fold; then she noticed that y'all acted different with her than you do with November or Liz, and that was okay with her. She understood that it would take some time to build a relationship, except no one ever tried, and now she feels like an outsider. Well, except Ma; she has made it clear from day one that she has Lilly's back." I smile; I love my mom.

"I know Liz has called her," Trevor says, and I nod.

"She did, and they talked and Lilly likes her a lot. She likes her and November both."

"I like Lilly," Trevor says, shaking his head and frowning.

"Yeah, but you all still act like she's going to wig out if you say or do the wrong thing when she's around. She can feel it, and so can I." I rub my face. "She is here all alone; her parents are in Alaska, and she has no one except Ashlyn, Jax, and me."

"We'll do better," my dad says, shaking his head. Then he turns as an officer starts coming towards us.

"Are you all here with Lilly Donovan?"

"Yes." I take a step towards him. His eyes go from me to my dad.

"Shit, James, is that you?" the officer asks, looking at my dad with surprise written on his face.

"Dan?" My dad steps forward to shake the man's hand.

"How the hell have you been?" Dan asks, pulling my dad in for a one-armed hug.

"Could be better. My son's girl was brought in for question."

"So you're seeing Lilly?" the guy asks, turning towards me.

"Yes."

"I know that this is hard, and I hate doing this, but it's not my decision. I'm sorry that she is going through this, and if it makes you feel any better, I don't believe that she did it. But the evidence is pointing in her direction," Dan says, looking at my dad.

"I know that it's a part of the job," my dad says, and Dan nods his head.

"I know she didn't do it," I speak up.

"I'm sorry, but until we get evidence that proves otherwise, we are forced to go with what we have. Now, I informed Ms. Donovan that she is not allowed to leave the state, and that it would be best for her if she got a lawyer."

"Done," I say right away.

"Also, it wouldn't hurt for her to have proof of her whereabouts on the days that the checks were cashed."

"If you can get me the dates, I'm sure we can come up with that information. She and my daughter are usually with my son and me," I say as Lilly starts heading back our way from the bathroom. Her face is pale, and her eyes are red and puffy from crying. I hate that she's going through this. Once she reaches our group, I wrap an arm around her shoulders, tucking her into my side.

"Lilly, here are the papers that I told you about, and there is also a list of affordable lawyers in there that you can contact."

"Thank you. And I know that the answer will probably be no, but do you think that I can get the address of the lady this happened to? I would like to see if she needs anything."

"I'm sorry, but I can't give that information out, but I can give her your information, and she can choose to contact you," he says with a shrug.

"Okay, well, thank you," she says quietly, taking the file folder from his hand.

"My card is in there as well, and if you need anything or have any questions, you call me."

"I will, thank you," she repeats, and I see the tears beginning to fill her eyes once again.

"Let's get you out of here, baby," I say softly, and then Trevor is there, taking her out of my arms and pulling her in for a hug.

"Don't worry, sis. We'll get this figured out," he tells her, rocking her back and forth. I hear another loud sob come from her before Trevor transfers her into my arms.

"You good riding with dad?" I ask Trevor before scooping Lilly up into my arms. She doesn't protest, just wraps her arms around my neck, laying her head against my shoulder.

"Yeah, man, call me tonight," he says, looking at Lilly once more before shaking his head.

"Thanks for coming, Dad," I say as we start making our way out of the building. Once outside, my dad holds open the door of the truck for me as I set Lilly inside, making sure she gets buckled in. When I'm done, I kiss her forehead, and then tilt her chin up to kiss her lips. "Give me a minute to talk to my dad, and then we can go." She nods, not looking me in the eyes. "Look at me, baby." She shakes her head. "Lilly, look at me." Her eyes come up and meet mine. "This will all be worked out; I promise you."

"Okay." The word sounds defeated. I press my mouth to hers in another quick kiss before hopping out of the truck and slamming the door.

"You're right; she didn't do this," my dad says, and Trevor nods in agreement.

"I know." I pull off my hat, running my hands over my hair and face.

"I'm going to call Dan tonight and see if he can tell me anything as a friend. In the meantime, I want you to call our lawyer and get him on the case. Any of the lawyers in that folder are going to be severely over-worked and underpaid, and it will show in their work."

"Thanks, Dad."

"You know I got your back, and I'm glad you finally got your girl, son. I know what you had to deal with, and it was wrong of me to add Lilly into the same category as Jules without giving her a chance."

"It's fine. Can you tell Ma that I'll come get the kids later, after I get her settled?"

"No problem," he says, patting my shoulder. "Take care of your girl."

"Call me if you need anything," Trevor says as I walk around the front of my truck.

"Thanks, T." I pull open the door to the cab of the truck and climb inside.

Once we pull up to the apartment, I look around realizing Lilly's car isn't in its usual spot. "Where's your car, baby?"

"It wouldn't start, so I had to get a ride with David from the school," she says, unbuckling her seatbelt.

"Why didn't you call me?" I feel my pulse start to speed up. I hate that something happened to her

119

and she didn't call me. And it pisses me off that I'm pissed she was in a car with another man. I shut off the truck and turn my body towards her, resting my arm on the steering wheel, trying to look casual, even with the blood pumping more rapidly through my veins.

"You were working, and I didn't want you to worry or hear you say that you were right about my car being a piece-of-crap." She shrugs, opening the door and hopping out.

"I wouldn't say that."

"Really?" She turns towards me, her eyes narrowing slightly.

"Okay, I may have said that your car was a piece of shit." I shrug and smile. Throwing my arm around her shoulders, I whisper into her ear, "Looks like you're getting a new car, baby."

"Um, no, I'm getting a lawyer. I am not going to have enough money for a new car."

"Okay, first of all, you are going to be using my family's lawyer, and second, I am paying for the car."

"I don't have the brain power to argue with you right now, but when I do, I will let you know that you're not buying me a new car. And as for the lawyer thing, if I can afford him, that's fine. If not, I will have to look somewhere else."

"What part of that didn't you understand?" I ask, pulling her to a stop and turning her towards me.

I place my hands under her jaw, tilting her head back slightly. "I'm paying for the car." I cover her mouth with mine before she has a chance to say anything. When I pull my mouth away, her lips are still close enough that they brush mine with each word I say. "You, our daughter, and occasionally Jax ride in that car. You three are the most important people in my life, and I will not have you riding around in a piece-of-shit car when I can easily get you something that is safe. And when the kids go to bed tonight, you're going to explain to me why the fuck you didn't call me when your car broke down. And you better come up with something better than you didn't want to bother me at work, 'cause as of right now, my palm is itching, and I plan on spanking you for that shit."

"Cash," she says, her eyes heating as she licks her bottom lip.

"Jesus, you want that, baby?" I ask, pulling her closer to me.

"We haven't—" she looks away without finishing, and I can't help but groan when her cheeks turn pink.

"I've been trying to be good. Do you know how many times I've had to jerk off because of the state you've left me in?" I shake my head. "It's too many to count." I lean forward, running my nose up the length of her neck to her ear, where I bite down gently on her earlobe. "I can't wait to be inside you. I can't wait to hear the sounds you make when you come. I can't wait to feel you squeezing my cock. I remember how wet you were when my mouth was on you and my fingers were deep inside you. I can't wait to feel that wet heat wrapped tight around me."

"Lilly," I hear a man call and my head comes up. Lilly's hands hold my t-shirt tightly in her fists. I look towards Lilly's apartment, seeing the guy from the police station coming down the stairs.

"Who the fuck is this guy, Lil?" I ask. Her eyes come to mine, and she blinks a few times like she's trying to clear her head before she looks over her shoulder.

"That's David; we work together."

"He's a teacher?"

"Yeah, he teaches second grade." She turns in his direction. "Hey, David."

"I was so worried, Lil. I didn't know what to do," he says, stepping closer and grabbing her hand. The fact that he used 'Lil' instead of Lilly and now has his hands on her is making me bite down on the inside of my cheek hard. *This is what Trevor was saying. Fuck me.*

"It's fine, just a misunderstanding. Thank you for stopping by, but I will see you after the weekend," she says, pulling her hand back to her side.

"Are you sure you're going to be okay?"

"Yeah, Cash is here, and we're going to go get our kids." My heart jumps at her words, and I want to pound my chest.

"Kids?" I see a slight flash of annoyance and anger cross his face before he hides it, and then his eyebrows draw together in confusion.

"Well, you've met Ashlyn," she says and he nods, "and Cash has a son named Jax."

"I see." He looks at me, then back at Lilly. "If you need anything, give me a call. Have a good weekend, and I will see you at school on Monday." He steps forward, pulling Lilly in for a hug. Her body goes ridged and she pulls away quickly, putting a small fake smile on her face.

I watch as David gets into a newer Nissan, and after he's in the car, he sits and watches us for a second before starting it up and backing out of the parking lot.

"He only works with you?" I ask her, because the look on the guy's face when she told him that we were together was one of jealousy.

"Yes." She pulls away and starts up the stairs to her apartment.

"Has he ever asked you out?"

"Once," she mumbles before shoving the key in the lock and opening the door.

"Just once?" I ask, because when she's lying her words are always drawn out to sound more like a question than an answer.

"Okay, fine, a couple of times." We make our way back to her bedroom. She goes to the closet, pulling out a bag, and starts shoving clothes into it. I stand next to the bed, trying to think of something to say. My mind is turning over; I used to get jealous before when we first started dating, but it was nothing like the feeling I have right now.

"You said no, right?" My fists clench at the thought of her seeing David—fuck, seeing *any* man who's not me.

"Is that a real question?"

"Yes," I say through my teeth, wondering why the fuck I'm doing this. I really don't want to know, and I'm acting like Asher or Trevor with their territorial, over-protective asses.

"I have never gone out with him. We work together, and he is kind of a friend."

"How is he 'kind of a friend'?"

"You know, Cash, you're starting to make me feel like you don't trust me. I told you we never dated. I told you we work together, and I told you he is a friend. Now unless you want to give me a polygraph, you're going to have to take my word for it."

"I hate knowing that you called him instead of me," I tell her the truth.

"I never called him." She shakes her head and looks at me like I'm crazy. "We left the school at the same time; he was parked next to me, and when my car wouldn't start, he offered to give me a ride home. I knew your mom had Ashlyn, so I was planning on coming home, changing, and calling you, that way you could take me to my car later and look at it. But when I got home, the police were here waiting for me, so that kind of ruined all of my plans."

"Will you promise me not to go anywhere alone with that guy?" This is not about me being a jealous asshole...okay, maybe it is a little bit...but there is something about him that sets my teeth on edge.

"Cash." She shakes her head.

"Baby, it's not that I don't trust you." Her eyes narrow, making her look adorable. My hands go under her jaw, titling her head back. "Something about him doesn't sit right with me."

"Is it because he has a penis?" she taunts. I smile and lean in to kiss her.

"No, smart ass, it's not because he has a penis," I say against her mouth.

"Cash," she says softly; my eyes go from her mouth to her eyes. "He has been nothing but nice. Just, please, trust me."

"I do trust you," I tell her honestly. Not only do I trust her, I love her. Maybe Trevor is right in a fucked-up kind of way, and I need to tell her that I love her...put it out there.

"So just know that I will not put myself in a situation that something could happen to me," she says, running a hand through my hair. My eyes close when her soft hand travels down my neck and up my jaw.

"Do you know that I love you?" I ask as my eyes open, looking into hers. I hear her quick inhale and she shakes her head, her eyes searching my face. "I never stopped loving you. I didn't know how much of the old you was in this newer version," I smirk, "but I found out that I love the new you just as much, if not more. I don't want anything to happen to you." I pull her against me, resting my cheek on top of her head.

"I love you too," she says, making me smile and feel lighter than I've felt for the last two months—hell, the last few years.

Chapter 5

Lilly

I look down at my lap. Cash's large hand is entwined with mine, his thumb moving slowly back and forth against my skin. The roughness and strength in his hand makes mine feel small and delicate. I can't believe he told me he loves me. I knew it would come eventually. He shows me every day that he cares not only for Ashlyn, but for me as well. I have finally accepted that he is not going anywhere. Part of me is still hurt that he walked away from me when I needed him, but the other part understands why he did what he did. I would do anything for my daughter, just like he did for his son. "I think you should meet my parents," I say, looking over at him. His eyes come to me for a second before going back to the road.

"Sure, we can go during your next school break." He squeezes my hand before bringing it to his mouth and kissing my knuckles.

"I won't have another break for a few months." I try to think of a way to have my parents come out here, but right now, getting out of Alaska is like trying to get out of Alcatraz—nearly impossible. The only way in or out of the place I grew up is by boat or plane, and when the weather is bad like it has been, there is no way. "I was going to Skype my mom tonight so she could talk to Ashlyn. You can meet her then."

"What's Skype?" I look over in shock. Who in the world doesn't know what Skype is?

"You're joking, right?"

"No." He shakes his head.

"Skype is only the best invention ever. You use your computer and the other person uses theirs and you call them then they are sitting there in front of you."

"Like teleporting?" he asks and I burst out laughing.

"No, I'm explaining it badly. You see them on the computer like a live video feed. I got my mom hooked when I was home. Her sister lives in Hawaii and they hadn't seen each other for over four years. Then my aunt was on Facebook one day telling everyone that she got Skype. My mom, who had become addicted to Facebook because of my aunt, wanted to know what Skype was so I took her and got her a camera to hook up to her computer. Now during the winter, when Mom's stuck inside because there is normally ten-feet of snow outside, she Skype's with my aunt. They also they play all those annoying Facebook games and send everyone they know invites." I take a deep breath when

I'm done talking and he looks over at me and smiles.

"I don't know what that is. I don't have Facebook."

"You don't have Facebook?" I gasp. "How in the world do you know what's going on with your friends if you don't have Facebook?"

"I call them and say 'hey, what's going on? How are things? Anything new?'"

"Oh, yeah, I guess you could do that." He squeezes my hand and chuckles.

"So, you want me to meet your mom over Skype? I'm not sure if I'm ready for such a serious step in our relationship."

"Very funny." I roll my eyes. "I'll see if she can get my dad to sit down long enough to meet you as well." I notice him shifting in his seat and squeezing my hand a little tighter. "Are you okay?"

"Yeah, I mean, I'm sure your dad hates me." I want to say, 'no, of course he doesn't hate you," but that would be a big fat lie. I'm Daddy's little girl, have been and will always be. When I came home with Ashlyn, my parents fell in love with her and couldn't understand why anyone wouldn't want her.

"My parents know that you didn't send those texts," I say gently.

"I know." He takes a deep breath. "I'm sure they don't believe that."

"My mom thinks your ex sent them."

"She's the only person who could have," he says, and I can feel my pulse speed up. I have never hated anyone in my life, but what I feel for her is close.

"Well, I know once my dad gets to know you, he will love you," I tell him. He is honestly my dad's dream-son, and I hope he gives him a chance.

"I'm sure it will be fine," he says, and my stomach flips, wondering if this is a huge mistake.

"Honey, you have to move that out of the way, at least until I can get the camera turned on," I hear my mom say. I look over at Cash, who is sitting next to me at his dining table. The computer is in front of us, the screen black, but we can both hear my parents arguing back and forth. Cash smiles, and I laugh when I hear my mom yell to get the damn thing out of her face. Finally, the screen turns on, and I see my mom sit down hard in her chair and glare off camera.

"Hi, Mom."

"Hey, honey." My mom smiles then looks over at Cash, and her eyes get big before coming back to me. "Well, at least he's hot, even if he is a prick."

"Mom," I snap.

"Oh, please, now I see why you went all gaga over him." She waves her hand back and forth, and then I see a shadow over her right shoulder before my dad sits down next to her in one of their kitchen chairs. I suck my lips into my mouth, trying not to bust out laughing. My dad is wearing his hunting gear. His short hair is slicked away from his face, and under his eyes are black smudges of paint. He also has his shotgun out and his hunting knife in a knife holster under his arm.

"Hi, Dad." I give a slight giggle. He glares at me, looks over at Cash, and I look over at Cash as well. His face is slightly red and he looks like he is trying not to laugh. "Dad, Mom, this is Cash. Cash, these are my parents, Frank and Tina Donovan," I say.

"Nice to meet you, sir and ma'am." He nods at both my parents, and we can hear my mom mumble something under her breath about manners and good looks.

"Dad, why are you wearing that?"

"Well, I thought that I should let this young man here know that I was a Seal. I know how to go into places and get out unnoticed. I know how to kill someone before they even know I'm there. And I know how to—"

"Yeah, yeah, I know, but what does that have to do with your hunting gear?

"He can't fit into his uniform," my mom chimes in. "Trust me, honey, he tried. Even tried to have me button him up, and it was still a no-go." My mom shakes her head, and then smiles when my dad turns to look at her and glare.

"Woman, I told you to stop baking all the damn time."

"Oh, stop. Don't blame your weight on my baking."

"Mom, Dad..." I sigh.

"Fine," my dad says, still looking at my mom. "Know that you're going to pay for that later," he says quietly, making my mom blush.

"Gross, can you both please act like normal parents for five minutes?" I shake my head.

"Memaw!" Ashlyn shrieks climbing onto Cash's lap and waving into the camera.

"Hey, baby." My mom sits forward, smiling.

"Papa, look! My daddy's here!" Ashlyn looks at my dad then leans back, looking up at Cash. He leans forward, kissing her forehead.

"I see that, angel." Dad's face transforms into a smile. Ashlyn looks away from Cash, back to the computer.

"Oh wait! You hab to meet my brother!" Ashlyn squeals, climbing down from Cash's lap. I can hear her in the other room yelling for Jax to come meet her Memaw and Papa. Cash and I look at each other and laugh. Cash slips his arm around my shoulders, pulling me into his side. I feel his lips at my temple, and then Jax and Ashlyn are running into the room. Ashlyn climbs back onto Cash's lap, and Jax looks at me for a second, seeming unsure. I hold out my arms and he smiles before jumping up to sit on my lap.

"Fuck me," my dad says, looking between Jax and Ashlyn.

"Daddy!" I scold, covering Jax's ears. Jax starts laughing, and then Ashlyn joins him. I look at both of them and shake my head. "Do not repeat what you just heard."

"They could be twins," my mom says, and I look up from the kids' smiling faces to see tears in my mom's eyes. "Nice to meet you, Jax. You can call me Memaw or Grandma," my mom says, "and you can call this guy here Papa or Grandpa." She points to my dad.

"Hi," Jax says, giving a small wave before leaning back into me. I wrap my arms around him and kiss the top of his head. We have gotten closer over the last couple months, but it's rare that he will cuddle. Just like Ashlyn, he likes to be off running around creating havoc and chaos.

"So how are you, angel?" my dad asks Ashlyn, who is cuddled back into Cash.

"Good! Daddy says I can get a dog," she says randomly, and I look over at Cash and glare.

"I didn't say it was going to happen today." He looks a little sheepish.

"I want a dog," Jax says, leaning back to look up at me.

"Um...I...well, one day."

"Do you think that Spike will like having a dog?" he asks. I know, I know...I kinda ended up liking Spike; he's cute. But I wonder if dogs eat ferrets.

"I don't know."

"I don't want Spike to get hurt," Ashlyn says.

"Who's Spike?" my dad asks.

"My ferret," Jax says, looking over at Ashlyn. "We should go get him." Ashlyn nods before they both jump off our laps, running to the back of the house where the bedrooms are.

"Seems you two have your hands full and a good reason for birth control," my mom says, and I laugh.

"Yeah, but they are both really good kids," I say, leaning into Cash.

"So, what are your intentions with my daughter?"

"Dad!"

"Don't you 'Dad' me; I want to know what his plans are."

"Well, I would like Lil and Ashlyn to move in with me—" Cash starts to say something else, but my dad cuts him off.

"So you want to get the milk for free?" my dad asks with narrowed eyes, and Cash looks confused.

"Sorry, I'm not following."

"You know, why buy the cow when you can get the milk for free? You want my daughter and granddaughter to live with you, and you don't want to marry her.

"No disrespect, sir, but that is something that I will be discussing with Lilly first before anyone else. And when the time's right, I will come to you like a man and ask for your permission, not that it will change my mind about asking her," Cash says, and my dad's eyes flash, not with anger, but approval, and my tummy flips. *Cash said when the time was right, he would ask me to marry him. Oh, my God.*

"Well, I know what Lilly has told us about your situation and what happened in the past," my dad says looking at me, his eyes going soft. "She believes you, so I'm going to give you the benefit of the doubt, but just remember what I said earlier about being a Seal."

"You're not a Seal; you're a Papa Bear." Ashlyn laughs, climbs into my lap, and Dad smiles. I look over at Jax, who has Spike in his arms as Cash picks him up to sit on his lap.

"This is Spike," Jax says, holding the ferret out in one hand, his long body swinging back and forth.

"Isn't he cute, Memaw?" Ashlyn cries, looking at my mom.

"He is something." My mom makes an eeek-face at me, then smiles at Jax.

"So, has anything new happened?" my mom asks, and I want to tell her about what happened today with the police, but I don't want her to worry about it. I know the cop said he believed me, so I just hope he finds who really did this and clears my name.

"Nope, nothing new at all." Cash squeezes my shoulder. I smile, and my mom's eyes narrow on me. *Dammit, I need to work on becoming a better liar.*

"So, Lilly says you do construction," Dad asks Cash, and they start talking about Cash's job, then about hunting and fishing, and my eyes start to feel heavy.

"All right, love bug, you need to go get ready for bed," I tell Ashlyn, and she sighs loudly.

"Bye, Memaw. Bye, Papa." She blows them each a kiss before getting down and walking into the bathroom.

"You too, little dude," Cash tells Jax, who waves bye to my parents.

"Love you, Mom and Dad," I say, leaning towards the camera.

"Love you too, honey. If you need to come home, you just say the word," my mom says, and I feel Cash's arm go tight around me.

"We're good, Mom. I promise," I tell her, giving her a genuine smile.

"All right, it was nice meeting you, son. You take care of my girls," Dad says, looking at Cash, and then his eyes come to me. "Love you."

"Love you too, Daddy," I say softly, feeling his words deep inside my soul. My parents are the best.

"Nice to meet you both," Cash says before the screen goes black on the computer and my parents are gone.

"I like your parents," Cash says, and I look over at him.

"They are pretty awesome parents."

"So what do you say we get the kids to bed and find a movie to watch?"

"Sure." I start to stand and Cash stops me, dragging me down onto his lap.

"And tonight, you're sleeping with me. No more sleeping in the room with Ashlyn," he says, his eyes turning a shade darker, and then dropping to my mouth. We have only stayed over a couple of times, but I always sleep on the pull out in the room Cash fixed up for Ashlyn. I bite the inside of my cheek and give a slight nod. "Good. Now, let's get the hellions to bed so I can get you alone."

"Okay," I breathe and feel his fingers flex into the skin at my waist.

"Okay," he says, and his lips touch mine. His mouth opens, pulling my bottom lip between his teeth. I feel his tongue run over it before his hand slides up my back and into my hair, tilting my head further to the side. I press my tongue into his mouth; his teeth release my lip, and he puts more pressure on the back of my head, kissing me harder. My arms go around his neck, one hand in the back of his hair, running my fingers through it. When our mouths finally part, we're both breathing heavily. I lean forward, resting my head in the crook of his neck. "The kids are quiet. We should go make sure they're not trying to find out how many things they can flush down the toilet before it backs up," he says after a few minutes. I start laughing. It wouldn't be the first time, and he is right; when the kids get quiet, they are normally up to no-good.

"All right," I sigh; I would much rather stay curled up in his lap for the rest of the night, but parenthood is a never-ending job. Cash stands, taking me with him. Once we're up, we go down the hall to where two of the four bedrooms are located. Jax's room is on one side of the hall, and Ashlyn's is on the other. I stop before Jax's room when I hear both of the kids' voices. I can't make out what they are saying, so I creep forward until I can peek my head around the door. I feel Cash's hands at my waist and we both stand there in silence, listening to Jax and Ashlyn's conversation.

"Daddy said that it's my job as your big brother to take care of you."

"Well, if Mommy and Daddy have another baby," I feel Cash's hands squeeze me, "I will be bigger than them," she says, and I can see her putting her hands on her hips like a total diva.

"I will still be bigger." He sighs like he is annoyed, making me giggle. I step into the room when Jax's head comes up.

"What are you guys doing?"

"We were going to listen to a story," Ashlyn says, picking up the Kindle Fire from the bed.

"Oh yeah? Did you both brush your teeth?"

"Yes," they both say at the same time.

"Did you put Spike back and make sure that you locked the cage?" Cash asks, and I'm so glad he thought of that. I, for one, didn't want to wake up with Spike in bed with me.

"Yes," they both say at the same time again, looking at Cash and me like we're annoying them.

"One story for both of you. Then it's bed time," Cash says.

"Fine," they grumble. Ashlyn crawls up onto the bed with Jax, and they pull the Kindle between them and start an audio-story about the Bernstein Bears.

"We will be back to tuck you in," I say, but may as well be talking to air because neither of them are listening to anything I have to say.

"So what do you say we skip the movie and go straight to the credits?" Cash says against my ear, his body wrapping around mine from behind as we walk down the hall.

"Who watches credits?" I moan when I feel his fingers slide just under the top of my jeans against my stomach.

"No one." He bites my neck. I then feel his tongue licking the abused skin. My pussy jumps and wet heat floods my center. My head falls back against his shoulder, my arms going over my head and around his neck. The fingers of one of his hands travels down the front of my jeans, while his other hand comes up to cup my breast under my shirt and over my bra. Goose bumps break out over my skin when I feel the tip of his finger slide between my folds and over my clit.

"Yes," I whisper, arching back as my eyes close.

"As much as I want to tear open your jeans and make you come, we can't do anything until the kids are asleep," he groans, flexing his hips into my ass. I can't help but pout when he pulls his hand out of my jeans. When I turn around, his eyes look over my face and he smirks. "My poor baby. I left you all swollen and wet." His words send a shiver down my spine, and my pussy contracts. "I hope you don't plan on getting much sleep tonight." He pulls me against him, and I feel the hardness of his cock against my stomach. "And I hope you didn't have anything important to do tomorrow, because there is no guarantee you're going to be able to walk." I feel my pulse speed up, and I take a deep breath. "I love that look, baby." He leans in kissing me.

"Take off your clothes." I jump and spin around at the sound of Cash's voice. I'm standing in front of his dresser, grabbing a t-shirt to put on after I get out of the shower I am about to take. I had left him a few minutes ago when he was going to "shut down the house" as he put it, and check on the kids one last time before coming to bed. I was nervous. I wanted Cash in the worst way, but I still had no experience except for him that one time, and my LELO, which I used to get myself off.

"Wh-what?" I stutter out. The look in his eyes is so primal that I start to take a step back.

"Lil, I'm not fucking around." He runs a hand through his hair, making it look messier. "Lose the clothes."

"Um..." I start to say that I was going to shower, but before I know it, he's in front of me, his hands ripping my shirt off over my head. I'm caught off guard, but also turned on by how badly he wants me.

"I'm sorry, baby, but this is going to be fast. It's been too long, and I want you too much." His teeth sink into my neck, and I notice he does that a lot, almost like he's marking me. His hands are at the button of my jeans, and then I can hear my zipper sliding down. My hands go under his shirt, running along the smooth hot skin of his back. I pull it up, his hands leaving me long enough to put his arms up over his head, pulling his shirt off. My hands automatically wander to his abs, feeling the ridges and valleys under my palms. His body is like a living work of art. "Baby," he growls, "you have to stop touching me or this is going to end before I even have a chance to make you come or slide inside of you." His mouth slams down onto mine as he starts walking me backwards. My hands go to his hair. *God, I love his hair.* I feel the back of my knees hit the edge of his bed. I feel my jeans tugged down over my hips. Then his mouth leaves mine as he pushes me gently so that I fall onto the bed behind me. He pulls my jeans the rest of the way off. His hands go to my knees, spreading my legs wide. They then slide up my inner thighs where I can feel his thumbs on the outer-edge of my panties. I come up on my elbows so I can see what he's doing. His eyes meet mine before his face lowers and he runs his nose up the center of the lace that is covering me.

"Cash." I can hear the uncertainty in my own voice.

"What, baby?" His mouth is hovering over me.

"I...I..." I try to close my thighs. His hands tighten on my legs. I can feel his fingers imprinting into my skin.

"Don't." He turns his head, and I can feel his mouth open over the skin of my inner thigh and suck deeply.

"Oh." I fall back, covering my face. I can feel my pussy contract as his hand on my other thigh travels up and under the edge of the lace, his thumb sliding over my clit, then inside.

"Fuck, I'm not going to last," he says again, taking his mouth away from my thigh. He stands, pulling off his jeans. His hands go to the bed on each side of me. "I'll make it good for you next time, baby," he says, pulling me up so I'm in the center of the bed. He rips the delicate lace away from my body, tossing it across the room. Then his mouth is on one of my nipples, then the other. His fingers slide down my belly, and I feel one enter me and pull up, then out, and suddenly two are filling me. My head starts to thrash back and forth. "I can't do this," he grits out. My eyes fly open when he lifts one of my legs up and over him, turning my body so that he is sitting between my legs. I look down and see his very large erection and his fist wrapped around it.

"Condom," I say, and he holds one out and smiles before ripping open the gold package with his teeth. His other hand is slowly stroking up and down his cock while his eyes are looking between my legs. His eyes come to mine before dropping to his cock, holding the tip of the rubber before sliding it down over his length.

"I can't wait," he growls as he leans forward, filling me in one stroke.

"Oh, God!" I cry, my back arching and my nails digging into his biceps.

"Shit. I'm sorry, baby." He stills, his hands going to my face as he leans in and kisses me gently.

"Don't stop," I moan, wrapping my legs around him. I'm not in pain; I just feel full and stretched. My nails scrape down his back when he pulls out.

"Jesus, you're so fucking tight." He leans forward, my mouth meeting his as I dig my nails into his scalp when he pulls out and slides back in quickly.

"Yessss," I hiss. My fingers go between our bodies and slide over my clit, making my hips surge up.

"Fuck yeah, touch yourself." He sits back on his calves, pulling my knees up as his eyes smolder, watching our connection and what my fingers are doing. I can feel heat pool in my belly, and I know that I'm going to come.

"Please, harder," I moan and feel him slam against me. I can feel that heat in my belly start to turn into a delicious weight.

"You're so beautiful," he says, his voice strained. My eyes open to look at him. His head goes back, his jaw tight, eyes closed, and I can tell he's trying to hold off until I come. "I need you to come, baby," he says, and his eyes open as he leans forward, pulling one nipple into his mouth before biting down on it. And that's all I needed to send me over. My legs tighten, my hips raise, and that heat and weight turn into a tingle. Then I shatter, seeing a million colors dance behind my closed eyelids. I moan out his name, shoving my face into his neck.

"Shit," I hear Cash say as his hips jerk before leaning forward and biting onto my shoulder. His movements slow and I can feel myself still convulsing around him, trying to pull him deeper. "That went better than I expected." The skin of my neck muffles his words.

"What?" I run my hands though his hair and wrap my legs a little tighter around him.

"I didn't think I would be able to hold out until you came." He licks my shoulder where he had bitten it. His head leans back so I can see his face. "Hey." He smiles, and both of his dimples make an appearance. His finger runs from my forehead to my chin.

"Hi," I say softly back; he is so handsome, and I can still feel him inside me, and I know that it's stupid and immature, but I want to stand up and jump on the bed while yelling 'I just had amazing, mind-blowing sex with Cash Mayson!'

"What's that smile?" he asks, leaning in to kiss me.

"Just happy," I say, tilting forward to kiss him. His cock twitches inside of me, and he groans before slowly sliding out. My eyes close slightly, and a soft mewl climbs up my throat at the loss of him.

"Let's shower." He kisses my lips, then my chest and belly, as he climbs off the bed. Once he's up, he pulls me up so we're both standing next to the bed. "Then we can come back here and do that again." His smile is wicked before he kisses me, leading me into the bathroom. I stand behind him, watching his muscles move as he tosses the condom into the trashcan and leans in to turn on the shower. Once he has the temperature right, he looks over his shoulder at me, his eyes traveling down my body. "I have wanted to see you naked, soapy, and wet since we were in Asher's shower. I guess sometimes wishes do come true." He smiles, taking my hand, pulling me in and under the showerhead. His hands work warm water through my hair, then shampoo and conditioner. I close my eyes, relaxing into the feeling of him touching me. "Am I putting you to sleep?" He chuckles, and I open my eyes to see him with a big, pink loofa that is covered with bubbles. I raise an eyebrow, looking at it. "It's the only color they had." He shrugs and starts washing me slowly. When he's finished, he kisses me, and then pulls me behind him and starts washing his own hair. I pick up the same loofa and dump tons of soap on it, washing his back and watching the bubbles slide down his skin and onto the floor of the shower. When he turns around to face me, he's hard again. He takes the loofa from me.

"Hey, I was doing that." I pout, feeling like he just stole my candy.

"I know, baby, but with your hands on me, I can't control myself, and I didn't bring a condom in here."

"Oh," I say, looking him over, my hands tingling with need to touch him.

"You need to get on birth control," he says, and my eyes go to his.

"I'm on birth control. I got on it after Ashlyn was born because my cycle went all wonky," I say, and I can feel my eyebrows pull together.

"You are?"

"Yes. But that doesn't protect against other things."

"I haven't been with anyone else, Lil, not since long before my divorce. Even when I was married, I used a condom."

My stomach rolls, and I hide my face with my wet hair. "Oh." I bite the inside of my cheek. I hate that he was married. I hate that I forget about it all the time, and then something reminds me that this hasn't always been mine.

"Hey, what's going on in there?" he says, tapping my forehead.

"I just hate it so much. Can we not talk about you sleeping with her? Like, ever?" I say, feeling like I want to cry.

"I hate it too." He nods, pulling me into him. "We can use protection until you feel ready not to, okay?" He rubs his hands down my back. "I'm clean. I get tested every year with my physical for insurance." His body stills, then he pulls me away from him. "What about you?"

"What about me?"

"Have you?" His jaw clenches. "I mean, have you been tested lately?"

I shake my head. "Cash, you're the only person I've ever slept with. Before a few minutes ago, the one time we did it, when I gave you my virginity, was the only time I've ever made love. I was too concerned with Ashlyn. I didn't have time to date...or even really want to."

He looks at me with a mixture of shock and awe. "I'm so happy I'm the only one you've ever been with. I don't think I would be able to handle it as gracefully as you do, knowing I've been with others," he says gently. I lay my forehead against his chest. "I don't mind not using condoms. I mean, I got pregnant with Ashlyn when we used a condom before."

"Yeah, and the same thing happened with—" he starts to say her name but stops, and his arms around me tighten so much that the air rushes out of my lungs.

"What's wrong?" I say when I'm able to take a breath.

"Nothing, baby, let's get out," he says abruptly, turning away from me to turn off the water and get out of the shower, pulling a towel down from the shelve and wrapping it around me before getting one for himself.

"Are you sure you're okay?"

"I'm good. You're here; my kids are here. I couldn't be better." He smiles, but it doesn't reach his eyes, and I want to ask again but know it will be pointless, so I just sigh and let it drop.

Once we're back in the bedroom, I start to pull out one of his shirts from the dresser. I squeak when he picks me up, carrying me to the bed and tossing me onto the mattress before ripping my towel from my body.

"What are you doing?" I don't know why I ask; I can tell by the look in his eyes exactly what he has planned.

"I'm going to explore you." He smiles, climbing up the bed.

"Oh," I breathe when I feel his hands at my feet start to move up my legs.

"Yeah, I missed you. I missed the way you laugh." He pulls my leg up, kissing the inside of knee. "I missed your smell." He pulls my other leg up, kissing that knee as well. "I missed your touch." He runs his hands up the tops of my thighs. "I missed the way we could talk for hours about nothing and everything." His hands go to my stomach, then up my rib cage. "I missed your kisses." His knees spread my legs wider. "I missed your mouth." He leans forward, his mouth landing on mine. "I love you, and I'm so glad I have a second chance," he whispers against my lips, his forehead touching mine before sliding back inside me. And for the rest of the night, we make love, touch, talk, and share. He explores me and lets me return the favor. When I close my eyes to go to sleep, my body is tucked tight next to his, my head on his shoulder, my leg between his, and his arm wrapped around my waist. I love him, and I'm happy to have a second chance too.

Chapter 6

Cash

"Shit." I run across the kitchen into the living room when I see Spike is making a run for it. I grab him just as he starts to get behind the entertainment stand. "Jax," I call down the hall towards his room where he and Ashlyn are playing, waiting for breakfast.

"Yeah, Dad?" he yells back, and I shake my head. I really must have worn my woman out if she's sleeping though this craziness. I smile and feel my dick jump knowing she's in my bed with only my t-shirt on, my marks all over her body. Damn, I love my kids, but right now, I want them gone. *If they were older, I would give them keys to the car and a wad of cash to get them out of the house*, I think as I walk down the hall towards the bedroom.

"Hey, when I call you, you come to me; don't yell. Got it?" I ask as soon as I enter the room and make eye contact with my son.

"Yes, Dad," he grumbles, looking at Spike in my hands, then over to Spike's cage that is now hanging open. "Oh, he got out."

"Yeah, he got out," I say, handing him the damn ferret. "You need to make sure you lock that up when you're not playing with him." I point to the cage.

"Sorry," he says, looking at me before going over and putting Spike away.

"Daddy, I'm hungry." Jesus, I love hearing her call me Daddy. I look down at my daughter.

"I'm making breakfast now, beautiful." I run my hand over her soft hair.

"Okay," she sighs before picking up her doll, sitting down on the ground, and brushing its hair.

"I'll call you two when breakfast is ready," I tell both of them and ruffle Jax's hair before leaving the room. I was nervous about him taking to Ashlyn and Lilly, but he has been awesome, and there haven't really been any jealousy issues. I wonder if that's because of how much Jax has taken to Lil; there are times when he seems unsure, but she is always affectionate with both of the kids. I walk back into the kitchen and finish putting the stuff together for making pancakes...well, I add water to the mix. I'm getting ready to start putting pancakes on the griddle when out of the corner of my eye I see Lilly come around the corner, looking adorably sleepy. Her hair is up on the top of her head, her face rumpled with sleep. She still had my t-shirt on, but I can see she's put on a pair of sleep shorts underneath. We both just stand staring at each other. All I can think is that I want this every day, and I would kill to have it. I watch fascinated as her hand goes to her neck and her cheeks turn a light pink. I know she has seen the marks I left on her. I couldn't help it; she makes me crazy, and I want her to always know that she belongs to me. My eyes drop to her mouth, then to her breasts. I can see the tips of her nipples through my shirt. When my eyes make it back to hers, the pink of her cheeks have darkened. "Hi," she says quietly.

"Come here." I hold out my hand. She looks at it for a second before taking a step towards me.

"Um...where are the kids?" She starts to look around, but before she has a chance to take her eyes off me, I wrap my hand around the back of her neck and pull her closer so her body is fully against mine.

"The kids are playing." I wrap my other arm around her waist, dragging up the back of my tee so I can run my fingers along her skin. "How are you feeling?" I ask, leaning down to press my mouth to hers.

"O-okay." Her stuttered word is said against my lips. I smile, pulling her closer, my face going into her neck, and her subtle smell of lavender makes me groan.

"Are you sore?" I ask against her ear before licking her lobe and pulling it between my lips.

"Or can you still feel me here?" I run my hand down her back, over her ass and in-between her legs from behind. She gives a soft moan and I lean back so I can see her face when she answers me.

"I'm okay." I can feel her hand on my arm tighten, and the nails of her other hand sink into the skin of my side. My fingers that are resting between her legs flex, and she comes up on her tiptoes. "The kids," she says as her mouth comes to mine. I put my mouth on hers, licking her lips, making her open up for me. I love the way she tastes. And I love that she gives just as good as she gets. Her tongue chases mine. I feel a rumble start up my chest, and I know I need to stop this before it gets out of hand and I put her on the counter, spreading her out. I reluctantly pull my mouth away from hers, shoving my face into her neck, trying to get my control back.

"You want coffee?" I ask into her hair, not moving my hands from her neck or her pussy.

"Yes," she hisses out, and I know she's not saying yes to coffee, but to the feel of my hand. I can feel her heat through the thin material of her shorts, and I fight with myself about sliding my hand up the leg of her shorts so I can feel how wet she is.

"Come sit with me while I make breakfast." I remove my hand from between her legs, moving her so that her back is to the counter where I can easily pick her up, setting her next to the stove. I move around, getting her a cup of coffee before coming back to her. "How did you sleep?" I ask, handing her the cup of coffee and stealing a quick kiss.

"Really well." She smiles, tilting her head to the side like she's studying me. "How did *you* sleep?"

"Better than I have in years. I like knowing that my family is all under one roof. I like waking up to the feel of you tucked in next to me." I watch her face turn soft, and I can't help but kiss her again. "Do you feel up to going to look at cars today?" I ask, pouring pancake batter onto the griddle.

"Cash." The way she says my name is like a full conversation; she doesn't even have to say anything else, and I already know exactly what she is thinking.

"Okay, that came out wrong," I say and look over at her. "It sounded like a question, and it wasn't. We're going to go look at cars today."

"I knew it," I hear her say under her breath, and I chuckle.

"Babe, you're not driving that piece-of-shit anymore; it's not safe or reliable." I pull out a spatula from the drawer and start to flip the pancakes. "Honestly, I'm surprised I lasted this long. I was thinking about slashing your tires; I hate that fucking car.

"Fine, I know I need a new car. I will just use some of my rainy day money for a down payment."

"Were you not here when we had this conversation before? I know I told you I'm buying you a new car."

"Cash," she says again, then shakes her head, "I need to help."

"Lil, you have done more than your fair share over the last few years."

"You can't just come in and take over, Cash."

"I'm not taking over, but if there is a way that I can make things easier for you and Ashlyn, then I'm going to do it." I watch as she rolls her eyes before taking a sip of coffee. "That's one."

"What?" she asks, looking all confused.

"One spanking for rolling your eyes."

"You do know that I'm a grown woman, right?"

"And?"

"And you can't threaten me with spankings."

"First, it's not a threat. Second, I can see that you want it. Every time I tell you that I'm going to spank you, your eyes light up and you wiggle around."

"I do not," she huffs out, wiggling on the counter, making me laugh as she glares.

"Breakfast is ready," I yell down the hall a few seconds later. I hear the kids' feet pounding down the wooden floor before coming around the corner into the kitchen.

"Yay, pancakes!" Jax yells.

"Yippieee! Can I have chocolate chips in mine?" Ashlyn asks, and Jax looks at her like she's a genius.

"And mine," he says, climbing up onto one of the stools.

"Sorry, guys, we don't have any, but we can get some for next weekend," I say, putting pancakes on plates for both of the kids. Lilly jumps down from the counter, goes to the fridge, and pulls out orange juice, pouring it into two plastic cups and setting it in front of each of them. Then she takes a banana and cuts it in half, putting a section on each of their plates before doing the same with an orange.

"What?" she asks when she catches me watching her closely. She is such a good mom. Last night in the shower, when she brought up the fact that we had used a condom when she got pregnant with Ashlyn, got me thinking. What are the chances that I could have used protection with two different women and gotten them both pregnant? That shit is as unlikely as winning the lottery. And as much as it pisses me off that it happened, and that Jules is most likely behind that shit, I have a hard time being pissed about it.

Or at least being pissed at the situation. If Lil didn't get pregnant, Ashlyn wouldn't be here. Lil would probably be married to some dude, having his kids, and I would have never heard from her again. She would have been the one who got away.

"Nothing." I pull my eyes off her, adding more pancakes to the griddle before pulling down a plate for the two of us.

"Can we go to the zoo?" Ashlyn asks, and I throw my head back laughing; she always wants to go to the zoo.

"Not today. Today we're going shopping for a new car for your mom."

"Oh." She pouts before shoving more food into her mouth. Just then, the doorbell starts to go off. I look over at Lilly and she shrugs. I'm not expecting anyone. Even before I make it to the door, I can hear kids yelling and people talking. "Shit," I mutter to myself, unlocking the door.

"Took you long enough," Trevor complains, shoving his way inside.

"What the hell are y'all doing here?" I watch as every person in my family files into my house.

"Put a damn shirt on." Asher shoves past me, covering November's eyes, making her and I laugh.

"You know this is my house, right? And it's a Saturday," I tell him, locking the door behind Nico after he comes inside.

"Yeah, but we thought that we could all plan something to do for the day," Trevor explains, going into the kitchen. I see Lilly's eyes get big; she's standing behind the counter, pulling at the hem of my shirt.

"I'm sorry, you guys. I'll be right back," she says, running off. I groan; I don't want this. I want to have a relaxing day with my woman and kids.

"Can ya'll watch the little ones while I go get dressed?" I don't even look at my brothers; I look at Liz and November when I ask my question.

"Sure," November says, and Liz nods. I make my way into my bedroom just in time to see Lilly taking my shirt off and a bra in her hand. She jumps when she hears the door close behind me.

"Do you think you may have gone a wee bit overboard?" she asks, holding her arms out to the side but gesturing with her hands to all the marks I left on her.

"Nope." I bite my lip, looking her over. Yeah, okay, it may have been overkill, but fuck if I care. If anyone were to get her clothes off, they would know that she is taken.

"It's a good thing it's cold and I can wear sweaters and jeans," she mumbles under her breath, putting on her bra. When she pulls down her shorts, her eyes meet mine. "It looks like I got attacked even between—" she starts to say between her legs, but points instead.

"I would say I'm sorry, but I would be lying." I walk over to the dresser, grabbing a shirt and a pair of jeans. I toss the shirt on the bed, kick off my sweats, and step into my jeans, making sure to tuck myself in so I don't zip my dick—that shit is never fun. When my head comes up, Lilly is watching me closely. "Are you okay?"

"You're not going to wear underwear?"

"No, for what?"

"I don't know." She shrugs, looking at the piece of satin in her hand.

"Don't even think about it," I groan, seeing her intentions.

"What?"

"Put them on."

"Why? If you can—" I cut her off, pulling her close and putting my mouth on hers.

"As it stands right now, I'm going to have a hard enough time being around you today, if I know you're not wearing underwear that is going to do me in. And you're likely to end up bent over in every small room with a little bit of privacy that we come across," I tell her, biting down on her bottom lip before licking it. Her mouth forms an O before she gets a small devious smile on her face. "Shit." I press my now-hard cock into her belly. "Don't fuck with me, baby." I wrap my arms around her, hugging her before kissing the top of her head. "Let's go see what everyone is up to, then figure out a way to ditch them," I say, kissing her once more on the mouth before stepping away and putting on my shirt.

I make my way out of the bedroom after feeling Lilly up and helping her put on her panties. I smile thinking about the way I got her to put them on. I fix my face into a firm mask before walking into the kitchen. Asher is now standing in the kitchen in front of the griddle, flipping pancakes.

"What are you guys doing here?"

"We wanted to come and see what you guys were doing today," Trevor says, and I almost laugh. "Well, we're not going to be here; we're going to get Lilly a car," I tell them all before picking up my plate off the counter and finish eating.

"So we can all go," Nico says, and everyone else agrees. I look around, seeing that there is no real way to get out of this, so I may as well just have them tag along. Who knows, maybe if they are there with me, Lilly will be more agreeable. I know she won't argue in front of everyone. I rub my hands together thinking I couldn't have planned this better if I tried.

"All right, we'll leave after Lilly finishes eating breakfast," I tell everyone.

"You're not buying me a brand new car that costs more than I make in a year," Lilly yells, walking back and forth in front of all of us. We're all standing outside the dealership. Phil is looking around nervously; I don't blame the poor guy. When we first got here, I told him what I wanted for her, and he of course, being a salesman, took us to the top-of-the-line model with all the bells and whistles. The newest model GMC Acadia was nice; actually, it was perfect, and she was getting it whether she wanted it or not.

"Baby, I am. It's safe and good on gas," I tell her.

"I will have to sit on a phone book just to see over the damn steering wheel. How the hell is that safe?"

"Actually, the seats are completely adjustable," Phil says, earning a glare from Lilly. And laugher from our group.

"This is not okay." She stomps her foot.

"Look, maybe we can compromise?"

"Compromise?" she yells, throwing her hands up in the air. "Like what? I say you're not going to buy me a car, and you force it on me? That kind of compromise? Yeah, no thanks."

"Calm down, okay? I want you to be safe, and this is one of the safest cars available."

"Actually, we have a Mercedes Benz tha—" I look up and narrow my eyes on Phil. "Never mind," he mumbles before walking off.

"Take a deep breath."

"I don't like this," she whispers, and I see tears in her eyes. "I didn't want a car to begin with, and I don't want that thing." She point at the Acadia.

"Why don't you want it?"

"I just don't. And I don't want you to spend that kind of money on me."

"You know, if you were to sue me for back child support, you would be rolling in the dough."

"I would never do that," she gasps.

"Lil," I laugh, running my fingers along her jaw, "I know that you wouldn't, but the point is that you could. I haven't been around since Ashlyn was born. I wasn't there to help you with bills or expenses. I want you to have nice things. There is no reason for you to struggle anymore. So please, let me do this for you," I beg. It's not lost on me how different this situation is compared to the one I was in with Jules. Jules wanted everything; she was never satisfied, and if I took her to a car dealership and told her to pick out a new car, she would have left me filling out the paperwork while she took off in her new ride.

"I don't like it."

"I know, but can you just do this one thing for me? I want to know that you're safe, and that when you have my kids in the car with you, they're safe too."

"You say 'this one thing', but I know that you're going to have a million other things." She pouts.

"You know you're really fucking cute when you're upset?"

"You're so..." she stops, like she's trying to think of a word to use to describe me.

"Annoying," Liz supplies, laughing.

"Yes," Lilly says, looking at Liz. "Thank you."

"You are so annoying," she says, looking back at me.

"But you love me."

"Don't remind me," she grumbles, so I bend her back and kiss her until I feel her body relax, and I know I have her right where I want her.

"Let's go get your new car," I say kissing her again before swinging her up into my arms. "Get the paperwork ready, Phil."

"On it." He smiles.

"Yay!" I hear Ashlyn yell.

~~*

It is official. My family is fucking crazy. Yes, they mean well, but they need to leave; I want to be alone with my woman and kids. I look around the room, realizing that everyone is settling in, getting comfortable like they plan on staying all fucking night.

"What the fuck is your problem?" Nico asks, making my eyes narrow.

"What the hell is going on? You guys have never all stopped by on the weekend. And now it seems like you're never going to leave."

"We wanted to come show our support and prove that we do like Lil," he says, looking into the kitchen where she and November are standing.

"First, don't call her Lil. Second, since when have you liked her?" I ask, watching Lilly laugh at something that November says.

"She's grown on me, and I know that it's not some game or a show that she's putting on for us."

"Lil's not like that," I tell him, taking a pull from my beer.

"So you can call her Lil, but I can't?"

"Pretty much." I shrug.

166

"Daddy, can we go outside?" Ashlyn asks, coming to stand in front of me.

"Yeah, baby, let's go get your coat."

"I'm coming too," Asher says.

"Me too," Trevor says.

"Oh, me too," Nico says in a high-pitched girl's voice.

"You're silly, Uncle Nico," Ashlyn says giggling, making Nico smile. He bends, picking her up and holding her upside-down.

"Do you still think I'm silly?" he asks, bouncing her up and down, making her laugh louder. I look up and see Lilly watching; our eyes meet for a second before hers go to Nico, going soft. She loves that Ashlyn is able to experience this; being an only child and her parents' siblings living so far away when she was growing up, she wasn't able to spend much time with her aunts and uncles.

"Okay, you're not silly-y-y-y," Ashlyn squeals before Nico rights her and sets her feet on the ground, making sure she is stable before letting her go and ruffling her hair.

"All right, get your jacket and see if Jax wants to go out with you," Lilly says, walking into the living room.

"You good, baby?" I put my arm around her waist, kissing her hair.

"Yeah." She leans in, wrapping her arm around my back. "Should we order pizza for everyone?"

"No," I say, just as everyone else says yes, and all the kids start yelling, "PIZZA!"

"Honey," Lilly whispers, her fingers digging into my side. I look into her eyes and shake my head.

"Jesus, fine, you girls call it in, and me and the boys will go pick it up," I tell her, kissing her forehead before dipping my head to the side and whispering into her ear, "You owe me later." I watch her face turn a light pink before hiding it against my chest. "Love you, Lil," I say into the hair at the top of her head.

"Love you, too," she says, her words muffled by my shirt.

"All right, I'm going to take the rug rats outside. Let me know when you guys order the pizza so we can go pick it up."

"Sure," she mumbles. I tilt her head back with a thumb under her chin so I can kiss her. The second my lips touch hers, I pull her a little tighter against me, wanting to absorb as much of her into me as I can.

"Stop being gross!" Jax yells.

"Yeah, that's icky," Ashlyn says, and Lilly smiles against my mouth.

"Get used to it," I can hear my oldest niece July say, and I smile, rubbing my nose against Lilly's before pulling away.

"All right, let's go." I throw out a hand towards the door and watch as all the kids start to run outside.

"So I did a background check on Lilly," Nico says once we're outside and all the kids are running around screaming. His words catch me off guard and I turn to look at him.

"Say what?" I ask. I can feel my body preparing to attack.

"Look, I did it a while back after the first time you saw her. I wanted—" That was it; I couldn't take anymore. I looked around, seeing if anyone was watching us before putting him in a headlock. We have all been fighting since we were kids; yes, we all love each other, and yes, we are close, but we *are* male, and sometimes you had to let that shit out through your fist. I pull his head down low so that if any of the kids were to see us, they would think that we are just horsing around.

"I'm going to say this one fucking time, and I want to make sure you hear me, so I'm going to speak really slowly." I tightened my arm around his neck, and it barely registers that he isn't fighting back. Nico is as big as Asher and has filled out even more since working for Kenton, and I know if he wanted to, he could put me on my ass any other time, but right now, I'm so pissed that I feel like The Hulk. "Lilly is off limits. She is not Jules; she's not some chick that I'm just fucking with. She is someone I have history with. And the person I plan to spend the rest of my life with. So I'm gonna tell you like I told Dad—if you're not on Lil's side, you're not on my side. Do you understand?"

"What the fuck?" I hear before I'm being pulled away from Nico. I brush Trevor and Asher off and right myself.

"It's cool; we're cool," Nico says, holding up his hands.

"Are we cool? Tell me what I want to hear." I look at all three of my brothers. "You three all need to tell me that you're on her side."

"Dude, chill, we're all on Lil's side," Trevor says softly.

"Don't fucking call her Lil," I growl, and Nico laughs.

"Look, we get it, and we're all sorry," Nico says smiling.

"So why the fuck did you have a background check done on her?"

"I wanted to see what she's been up to," he mumbles, and I run my hands down my face.

"I love you all, but I know what I'm doing. This situation with Lil is stressful enough for her. If

170

she finds out that you're running background checks or anything else," I tug my hat off and run my hands though my hair, "that might send her running." I close my eyes and shake my head. When I open my eyes back up, I look at the three of them. "I have to tell you, if she runs, I'm following her. Even if that means moving to another state."

"The only reason I said anything was because I wanted you to know that I didn't think she would commit check fraud," Nico says, looking worried.

"I already knew that without you telling me you did a background check, dick. It's called trust."

"You know, if you ever did something like that to November, I would kick your ass!" Asher says, glaring at Nico.

"Yep, I would fuck you up if you did that shit to Liz."

"Just don't do anymore shit like that," I say.

"You have my word." Nico nods. "She's good for you. I see that, and I can tell she loves you and Jax," Nico says.

"Just, all of you, stay out of my love life."

"You haven't had a love life in a long time; we're all waiting to see what happens," Asher chuckles.

"This isn't *The Real Housewives*; this is my life!" I shout.

"Hey, that's a good show," Trevor mumbles.

"You're all idiots," I toss over my shoulder as I walk off to join the kids. A few hours later, after everyone has left and the kids are in bed, Lil and I are cuddled up on the couch watching *Ridiculousness*, laughing our asses off at the stupid things people do, when she reaches over, grabbing the remote and pausing the TV.

"Thank you for having everyone over today," she says, turning towards me.

"I didn't want them here," I tell her, and her eyebrows come together.

"What?"

"I didn't invite them. They just showed up. All I wanted to do today was relax with you and the kids."

"Oh," she says, her eyes searching my face.

"They wanted to prove to you that they've got your back. They do care about you, baby."

"But—"

"No buts." I cover her lips with my finger. "They know that they shouldn't have placed you in the same category as Jules. They wanted to show you that we are all family, and we all stick together."

"I really like them all. And I'm happy they have been here for you," she says, leaning in and kissing my chest before turning her body back around and laying her head against my chest. Then she lifts the remote in her hand towards

172

the TV and the sound of Rob Dyrdek's voice fills the room. I sit watching the show, but not really seeing it. My mind is full of thoughts about the past, and if I'm lucky, what the future will hold for all of us. I hold Lil a little closer when I hear her laugh. This is my boom. I knew it years ago, and I know it now.

Chapter 7

Lilly

"Stay away from my husband." I look up, along with every child in my classroom.

"Can I help you?" I stand up from where I was sitting on the floor in a beanbag chair having story time.

"You need to stay the fuck away from my husband!" It takes a second for me to realize who she is and who she's talking about. She looks different from the last time I saw her at Cash's parents' house; her once brown hair is now blonde, and she's wearing jeans and a sweater that is cut low, showing way too much cleavage and it looks like she has lost twenty pounds.

"Let's talk in the hall," I say softly. I have a classroom full of seven and eight year olds; I don't need her to start yelling and screaming in the middle of my classroom.

"I don't want to talk to you in the fucking hall. I want you to tell me that you will stay away from my husband." I walk to the door of my classroom. Once there, I turn slightly to look at my students.

"Molly, will you please finish reading the rest of the story to the class?" Molly stands, picking the book up off the floor before sitting in my chair. Once I see that she is seated, I turn to face Cash's ex.

"Let's just step out into the hall." I step out, hoping that she will follow me and not cause a scene in front of my students.

"I told you already, I'm not talking to you in the fucking hall. I am not talking to you at all. The only thing that I want is for you to tell me that you are going to stay the fuck away from my husband."

"Can you please calm down? There are children here and you are scaring them," I say quietly, stepping further into the hall. She finally steps out with me. I take a breath, feeling better knowing that she is away from my kids. I pull the door closed behind me, turning to face her.

"So, tell me that you are going to stay away from him." She crosses her arms over her chest, glaring at me. I am not going to stay away from Cash. I love him. He is amazing with Ashlyn and Jax. He makes me smile, and I am really happy for the first time in a long time.

"You and Cash are divorced, and if you have a problem, you need to talk to him about it," I tell her, using the same tone I use when speaking to students that are misbehaving.

"He will always be mine, and when I want him back, he will come back to me." It was on the tip of my tongue to ask her why she did what she did to me—making me believe that Cash had wanted me to get an abortion while holding her own pregnancy over his head. "I will talk to him." She leans forward, forcing me back. "I am going to let him know that if he doesn't stop seeing you, I will make it so he won't see his son."

My stomach drops. "You can't do that." I do not understand why she is so hateful.

"You, bitch, do not get to tell me what I can do. Just stay the fuck away from him!" she yells.

"Lilly, are you okay?" My eyes fly to the door across the hall from mine. David has his head peeking out, looking between Jules and me.

"Yes, fine. Sorry about that, David. She was just leaving."

"I'm not leaving until you say the words I want to hear." I look down the hall, watching as the principal starts heading our way. My pulse speeds up; she looks mad—really mad. Oh God, I was going to get fired. I knew right then that my job had just been lost because of Jules.

"Lilly, what's going on? You have students, and I have gotten three calls from different teachers about cursing and yelling in the hallway."

"I'm sorry, Mrs. Jennings. She was just leaving." I look at Jules and her face completely changes;

her eyes start to tear and she points at me. "She was yelling and cursing at me. She is having an affair with my husband. I came here to talk to her, to try to get her to understand that I have a child." She breaks down sobbing. I am stunned. I cannot believe that this is happening.

"Oh, my God," I whisper in shock. Mrs. Jennings looks at me with complete disgust, and she would believe it; rumor has it that her husband had been caught cheating on her with a close friend.

"That's not true." My voice is so quiet it can hardly be heard over the sounds coming out of Jules's mouth.

"Lilly, I am going to have to ask you to wait in my office while I find someone to take over your class for the day."

"Mrs. Jennings, please." She glares at me, pulling Jules into her arms.

"You need to get your bag from your classroom and wait for me in my office. I will be there shortly." I look between her and Jules before walking into my classroom. I know it's pointless to argue with her right now. I turn away from them, walking back into my class where my students are all talking quietly around the reading rug.

"I'm sorry, you guys, but I am going to be leaving for the day. Mrs. Jennings is going to be sending in another teacher to take over. Until she gets here, pull out your solar project and start working on that." I watch as they all get up off the ground, going to their desks to start working. I go to my desk and grab my bag, along with a few personal items that I keep in my desk. I want to tell my class how much I have enjoyed teaching them, but I know that they are already upset about the way Jules was acting, and if I say the wrong thing, it could upset them even more. I leave the class, closing the door softly behind me. I walk around Jules and Mrs. Jennings, and head straight for the principal's office—*what a cliché*. When I get there, her secretary shows me in and I take a seat, waiting for my execution. It takes about fifteen minutes for Mrs. Jennings to enter her office, and I know the second I see her face that my job is not salvageable.

"Mrs. Donovan, what happened today is unacceptable," she says in a tone that makes me shift in my seat.

"Yes, I know, but if you—"

"I am going to be turning your case over to the school board," she cuts me off.

"But if you would—"

"You will be put on leave until the board is ready to hear your case. You will be assigned an advisor from the union." She wasn't going to let me speak; her own situation wasn't allowing her to. I shake my head.

"Mrs. Jennings," I try again.

"You're dismissed until further notification. Your belongings will be packed up and waiting for you in the attendance office. You can pick it up any time after tomorrow." I sit there for a second, trying to come up with something to say, but no words are making it from my brain to my mouth. "That will be all, Ms. Donovan." She waves her hand, then looks down at some papers on her desk and starts writing. I'm dismissed. I stand on shaky legs, trying to keep it together, at least until I'm in my car. Once outside, the cool air helps make it easier to breath. I dig around in my bags until I find my keys, fumbling with them until the door unlocks. I sit behind the wheel, laying my head against the headrest. I have no idea what I'm going to do. I open my eyes when there is a tapping on my window. I turned my head, seeing Jules. I'm not going to roll down my window or open my door. I'm done dealing with her. I put my key in the ignition and turn my car on. She starts banging on my window harder, yelling at me to open the door. I don't even look at her when I click my seatbelt into place before putting the car in drive. That's when my window shatters. I scream, looking up at Jules as she reaches her hand in, grabbing a handful of my hair. I hit the gas. Pain rips through my skull. She runs with my car for a second before being forced to let go. Tears start streaming down my cheeks from the pain at the back of my head and the stress of the day. I look in my rearview mirror, seeing if I can spot her following me, but she is nowhere in sight. When I pull into a large parking lot, I put my car in park, digging out my phone. I need to talk to Cash and tell him what happened. Once I finally get my phone and call his number, his phone rings once before going to voicemail. I lay my head back for a second before deciding that I may as well go pick up Ashlyn from Susan. When I call her, she tells me that she and Ashlyn took lunch to the jobsite, and to meet her there. I hang up, putting my car back into drive. My hands are shaking the whole way; I don't even remember driving when I pull up next to Susan's car. I don't even think; I hop out of the car, glass falling to the ground at my feet. Nico walks around the corner at the same time, his eyes going from my face to the window, and then to the glass that is now littering the ground.

"What the fuck happened?" he growls. Tears fill my eyes. I shake my head, not knowing where to start. He pulls me into his arms, rubbing my back.

"What the fuck are you doing?" I hear Cash's voice, and I want so badly to see him, but I can't lift my head. I think I am in shock; it's so hard to take a breath.

"Breathe, Lilly. Breathe," I hear Nico plead, right before I am turned and arms wrap around me, and the smell that is all Cash washes over me.

"Baby, what the fuck is going on?" Cash says softly into my ear. I pull at his shirt, needing to be closer to him. I start to cry harder. "Baby, I need you to tell me what's happened."

"I got fired," I breathe out, stepping out of his arms. I bend over, putting my hands on my knees, trying to catch my breath.

"You got fired?"

"Yes, Jules came to my classroom and told me to stay away from you, and then my principal showed up. Jules started to cry, and then I got fired." I try to get all the words out in-between harsh breaths.

"Why is your window broken?" Nico asks. I look up to see Cash's concerned eyes on me.

"Jules broke it before I could get away," I tell them.

"Jules broke your car window?" I nod, hugging my waist. I want to sit down before I fall over. Cash takes two steps, pulling me into him; his hand goes to the back of my head to tuck my face into his chest, and the pain has me crying out. "What the fuck?" I put my hand to the back of my head. There's not a bump, but I can feel a slight bald spot, along with heat coming off the area. "What's wrong with your head?"

"She had a handful of my hair when I drove off."

"I'm going to fucking kill her!" Cash growls, holding me tighter.

"You need to press charges," Nico says looking at me, and I can see that he is barely holding on to his temper.

"I don't want to make it worse," I say, looking up at Cash.

"If you don't press charges, there will never be any proof of what she did," Cash says.

"I hate this. Why is she doing this?" I ask, laying my forehead against his chest.

"She's crazy, baby. I don't think there is a reason for anything she does."

"Why did she let you divorce her if she was going to act crazy?"

"She didn't *let* me divorce her. She tried to contest it, but her plan fell through when she saw how much money it would cost her to keep playing games. She tried to get custody of Jax, but the judge who had the case, didn't believe he would be in good hands if placed with her."

"I think she needs medication," I say quietly. There is no way someone can act like she does and not need serious help. I pull my head up and look between Cash and Nico, and I can tell they are having a silent conversation. "What?" I ask, looking at Nico.

"I'm going to call the cops and they can meet us here. When they leave, Cash and I can take your car to get fixed."

"Are you sure about this? I mean, do you think if we ignore her, she will go away?" I ask, looking between the two of them.

"Fuck no. That bitch is like crabs—you ignore them and they spread," Nico says. A laugh bubbles up my throat, and I am just about to ask him if he is speaking from experience when he says, "No, I have not had that shit, so don't even ask."

"Alrighty then." I bite my lip when he glares at me. I know that on the inside he is a big softy, but there are times when I can see an edge of darkness about him. It was the same thing I saw in their cousin Kenton when I met him at a bar-b-que we had a while back, but Kenton's darkness is right there out in the open. I don't know if it's because of the job he does, or the people in his life, but something about him scares me in a way I would never want to be on his bad side. I watch Nico pull out his phone; he walks off before he puts it to his ear.

"I'm really sorry about this," Cash says, and my eyes go to him.

"It's not your fault." He raises an eyebrow. "Okay, she's your ex, but it's still not your fault. I just can't believe that she went so far."

He sighs, laying his forehead against mine. "Me either, honestly."

"She said that she is going to get Jax."

"I have full custody. She's just spouting bullshit." I wrap my arms around his waist, trying not to think about the chance that Jules could ever get custody of Jax. I know how much Cash has

183

sacrificed for his son; I don't want anything to jeopardize that.

"Cops are on the way," Nico says, walking back over to us. "When they get here, I want you to make sure that you tell them everything that happened. And I want you to tell them that you are pressing charges and applying for a restraining order."

"Okay." I take a breath, letting it out slowly. It takes about thirty minutes for the cops to arrive. They ask a few questions and take pictures of my car window, and then the back of my head at Cash's demand. After they leave, I look at Cash and Nico. I can tell that they are up to something. "What's going on?" I ask impatiently.

"Nothing, sugar. Why don't you go see Ashlyn? She's in the trailer with Mom. Me and Cash will take your car and get the window replaced."

"But—"

"Baby, go inside. When you're ready, I want you to take my truck and the kids to my house. I will be home later."

"But—" I try again, getting sick of people not letting me get a word in. He shakes his head, and then wraps his arms around me, pulling me flush with him. His face goes into my neck, and I can feel him taking a few deep breaths.

"I want you to go inside and sit with Mom until you're ready to take the kids home," he repeats.

"What are you going to do?"

"I'm going to get your car fixed. Then I'm going to meet up with my dad."

"And that's all?"

"That's all," he says, avoiding my eyes.

"Please, don't do anything stupid. And you," I say, pointing at Nico, "if he gets in trouble, I'm going to hurt you."

Nico smiles, and then looks at Cash. "Whatever you say, sugar," he says, walking off to my car.

"Please be careful," I say, standing up on my tiptoes, pressing my mouth to his. Cash groans, wrapping his arms around me and plastering me against him.

"I won't be long. Hang out with Mom for a while, before you take the kids home. We can order in food if you want."

"So, you don't want fish sticks and tatter tots?" I ask, knowing that was the only thing left in our freezer.

"No, thanks." His face looks disgusted at the idea of fish sticks, making me laugh.

"Okay, I will see you in a little while."

"See you," I say, taking a step back. He starts to walk off, and then turns abruptly, walking back to me. His hand goes to the back of my neck and pulls me forward, being mindful of the back of my head, and this time, the kiss is all tongue and teeth, and when he pulls his mouth from mine, I'm completely breathless. "What was that?"

"Love you. See you when I get home," he says. His eyes flash before he turns and walks to my car, climbing inside. I go up the steps of the work trailer and watch as he pulls away. Once I can no longer see him, I go inside and sit with Susan for a while, watching the kids finish a project she has set up for them. While they are occupied, I explain to Susan what happened with the police, and why they took me in for questioning last week. I'm so worried she won't believe I didn't do what they accused me of, until she pulls me in for a hug, much like my mother would do. When she pulls away, she puts her hands on each side of my face, holding me gently.

"You know I wouldn't believe you could do something like that." She pushes my hair away from my face. "You are an amazing woman, Lilly, and I know you are a good person. You're good for my son, my grandson, and my family. I hate that I have missed so much time with you and my granddaughter, but now that you're here, I will do everything in my power to make sure you stay right where you are. You and Cash both deserve to have something good, and it's not very often that God offers you a second chance at love. I know Cash has told you some of the stuff that went on with Jules, but I'm sure that my son has kept most of that bottled up. I doubt any of us really know everything he went through. He

186

doesn't like people to feel sorry for him. But as God as my witness, I hope that woman burns in hell for what she did, not only to you and Ashlyn, but for the pain that she has caused—and continues to cause—my son and grandson. I know I shouldn't wish something like that even on my worst enemy, but she deserves it," she says, looking over at the kids. "You both have a lot to be thankful for."

"Thank you," I mumble over the giant lump that has invaded my throat.

"You don't need to thank me. That's what family does. We may all fight and argue and get on each other's nerves, but if one of us stumbles even slightly, there is always someone there to lend them a hand." Her eyes search my face before turning serious. "Be strong for my boys; they need a woman who will not only show them what the power of a strong woman's love is capable of doing for the soul, but they need a woman who will fight to keep them."

"I love them, both," I tell her, looking down at Jax, who is helping Ashlyn with the glue bottle. "If I could adopt Jax as my own son, I would do it in a heartbeat. He is so much like Cash that it's scary. He has a big heart for such a little guy."

"That's all I need to know," Susan says, and my eyes go back to hers, seeing tears fill them. I reach out and pull her in for hug. When we pull away, we're both a mess with mascara running down our cheeks. The kids both look at us like we're crazy, and then Jax makes me crack up when he tells us that his Uncle Nico said that girls are weird, and that's why he doesn't want one.

"Nico isn't going to know what hit him when he finally finds his girl," Susan says, and I agree completely.

~~*

"I have a question, and don't be afraid to say no," I say later that night when we're in bed. "I won't be mad; I promise," I say, and feel my stomach roll at the thought of him not wanting us.

"What is it?"

"Um...do you, um...doyouthinkthatAshlynandIcouldmoveinwithyou?" I ask quickly, trying to get it out. I won't be able to sleep until I know my daughter and I won't be homeless. I love Cash, and have wanted him to ask us to move in with him for a while now, but I don't want to pressure him about it. And Cash is Cash. I figure if he wants us here, he would find a way to make that happen. I feel his body start shaking, and I know he's laughing. I just have no idea what could be funny about this.

"Are you laughing?"

"Baby, I have wanted you to move in since I walked you and Ashlyn to your car outside of the Jumping Bean," he says laughing. Then his eyes

188

search my face and grow serious. "I hated knowing I would have to wait to see you again. And it's only gotten worse over the last few months. So yes, I want you to move in. I just didn't want to push you too fast," he says softly, and I can hear the vulnerability in his words.

"Do you think it's too fast?" I ask, rubbing my face against the skin of his side.

"It's not too fast." He squeezes me.

"The kids?"

"Will be fine. Ashlyn loves being here. Jax loves having you both here. Don't worry about this right now." He pulls me so I'm almost fully on top of him. "The kids are their happiest when we are all under one roof. Right now, I want you to sleep. Tomorrow, we will sit down with the kids and talk to them and just make sure that they are good with us all moving in together, okay?" he asks quietly.

"Yeah," I sigh, laying my head down against his chest and snuggling closer.

"I'm really sorry about all of this, Lil." My eyes fly open, and I lift my head to look at him. His eyes are full of pain, and I know that he thinks this is all his fault, but it's not. His ex is crazy and needs serious help.

"This isn't your fault."

"It is."

"It's not," I say, sliding one of my legs over both of his and rolling so I'm sitting on top of him. My hands go to his chest; feeling the hardness of his muscles under my palms makes me rock against him. "This isn't your fault," I repeat as I rock against him again. I moan when I feel him harden beneath me. His hands slide from my thighs up my waist, under the edge of his shirt. I want to forget about today. All I want is to feel him inside me, and feel the delicious sensations I experience when he takes it over.

"What are you doing?" he asks as his hands move over my skin, leaving a path of fire in their wake.

"If you have to ask, then I'm doing it wrong," I say, grinding down onto him. One of his hands squeezes my ass, the other goes to the back of my neck, pulling my face down to his.

"You're doing it right," he says as his mouth takes mine in a deep kiss, my fingers digging into his chest. I pull my mouth away from his, kissing my way down his chest to the edge of his boxers. I pull them down and lick up his length with one long stroke of my tongue. I want him in my mouth, but I really want him inside me, so I roll to my back, lift my hips off the bed and my legs into the air, pulling my panties off and tossing them away. I start to roll back when my ankles are grabbed and crossed above me, then pushed down towards my head.

"What are you doing?" I breathe as I feel his mouth suck the skin at the back of my thighs.

"If you have to ask, I'm doing it wrong," he says, and I can hear the smile in his voice. Then he licks me.

"Oh." I try to move, but in this position, I'm immobile. He licks me again, and this time I can feel his tongue slide lightly over my clit. Before he licks me again, I try to push up to get more contact, but he presses my legs closer to my body.

"So pink." He blows against my wet pussy. I then feel one finger circling right outside my entrance. "How long do you think I can keep you on edge before you flip out?"

"Not long." I shake my head frantically as I feel him lick me lightly again.

"Humm." I feel the vibration against me before he licks again, this time with a little more pressure. He keeps teasing with one fingertip inside me.

"Cash," I moan, trying to free my legs.

"No," he growls, holding me down. Then his mouth opens over me. I feel like I'm going to come out of my skin if he doesn't do something...more. I don't know what comes over me, but his mouth and fingers giving me *some* yet not *enough* makes me crazy. Finally, I can't take anymore, and somehow, I flip him over onto his back and impale myself on him.

"God," I moan loudly, and Cash sits up, his hand coming up to cover my mouth.

"Jesus." I can hear the strain in his voice. His hand leaves my mouth, and then his mouth is on mine, my hips rolling as I grind down hard. "Fuck, just like that, baby. Fuck me hard," he groans against my mouth, his words making me take him harder. I'm breathing so heavily that I feel like I'm running a race. I feel warm heat begin to fill my lower belly, and then Cash's hands are at my breasts, lifting both, his fingers pinching one nipple as he drags the other to his mouth. His teeth closing around my nipple and then adding suction making me cry out, and my movements still as I feel my orgasm consuming me. Like a volcanic explosion, red-hot heat flows through my veins before settling and slowing to a lazy flow. I have had orgasms before, but with him, they feel like they are taking me over, so consuming that time stops. My head falls forward then his hands are on my ass, pulling me up before dropping me down his length. I can still feel myself convulsing around him as he grows even larger, and my nails dig into his shoulders.

"Lilly." He says my name in a deep growl that I swear I can feel in my soul. His movements stop dead, his arms wrapping tightly around me. My face buries in his shoulder. Both our breathing is erratic. "Are you okay, baby?"

"Ummhum." I breathe against his skin, my eyelids feeling heavy. He lays down with his erection still inside me, his body wrapped around me.

"Sleep," he whispers into the top of my head. I can hear the steady beat of his heart and feel the rise and fall of his breathing, and like a lullaby, the sound and feel of it puts me to sleep.

Chapter 8

Cash

I wake up with a start and look around. I don't know what caused me to wake up until I hear another loud bang coming from the kitchen or living room. My stomach tightens as a surge of adrenaline rushes through me. I lean over Lilly's sleeping body and whisper in her ear that she needs to wake up. She grumbles something, trying to burrow into my side before I shake her gently. "Lilly, someone's in the house. I need you to get the kids and take them both into Jax's room. In the back of his closet is a hidden door. Go in there and wait for me."

"What?" She rolls of the bed quickly, looking around.

"Look at me, Lil," I say quietly as another loud bang sounds through the house. I can see Lilly start to panic by the light of dawn coming though the bedroom window. Her face is pale as she comes around to my side of the room, her body shaking. I pull her closer to me. "Listen to me," I tell her a little more firmly. "Take my phone," I say, handing her my cell. "Go get Ashlyn, take her to Jax's room, and do as I told you. Get both of them and yourself into the room in the back of Jax closet, shut the door, and call the police. Tell them that there is a break-in. Do not come out no matter what you hear. Do not come out until I come get you, or until the police come get you."

"Okay," she says, looking at the door.

"It will be okay," I tell her, going to the closet and pulling out a baseball bat. For the first time ever, I wish I kept a gun in the house.

"Be careful," she says, and I nod and open our bedroom door, looking both ways before sending Lilly across the hall. I watch her as she makes her way down to where Ashlyn's room is, and once she clears the doorway I hear another loud bang. I make my way towards the living room and look around the corner into the kitchen. I hear a cry from behind me, and I know that Lilly can't find the kids.

She can't find them because they are both in the kitchen standing on chairs that they have pulled up to the counter, and they have a bowl between them, along with a bag of flour.

"Cash," I hear cried from behind as Lilly plows into me. "The kids aren't there," she says franticly.

"I know," I tell her calmly.

"What? I just said the kids aren't in their rooms, and you don't care?" she yells. I pull her around the corner and both kids are looking nervously at us; the flour that was on the counter in the bag is now covering both of them, and there is a white cloud of it filling the kitchen. "Oh, my God," she says, leaving my side, rushing into the kitchen, pulling both of the kids in for a hug, and covering herself with flour in the process. "What are you guys doing?" she asks them, looking around and seeing that they have made a huge mess.

"We're making you breakfast," Jax says sheepishly, looking at me then around the kitchen.

"It's five in the morning," I say, putting the bat down before I cross my arms over my chest, looking around at the flour-bomb they set off.

"It's your birthday," Ashlyn says, looking around before looking at me.

"Yeah, and we wanted to make you breakfast in bed as a surprise," Jax says with a shrug.

"That was very nice of you both," Lilly says, looking over at me with her arms wrapped around the kids. I can't even speak; all I can do is look at my kids and woman. "That was really sweet, right, baby?" she asks softly, the look on her face causing a slow burn to fill my chest. I nod because I can't speak. "What do you guys say we get this mess cleaned up while Daddy goes and lays back down, and we can still take him breakfast in bed?" she asks the kids.

"We're not in trouble?" Jax asks.

"No, honey, you're not in trouble," she says, kissing the top of his head, "but let's get all this flour cleaned up, okay?" They both agree, and then get down off the chairs. Jax goes and gets the broom, while Ashlyn goes and gets the dustpan. Lilly comes to me, wrapping her arms around my waist. I'm barely holding on to my emotions. "Go back to bed, Daddy, so the kids and I can bring you breakfast," she says softly, smiling. I nod again, kissing her forehead before I turn and walk back to our room and straight into the bathroom, where I turn on the faucet and splash cool water on my face. My hands gripping the basin, my head down, I take a few breaths before I look at myself in the mirror.

My hair is a mess, and the stubble along my jaw is darker than normal. My eyes are crystal clear, and I can see only happiness in them. There is no sign of self-hate in my eyes anymore. I used not to even be able to look at myself in the mirror without cringing away. I hated my life; my son was the only thing who made every day worth fighting for. Now, I have a family with the first woman I ever loved. The only woman I have ever loved, besides members of my family. Lilly is someone who I will never take for granted, because I know how it feels to be without her and the light that she brings into my life. When I looked into Lilly's eyes in the kitchen and saw the same happiness shining back at me, it almost brought me to my knees. I take a few deep breaths before turning off the water. I go back into the bedroom and sit on the bed. I can hear laughter coming from the kitchen, and I can't help but smile when I hear the sound. I sit back against the headboard, pull out my iPad, and start searching for engagement rings. I have known since the beginning that I would ask Lilly to marry me, but having her live here over the last few weeks has only solidified that thought in my brain. I know that she has been worried about her case coming up in the school board and finding a job, but I like her home with the kids while I'm at work. I like knowing that my kids are getting the same thing I had growing up. I finally find a style of ring that I think Lilly will love, but I'm going to take the picture to the jewelry store in town and see if he can have something custom-made with a few changes to the design. I close down the web page when I hear the sound of feet coming down the hall, then the door is swung open and Ashlyn yells, "Surprise!"

"He already knows we were making him breakfast," Jax says.

"So?" Ashlyn says back, sticking out her tongue.

"Hey, now, none of that," Lilly says, smiling and walking to the bed carrying a tray that has pancakes with chocolate chips, eggs, and bacon, along with a small box that is wrapped in blue paper and a card.

"Happy birthday, Daddy," Ashlyn singsongs, climbing up onto the bed.

"Thank you, baby," I say, pulling her up onto my lap.

"Happy birthday," Jax says, climbing up onto the bed as well, and I pull him into my other side and kiss the top of his head.

"Thanks, little dude," I say, my voice hoarse.

"Happy birthday," Lilly says, looking between the three of us before her eyes meet mine, and I can see that tears are filling them.

"Thank you, babe." I mouth the words to her because I can't seem to speak. She nods before setting down the tray.

"Can I have some of your pancakes?" Ashlyn asks, and I look down at her and laugh.

"Me too," Jax says, making me laugh harder.

"There's more in the kitchen. I'll be right back," Lilly says, leaving the room. She comes back a few minutes later with another tray, this one with three plates, two juices, and a coffee. She sets the tray on the bed before climbing up to sit facing us. We all sit on the bed eating breakfast, and once we are done, I set my gift and card on the bedside table and take the plates into the kitchen, telling them that I would be right back. When I come back to the room, I sit back down with a kid on each side of me. I put the gift in my lap so I can read the card. On the front of it is a guy in jeans and a shirt; there is a little window, and when opened, the shirt says Super Dad. I smile before putting down the card, picking up the box, and looking at it for a few moments.

"Are you gonna open it?" Ashlyn asks, looking worried. I feel Lilly rub my leg, and I look at her and smile. I start to tear the paper away slowly.

"Dad, just open it," Jax says, eyeing the box like he wants to take it out of my hands and do it himself. I finish opening it and pull the small box out, lifting the lid. Inside is a pendent on a ball chain. "It's backwards," Jax says. I use one finger and flip the pendent over, and on the other side are three stones going down the center of it. All three different colors each represent the three people surrounding me.

"Do you like it?" Ashlyn asks, sitting up on her knees.

"I love it," I tell her, looking up from the pendent into her smiling face.

"That one is Jax. This one is me. And that one is Mommy," Ashlyn explains, pointing out each stone.

"Are you gonna put it on?" Jax ask.

"Yes," I whisper, taking it out of the box, holding it up, and looking at it before I slide it around my neck.

"You look pretty," Ashlyn says.

"Boys don't look pretty; they look handsome or cool," Jax tells Ashlyn.

"Nuh-uh, Mommy says Daddy is the prettiest boy that she ever saw." My eyes go to Lilly and I raise an eyebrow; she shrugs before covering her mouth, laughing at the look Jax gives her.

"Boys aren't pretty, right, Dad?" Jax asks me, and I turn to look at him. I don't even answer him; I just drag him to me, tucking him under my arm and kissing the top of his head.

"Thank you, guys, for my gift. I love it," I say, kissing Ashlyn's forehead. She wraps her little arms around my neck, hugging me tightly.

"Lobe you, Daddy," she says, and my eyes start to burn.

"You're welcome, Dad," Jax says, hugging my other side.

"Can we go to the zoo?" Ashlyn asks, pulling her face out of my neck and making me laugh.

"You always want to go to the zoo," Jax says.

"The zoo is fun."

"The zoo is lame," Jax returns, and they both jump up so they are standing on the bed and proceed to argue back and forth. I lean forward, grabbing Lilly's hand, dragging her up to me.

"Thank you for this," I tell her, running my fingers down the side of her face.

"You're welcome; we love you," she says, laying her head on my chest, her fingers picking up the pendent to look at it.

"Thank fuck," I whisper into her ear.

"Dad, we're not going to the zoo, are we?" Jax groans, flopping down onto the bed dramatically.

"Not today, little dude."

"But, Daddy…" Ashlyn whines.

"Ashlyn Alexandra, no whining," Lilly scolds, and Ashlyn crosses her arms over her chest in a pout.

"But I want to see the wions."

"If you keep up the attitude, little miss thing, you won't be going to the zoo for a very long time," Lilly says, and I bite the inside of my cheek to keep from laughing at the look on Ashlyn's face.

"Come here, baby." I hold out my hand and she flops down on top of me, making me grunt.

"How about we go do something that *everyone* will like doing?"

"Like what?" she asks.

"Well, we could go fishing," I say. I haven't gone fishing in a while, and I know that it's something that Jax enjoys doing.

"Yay! Fishing!" Jax yells.

"Are we gonna fish for salmon?" Ashlyn asks.

"No, baby. Catfish," I tell her, pushing her hair away from her face.

"Catfish?" Her face scrunches up, looking adorable.

"Yep, catfish."

"Are catfish hairy?"

"Catfish aren't hairy," Jax says, laughing and rolling around on the bed.

"All right, guys, if you want to go fishing you need to go brush your teeth and get dressed," I tell them both and watch as they bounce off the bed and run out the door.

"So you guys are going fishing? That's fun," Lilly says, and I smile.

"We are *all* going fishing."

"No, you and the kids are going."

"Babe, it's my birthday, which means it's *my* day. So we're all going fishing."

"Fine." She pouts, and I know exactly where my daughter got her attitude.

"What did you tell Ashlyn about her attitude?"

"I don't have an attitude."

"Good, so get your ass up and get ready to go fishing."

"Cash."

"Lil." I say her name, bending forward so that I can kiss her until she's quiet.

"So when it's my birthday, I get to do whatever I want, right?" she asks breathlessly.

"Yes, that's a new rule."

"Good. Hopefully, the *Fifty Shades of Grey* movie will be out then and we can go see it," she says, hopping off the bed and making a beeline for the bathroom. It takes me a second to realize what she said and I walk to the bathroom, opening the door and catching her just as she's getting in the shower.

"We're not going to see that movie," I tell her. I know all about that shit; Asher told Trevor and me all about it.

"You said I get to do whatever I want," she says, and I can tell by the tone of her voice that she's smiling.

"Okay, let me clarify that statement. We can do anything you want, as long as it's something that the kids can be involved in."

"Fine, I will go see it with Liz and November."

"Are you interested in BDSM?" I ask her. When Asher broke the book down for us, he said this dude Grey had a bad childhood, and when he got older he had an urge to dominate the women he slept with.

"Your kink is enough for me, thank you," she says, laughing. I pull the shower curtain back so I can look at her.

"I'm not into kink."

"You're not?" She tilts her head to the side, studying my face.

"No, I'm not," I say firmly.

"Hmm...so what about the time you held me down and wouldn't let me come? Or the time you tied me to the bed? Or all the times you've threatened—which you haven't followed through, I might add—to spank me? Or what about the time you had me on my knees and—"

"Fuck me, I'm into kink," I breathe. I have no idea where this is coming from. With Lilly, I always feel a need deep in my soul to show her who's in charge. I glare at her when she starts laughing. "Keep laughing and I'm going to turn your ass pink," I growl. She moans then puts her ass in my direction.

"Jesus, I think it's you that's really into kink," I say, and I can't help but to run my palm over the curve of her ass. "We don't have time to explore this right now, but later, I will definitely find out how kinky you are," I say, smiling when her cheeks turn rosy. "I'm gonna go check the kids." I adjust myself before leaving the bathroom. Walking out of the room, I try to think of every baseball stat or piece of construction equipment I know, and not the fact that tonight I'm going to see just how kinky I can get with my woman.

~~*

"He's so ugly!" Ashlyn cries as I remove the hook from the catfish's tail.

"He *is* ugly," Lilly says, still holding the pole.

"Babe, I don't know how you keep hooking them in everything but their mouths, but this is your third one. I hope Fish and Game doesn't show up." I smile and she laughs. We have been fishing for over an hour and none of us have caught anything except Lilly, and every time she catches one, it's never hooked in the mouth; it's always through some part of the fish's body—like this one now. Somehow, she caught it right through the tail.

"You said when I felt a nibble to tug, and I did what you said," she counters.

"I did say that." I smile, and once I finally have the hook removed, I put another worm on her it for her and set up Ashlyn's again with the fish dough. She doesn't like to see the worm on her hook. Jax is sitting next to me, handling his own fishing hook while massacring three worms on it. "Dude, you don't need so many worms."

"If the fish are hungry, they will like it." His little face is scrunched in concentration.

"Good point," I say, finishing with Lilly's bait and watch as she walks down the long dock. Her tight jeans show off the curve of her ass and her long legs. Ashlyn runs off, following close behind her wearing her life jacket. A few seconds later, Jax follows behind them wearing his life jacket as well. After I get my pole hooked up, I start making my way down dock when Lilly yells that she's got another one. I watch as she brings it out of the water. The fish is hooked through the mouth this time, his body flopping around. Lilly starts screaming when the fish makes its way towards her; she keeps backing away from him but still has the pole in her hand, so the fish is following her the whole way. I'm laughing so hard, and so are the kids, until Lilly continues her backwards walk right off the dock. She cries out right before there is a loud splash. I have never in my life met someone as clumsy as she is. I shake my head and run down the dock just as Lilly comes back up and starts treading water. She wipes her hair out of her face laughing. Both the kids are cracking up, dancing around the dock.

"I can't believe I did that," she laughs. I reach down to give her a hand up; she takes it then tugs, and I'm falling over the edge of the dock into the water with her. When I come up, I'm sputtering. I look at Lilly, who is laughing her ass off, then up at the kids, who are looking down on both of us with giant smiles on their faces.

"You think this is funny?" I ask, and then start to splash water onto the deck at the kids.

"No, Daddy! There are fish in that water!" Ashlyn yells, running away while Jax looks at me, then Lilly, and jumps in.

"This is so much better than the zoo," Jax says, climbing onto my back.

"Come in, love bug," Lilly calls.

"Will the fish bite me?"

"No, they are all scared," Jax says.

"The water is icky, and it's too cold!" she says, looking at the water, then at us.

"You're such a girl," Jax yells, then tries to dunk Lilly.

"I know I'm a girl. I'm a princess. Right, Daddy?" She puts her hands on her little hips and glares at her brother.

"Right, baby," I say, putting my hands up on the dock and pulling myself up and out of the water.

"You two ready to get out?" I ask, putting a hand down to Jax, who kicks his way over to me. I take his hand and pull him out of the water, and once I've gotten him and Lilly out, Jax starts chasing his sister around threatening to hug her, causing Ashlyn to scream and run away from him.

"This is way better than the zoo," Lilly says, and I toss my arm over her shoulder, pulling her into my side. "It's a good thing that warm front came through or this would really suck," she says with a little shiver.

"Thanks for giving me this," I tell her, kissing the side of her head.

"It's been a lot of fun." We make our way to our blanket that we had laid out on the grass, along with our cooler full of drinks and snacks. Jax runs to the blanket, gets a towel and his extra set of clothes from the bag that Lilly packed. I have no idea how she knew that we would need all that; I guess it's a mom thing. I take him to the truck to help him get changed and bring back a jacket for Lilly to throw on over her wet clothes. We all sit down on the blanket and Lilly hands the kids each a sandwich before handing me one. Her eyes roll back before she sits forward and pulls out her cell phone from her back pocket.

"Shit," she mumbles, looking at her phone.

"You said a naughty word," Ashlyn informs Lil.

"Sorry," she says, smiling.

"Don't worry, babe; we can get you a new one," I tell her, pulling her phone out of her hand and looking at it. I can see water in the screen, so I know that it's not salvageable with a bag of rice.

"I can't afford a new phone," she says, looking at it.

"Will you stop doing that?"

"Doing what?"

"I didn't ask you to pay for the phone, Lil. You can get a line on my account. It's past time for you to get a Tennessee number anyways."

"But I really can't afford it. I still have to pay the lawyer," she says quietly, looking at the kids. And just like that, I'm reminded of the shit that is still happening around us. That shit, along with my ex, is something that I don't like to think about. Lucky for us, both have been quiet lately. The case against Lilly has been put on hold due to lack of evidence. And Jules has not made any contact since she went to Lilly's school and attacked her. The day Lilly showed up at my jobsite in tears from what Jules did to her, it took everything in me not to kill her myself. Not that I didn't track her down and make it known that if she continued her bullshit I would make her life a living hell. But even though she's been quiet lately, I know that she is up to something. I just don't know what.

"I love you, Lil. You and Ashlyn are mine, and it's my job to take care of you. So please, let me do my job."

"It's not your job," she huffs out, looking annoyed.

"Yes, it is."

"A job is something you have to do whether you want to or not." Her eyebrows come together, creating a small crease between them.

"Lil." I shake my head; she's so frustrating sometimes. I lean over, running my finger between her brows. "This is something I want to do. I love taking care of you guys."

"I don't want you to resent me," she says so quietly that I almost miss it.

"How could I resent you?" I run my hand down the side of her face.

"I don't know."

"Babe, you have to stop doing that. Are you happy?" I ask quietly, looking at the kids. They are now off running around in the grass, chasing birds that keep coming to them because they are dropping bread as they run.

"Yes." She watches the kids and a smile comes to her face. "I just don't want you to feel like I'm putting all this on you, you know?"

"Baby," I laugh, pulling her over to me. "If you told me that you were going to stay home from now on, that would fucking thrill me."

"Why?"

"I like knowing that you're at home when I get home, and that my kids are being taken care of by you."

"Cash—"

"Hey, I didn't say that you were going to stay home forever, but as long as you are, I'm cool with it."

"Just promise me that you will tell me if you get to a point where you're not cool with it anymore."

"Where's all this coming from?" I ask her, not understanding what's bringing all these doubts to the surface when we have been doing so well.

"I don't know. I'm just used to working, so me *not* working is messing with my head. I love being home with both the kids, but..." she trails off, shaking her head.

"But what?" I ask when her face pales slightly.

"Um...I...it's nothing." She shakes her head again and I know it's not nothing.

"Lil, please talk to me."

"Jules came by yesterday. The kids were down for a nap, and I answered the door not thinking, but I think she realized that I'm living there."

"Why didn't you tell me?"

"I didn't want you to be worried, and when she saw that it was me who answered, she left without really saying anything."

"Next time she comes by, you need to call me."

"Sorry."

"Its fine, babe, but I will not allow her to fuck with you or my kids." I take a breath, trying to calm down. And speaking of the devil, my phone starts ringing, with Jules' name coming onto the screen. "Yeah?" I answer on the second ring. Standing, I walk away from the where Lilly is and the kids are playing.

"So you moved in that chick?" she asks with venom in her voice

"Lilly is not a chick; she's my woman, the mother of my child, and soon, my wife. Second, you don't ever get to question what I do, or when or how I do it. And third," I growl when I hear her trying to cut me off, "you do not get to show up at my house unannounced *ever*."

"I think I have the right to know if there is a criminal around my son."

"Excuse me?"

"I heard that she is a criminal." I can tell she is smirking; I've seen her smug face enough to know what she sounds like when she's doing it.

"Who the fuck told you that?" I ask, my gut twisting.

"Don't worry about who told me, just know that I know all about her."

"You don't know shit. Why are you calling me?"

"I want to see Jax," she says nonchalantly.

"Not today."

"Why not today?" she whines, and I clench my fist. She never wants to see Jax, and she never calls to check on him. Even when he had to stay in the hospital with strep, she wasn't concerned enough to see him.

"It's my birthday. We're spending the day together."

"So you could come too," she says in what I'm sure she thinks is a sexy tone. All that shit does to me is make me want to punch something or cut off my dick.

"Have you lost your damn mind?"

"Please, I want to see our son."

"I will call you tomorrow and set up a time to meet up with you," I say, hanging up. I lean my head back, looking up at the sky through the trees. I hate that I'm going to have to deal with her ass for the rest of my life. I feel arms wrap around my waist, and my hands go to Lilly's on my stomach. I look down when I feel arms around each of my legs, and I know that no matter what bullshit Jules pulls, if I have this, I will be happy.

Chapter 9

Lilly

"Don't touch me," Ashlyn says from the backseat.

"I'm not touching you," Jax says.

"Don't touch me!" Ashlyn yells this time.

"I'm not touching you," Jax repeats, and I can hear it in his voice that he is smiling and really trying to piss off his sister.

"Mommy, Jax isn't touching me! Stop not touching me!" Ashlyn cries and I laugh. Looking through the rearview mirror, I can see that Jax has a finger close to his sister, but far enough away that he is not actually touching her.

"Jax, leave your sister alone," I say, trying to sound firm, but it's really funny so it's difficult. I never had siblings growing up, so I have no idea what it's like, but I love how Jax is with Ashlyn. I love that she has someone there for her. And I know that, yes, he picks on her, but let someone else try to pick on his sister and he turns into a twenty-year-old and lays down the law. No one, but no one, picks on his sister except him. Things have been good—no, that's wrong—things have been perfect...well, that is if you don't count getting accused of check fraud and losing your job.

The good thing is that I had my meeting with the school board and my case was dismissed. They were not happy about what happened, but after the union heard my case and saw for themselves the evidence against me was all false, they said I could return to work. And I would, just not at that school. I don't want to work somewhere where the principal didn't even give me a chance to speak, due to her own feelings and her own situation. I want to be somewhere that people know me and my character enough to realize I would never do what I had been accused of.

So for now, I'm a stay at home mom. I love having the kids, but I miss teaching. I have put in an application at the local middle school, and I'm waiting to hear back from them. So, things are going awesome, and we have all settled in. I'd thought that it would be weird living with Cash, but it isn't; I love it. I love that the kids have each other. I love that I get to wake up to Cash every day. I love him coming home to the kids and me, and having family dinners. I love that his family has started acting more comfortably around me. The only thing that I don't love is his ex. I know in my head that she is Jax's mother, but my heart doesn't like that very much. I hate seeing the disappointment on his little face when she is supposed to show up and doesn't. When he does see her, I hate the way he acts when he comes back to us. I hate that Cash is subjected to dealing with her when she wants to act like she cares about Jax, then how he has to put up with the aftermath of Jax, and trying to explain to him why his mom is such a bitch. So if not for his ex, things would be perfect, and that is one thing that worries me. When Cash and I were together before, things were like they are now, minus the kids. I'm concerned about getting too comfortable, but at the same time, he makes it so easy to fall back into a place where I feel safe and loved.

"Mommy, where are we going?" Ashlyn asks for the fiftieth time since we got into the car.

"I told you, love bug, we're going to the hairdresser."

"Oh, yeah," she sighs, making me laugh. I pull up out front of the salon, park, and hop out of my giant SUV. When I open the back door, both of the kids are standing and waiting for me to help them down. They each grab a hand as we make it into the building. The woman behind the counter greets us right away with a huge smile.

"Hi, I have a three o'clock appointment with Justin." She looks over her shoulder into the back of the salon.

"He is just finishing up with his client; if you could give him about five minutes, he will be right with you," she says, looking down at the kids. "Do you guys like to color?" she asks, and they nod. She ducks behind the counter and comes back up with some coloring books and crayons. We go over to the sitting area, and Jax and Ashlyn kneel in front of the table and start coloring.

"Lilly?" I look up when I hear my name being called. My eyes make contact with a very pretty Spanish man, and I say pretty because he has on more makeup than I do.

"That's me." I stand, looking down at the kids.

"You both be on your best behavior. I tell them, walking into the back of the salon. The reason I chose this place is because it is one of the only places around that allows you to bring your children with you, and while you are getting your hair done, they watch your kids.

"They will be fine," the girl who was behind the counter when we arrived says, looking over at the kids.

"Thank you," I say as my hand is grabbed and I'm dragged into the back of the salon.

"I'm Justin."

"Nice to meet you," I say as I'm sat down in a chair and a cape is tossed over my shoulders.

"I love this color, honey. Who is your stylist?" Justin asks, making me smile.

"That would be Nutrisse 6.60," I say, and smile when his mouth opens and closes like a fish.

"This is from a box?" he asks breathily, lifting my hair and letting it run through his fingers.

"It is," I confirm. "I came today to have you cut ten inches of it," I tell him. Watching him smile.

"Ten inches will leave you hair here," he says, holding my hair up to just below my shoulders.

"That's fine." I smile, looking at him in the mirror.

"Are you sure about this? I mean, your hair is so amazing," he says quietly.

"Well, I really just want a change, and I think that a new cut is a good place to start," I tell him.

"Let's do this then," he says, pulling a rubber band out from a drawer. I watch as he pulls my hair back into a ponytail at the base of my neck, and then pulls it down some before reaching over and grabbing a pair of scissors. "Last chance, love, then there is nothing I can do."

"Do it." I grin, watching as the scissors open over my hair and I hear the distinct sound of my hair being cut. Once he has gone through my hair, I watch as it falls down around my shoulders. My first thought is, *it's really short*. My second thought is, *Cash*. He has no idea that I planned on cutting my hair today. I wonder what he will think. Then I look at my hair in Justin's hand, then back at myself in the mirror, shaking my head back and forth. I already feel lighter. Once he's done, he stands behind me, gathering my hair before letting what's left run through his fingers.

"Now, love, on to the really fun part. When all is said and done, and I walk into the waiting area towards the kids, I feel hot. My red hair sits just above my shoulders in a mass of wild waves and flips. I feel sexy. I loved my long hair, but this cut...something about it just makes me want to hold my head a little higher.

"Mommy, you look so pretty!" Ashlyn yells as soon as she sees me. She jumps away from the table in front of her, running to me.

"Thank you, love bug," I say, crouching down in front of her. Her little hands automatically go to my hair, bouncing it. I look over at Jax, who is looking like he would rather be anywhere but here. "Are you ready to go, honey?" I ask, and he nods then hops off the chair, grabbing my hand. Once he has it, I stand, and he starts tugging me to the door of the salon. "Bye guys," I call over my shoulder, laughing as Jax drags me behind him. Once we're out at the car, he drops my hand and looks up at me.

"I'm starbing." His head is back and I can't help but to laugh.

"You had breakfast a couple hours ago," I remind him, opening up the door so he and Ashlyn can climb in.

"That was foreber ago," he says as he gets into his chair. He buckles in, and so does Ashlyn. I hop in the back to make sure they are both secure before getting out, shutting the door, and climbing into the front seat. "What would you like to eat?" I ask, reversing out of the parking space.

"McDonalds!" both he and Ashlyn say at the same time. I don't take them very often, but when I do, we end up spending at least a couple hours. The first thirty minutes is me trying to talk both of them into eating; the rest of the time is spent watching them play in the indoor play area.

"Okay," I say, and then wait a second for them both to stop yelling 'yippee!' "But if we go, you have to promise to eat before you go play."

"Promise!" Ashlyn claps.

"Promise," Jax says, and I know they are both lying through their adorable little baby teeth.

"Don't stop," I moan, my hands in Cash's hair. Between my legs, his mouth is on me, and his fingers are digging into my thighs. I'm close...so close. My hips try to raise, and his fingers press in deeper, holding me down. "Cash," I whimper, my head arched back as he pulls my clit into his mouth, sucking it. His hands travel down the length of my thighs, spreading my legs farther apart, then down under my thighs to my ass, lifting me up higher into his mouth. His head moves back and forth as his mouth devours me. My hands tug on his hair, trying to pull him off,

221

but all that seems to do is egg him on. "Cash!" I call again, using my feet to push up the bed. He growls low, and then wraps his arms around my thighs, putting his mouth back on me. He's keeping me on the edge; this is torture. It is my new haircut's fault. The minute he walked into the house when he came home, his eyes got dark and hooded; I felt my pulse speed up and between my legs get wet. He likes it a lot. After he said hi to the kids, he came to me in the kitchen, wrapping a hand around my waist, his mouth going to my neck, his tongue touching me there before his lips traveled up to my ear.

"Love the hair, babe," he said against the shell of my ear. "Tonight, I'm going to show you just how much I love it." He kissed the side of my head, his fingers digging into my hip and stepping away.

I'm brought back to the moment when he fills me with one thick finger. "Come for me, Lil," he grunts before his mouth covers me again. One finger slides out, and two slide back in. I do as I'm told, my head digging into the bed, my legs fighting to close. Behind my eyes, the world lights up; my body starts to sing and I convulse around his fingers. Before I have a chance to recover from my orgasm, I'm flipped to my stomach. His thighs spread mine a little wider and his hand comes down hard on my ass before he enters me in one long thrust. "Higher," his deep voice commands as I cry out and lift my ass higher up to him. His hand smoothes over my skin before coming down hard again, the sting from his palm hitting my skin making me tighten

222

around him, bringing me closer to the edge. "Higher, Lil," he says with another smack. I moan, my hands grabbing the sheets above me, my face going farther into the bed, and my ass tilting higher. "Give it to me, baby; fuck me back." Another loud smack lands against my ass. This one sets me off, making me pound back against him. My breath is coming in loud pants, my body slick with sweat. "Harder!" I press back harder, his hands grabbing my ass, pulling it up. "That's it, baby," he groans, slamming into me harder. I can feel myself being moved up the bed by the force of his thrusts.

"I'm going to come," I moan into the mattress. My thighs shaking, Cash brings down his hand yet again.

"Come for me," he says, spanking me on the opposite side. I feel the first waves of my orgasm begin to crash over me. My eyes close tightly; I feel like my body is catching on fire. My pussy starts to convulse, pulling Cash deeper. I cry out; his hands reach forward, wrapping around my breasts, lifting my upper body back so I'm kneeling in front of him. His fingers pinch my nipples. The feeling pulling me deeper under. My orgasm blinds me. His strokes become faster before his mouth meets my neck. I can feel his groan all the way to my clit as he finds his own release. His cock is planted deep inside me. His chest moves quickly up and down behind me, his hands still holding onto my breasts. My hands go to his at my chest, my fingers interlocking with his. I lean my head to the side, my body completely boneless. "I love the hair," he says, licking my neck.

"I think I got that." I laugh, and I can feel him smile against the skin of my neck. His hands squeeze my breasts before traveling down over my ribs, along my sides to my hips, pulling me even closer to him. One hand leaves my hip, following the same path before his hand closes around my neck. I can feel my pussy still convulsing around him with aftershocks.

"You wanna shower?" I feel his breath against my skin as he speaks the words, making me shiver.

"Yes," I tell him and groan when his hips pull away and I lose him and his warmth. I fall forward on the bed and laugh when he starts to tickle me.

"Let's go, baby. We need to get cleaned up. You and I know the kids are not going to magically start sleeping in until ten."

"God, when was the last time I slept past eight?" I ask out loud, not expecting an answer.

"How about tomorrow you sleep in and I will take the kids to my mom's?" he asks as his hands run up my calves and over my ass.

"I don't know," I sigh; his mom has been amazing, and I don't want her to feel like I'm trying to pawn the kids off on her.

"Ma loves having the kids over. Plus, I think she wanted to do something with them. There is supposed to be a storyteller at the library in town. I think she wanted to keep the kids overnight. And that would be perfect; I wouldn't mind taking you out on a date or just having you to myself."

"I don't know," I repeat, even though it would be nice to spend some alone time with Cash.

"It's done." He rolls me to my back then scoops me up, carrying me into the bathroom before setting me on my feet outside the shower. "I'll get up in the morning, take the kids to Ma, and then come back and we can spend the morning in bed before going on a date tomorrow night."

"I don't know why you try to make things seem like it's a question when you know your mind is already made up," I say, rolling my eyes.

"What, you don't want to spend some time with just me?" he asks, taking my hand and pulling me into the shower.

"You know it's not that."

"You're just using me for my body, aren't you?" he asks, and I can't help but to look over said body and admire every detail. His body is perfect. I watch as the water runs down and over every muscle; his chest has a little bit of hair— just the right amount—and down under his navel is a strip of hair, which makes a path to his perfect cock. "My eyes are up here, baby," he says, and I watch his cock twitch. I lick my lips and hear him groan. "You're not helping, Lil," he says, pushing me under the water. I sputter and wipe the water out of my face.

"What the hell?" I glare at him.

"You can't look at me like that. We need to shower and go to bed, and you can't look at me like that...looking how you do, with your body all wet and slick...*fuck*," he growls, his hands sliding along my hips to palm my ass. "Let's just say that if you look at me like that, neither of us will be getting any sleep tonight." His hands slide up my back and into my hair, tilting my head back, his mouth coming down on mine, stealing my breath. "Now, tomorrow you can look at me like that all day long." He smiles, showing off both dimples. "In fact, I plan on doing a lot of looking of my own." His eyes leave mine, trailing down my body. "But for now," he says, sounding like he's in pain, "for now we need to get washed up and go to bed."

"Okay," I agree, even though the space between my legs has begun to throb. I look over him again, my eyes catching on his massive erection.

"Lil," he growls. My eyes come up.

"Okay, okay." I take a step away from him, and grab my shampoo and start washing my hair quickly. I can hear Cash breathing heavily, but I don't open my eyes. I'm afraid of what will happen if I look at him. I turn around quickly and grab my conditioner to run it through my hair. Then I grab my body wash, washing up while I let the conditioner sit. Once I'm washed, I start to rinse the conditioner from my hair. My head is back, eyes closed, and without warning, I feel his mouth on my nipple and fingers sliding through my folds. My body is still primed from earlier, and it doesn't take much before I'm moaning my orgasm into the spray of the showerhead.

"We can't shower together anymore," he states, picking me up. My legs wrap around his waist and he slides inside me.

"Yeah, no more showering together," I agree as I use my legs to grind down on him. By the time we finish our shower, we're both exhausted, and it doesn't take long for either of us to fall asleep.

"Baby."

"Hm." I try not to speak; I don't want to wake up.

"I'm taking the kids to Ma's; I'll be back," I hear him say, but can't really process it because I'm still trying to sleep. Then I feel weight hit my forehead and something slide down my cheek.

"Mommy, I'm goin' to Grandma's," Ashlyn says, and I open my eyes to see her up on her elbows looking at me. Her long hair is pulled up in what looks like two lopsided pigtails.

"Okay, baby, have fun. Give me love before you go." I roll to my side so I can hug her. "Where's Jax?" I sit up to fix her hair.

"He was eating," she says, pulling her little head away from me.

"Hey, I want to fix your hair."

"Daddy fixed my hair," she says, jumping off the bed, her eyes narrowing.

"Sorry." I try not to smile. Cash can do no wrong, including her hair apparently. "Can I get a kiss before you leave?" I ask, and she belligerently climbs up onto the bed and gives me a kiss before jumping right back off the bed, leaving the room.

"You're awake?" Cash says, coming into the room.

"Yeah, Ashlyn was just in here," I tell him, getting up on my elbow.

"I wanted you to sleep," he grumbles, saying something else under his breath. He makes his way to me. His hands come down on each side of me on the bed. "You're going to go back to sleep." He kisses me, punctuating each word. "And when I get back, I'm going to climb back into bed with you." He runs his nose down my neck.

"Sounds good," I breathe, feeling my nipples get hard and between my legs dampening.

"Daddy, are we weabing?" Jax yells into the room before jumping up onto the bed. His presence is like a bucket of ice water on my libido.

"We are leaving, little dude," Cash says, standing. I sit all the way up; Jax jumps twice before plopping down on top of me, and his little hands come to my face.

"We're habing a sleep over with Grandma," he tells me, his tiny face titling back and forth, studying me.

"I heard; that sounds like fun," I tell him, running my hand down his soft hair. I have no idea how his mom can stand to be away from him.

"Daddy said that we're going to Awaska."

"We are," I tell him, looking up at Cash. I can't wait to see my parents. I miss them so much, and I know that Ashlyn does too. Jax has been chatting with my dad whenever we're able to Skype, and my dad has made Jax excited to come visit. I can't wait to introduce Cash to my parents and show him where I grew up.

"I can't wait to see a real life beer," he says, making me smile because I know he means bear.

"Well, next week at this time, we will be on a plane," I tell him. He hugs me quickly, making my heart melt. He jumps off the bed, running out of the room where I can hear him yell, "We're gonna see beers!"

Cash laughs and I turn to look at him. "I thought we weren't going to tell them that we are going yet," I say. We both agreed to tell the kids a couple days before we left so that we didn't have to answer 'are we leaving yet' questions a hundred times a day.

"I know, but they wanted to come in and wake you, so I told them I would tell them a secret if they let you sleep."

"That didn't work," I point out.

"Yeah, I got that." He smiles, leaning down and kissing me again. "All right, I'm going to go get the hellions to Ma's; go back to sleep," he says, and I don't think I will be able to go back to sleep, but I slide back down into the bed, pulling the cover up over my shoulder. He kisses me once more before walking out of the bedroom. I watch him leave, enjoying the view of his very firm ass in his Levi's. I can hear him talking to the kids. I hear the kids yell a goodbye and I smile before calling out that I love them. When I hear the door slam, I close my eyes, and before I know it, I'm asleep. I wake slightly when I'm pulled across the bed, and I feel weight and warmth behind me. I start to lift my head. "Sleep, babe. We're kid-free until tomorrow," he says, and I feel him kiss the back of my head, his warmth seeping into me from behind. I snuggle deeper into him before drifting back to sleep. I wake up feeling warm. I do not want to move, but I really need to pee, so I start to scoot off the bed when I'm tugged back. "Where are you going?" Cash asks, his voice rough with sleep.

"To the bathroom," I say, and his hand runs down my hip where his fingers squeeze in.

"Come back to bed when you're done." I roll out of bed, making my way to the bathroom. I make quick work of taking care of business so I can get back to Cash. Once I get back to the room, Cash is sitting up in bed, his back to the headboard, and his shirtless upper-body exposed. I crawl from the bottom of the bed, watching his eyes darken as I make my way up and straddle his waist. His hands slide up my thighs to my ass, pulling me tighter against him.

"So what are we going to do today?" I ask, leaning in to kiss the tattoo of Jax and Ashlyn's names on his chest. Unlike his brothers, he only has a couple of tattoos. This one has his kids' names intertwined with sharp lines and a floral vine wrapped around them, almost like it's holding them together. His other tattoo runs down his side along his ribs, and says, 'Experience is the hardest kind of teacher. It gives you the test first, and the lesson afterward.' The script is swirly and looks awesome against his skin. I can't help but get lost looking at him. His well-defined abs lead down to a deep V that I trace with my fingers.

"Did you hear me?" He chuckles, and I feel my cheeks get warm as my eyes meet his.

"What?"

"I said how about we have a naked house day?"

"A naked house day?" I repeat, studying his face.

"Yep." His hands run up my thighs, and then under my tank top, his hands skimming my waist and over my breasts as he pulls it off over my head. "Naked house day." His thumbs run over my nipples, making me arch closer to him. "The rules for naked house day are we stay naked all day, no matter what we're doing." His mouth covers one nipple; he pulls hard, then releases and blows a cool breath over it.

"Sounds like fun," I moan, my hands going to his hair as he gives my other nipple the same attention. "Did you just make this up?" I ask as he rolls me over, sliding inside.

"Yep," is all he says before I drag his mouth down to mine, wrapping my legs around him.

"No more!" I cry as I feel Cash come up behind me. I got away from him ten minutes ago. I thought naked house day sounded like fun this morning, but now it's seven at night and I'm starving, my legs feel like they are going to fall off, my body is covered in love bites, and all I want to do is sleep.

"Babe, you're naked standing in the middle of the kitchen looking sexy as hell. I can't help it," he says, his mouth coming to my neck.

"No more." I jump away from him, running to the other side of the counter. "I need food," I tell him, stepping back when I see that he looks ready to pounce.

"Okay, okay, you're right. I need to feed you," he says, holding his hands out in front of him.

"Thank you," I sigh, my head dropping forward.

"After I feed you, you're mine again."

"Did you take something?" I ask exasperatedly.

"What?" He smirks, showing off both dimples.

"It can't be normal for a guy to get hard so quickly after..." I say quietly, looking down at his very hard cock and waving my hand in its direction.

"*This* is all your fault." His fist wraps around his cock and begins moving in slow strokes. "All I have to do is look at you and I'm ready to go again."

"Food," I say, watching as he works himself. I lick my lips and feel my lower belly clench. I have no idea how I can still get wet after the amount of times I've orgasm today.

"I'll feed you," he says, taking a step closer to me. His free hand goes to my hip, turning me to face the countertop. "Put your hands flat on top and don't move them." I do as he says, my breasts pressing into the cold counter. He uses his foot to spread my legs farther apart; once he has me how he wants me, his fingers run over my clit, making my body jump at the contact. I feel like every nerve ending is exposed; the slightest touch is almost too much. "You're wet," he states, sounding almost surprised. I don't say anything, just nod my head. I feel his warmth hit my back, his legs bending right before he fills me, forcing me to stand on my tiptoes.

"Oh," I moan as my fingers dig into the countertop.

"I love being inside you," he groans. He keeps pulling almost all the way out before slamming back inside, each thrust causing my sensitive nipples to slide over the counter. His hand slides around my waist before traveling down and over my clit. I press back against him, trying to get away from his fingers. Everything that I'm feeling is too much. Without warning, I hear a loud smack and feel the sting from his palm against my ass. My body jumps, and I feel myself become even wetter. I cry out when his fingers pinch my clit, and my body bucks against his as I orgasm. I clench around him. My body burns from the inside out. Lights dance behind my closed eyelids. I know I'm dragging him over with me when I feel his fingers digging into my hips and his loud roar fills the room. His body collapses on top of mine. I can feel his heart beating wildly against my back, his chest heaving up and down.

"I think you're trying to kill me with orgasms," I say into the top of the counter.

"My dick is officially rubbed raw," he groans, sliding out of me.

"What are you doing?" I yell as he picks me up, walking towards the bedroom.

"Going to shower," he says, and I wiggle until I'm out of his arms.

"No! No way," I say, and I don't even look at him as I run to the room, slamming the bedroom door. I then run to the bathroom, shutting and locking that door as well.

"Babe." I can hear the laughter in his voice as he knocks on the door.

"Naked house day is over!" I yell before I jump into the shower, trying to wash as quickly as possible before he finds a way to break down the door. Once I'm done showering, I wrap myself in a robe, making sure to tie it tightly around my waist. I'm surprised to see Cash sitting on the side of the bed fully clothed, his hair still wet from his shower he must've taken in the kids' bathroom.

"What are you doing?" I ask, backing up when I see him stand and start prowling towards me.

"I'm going to kiss you and leave the room," he says, his arm encircling my waist. My hands go to his chest, trying to warn him off. "Just a kiss, baby, and then I want you to get dressed so I can take you out to dinner."

"We're still going to dinner?"

"I promised you I would feed you," he says, his lips moving softly over mine. I smile against his mouth. His face moves back, his eyes looking me over. "Unless you feel up to getting back into bed." He smiles when I growl. "Get dressed. I'll be in the living room." He turns me around, pushing me towards the closet. I jump when he smacks my ass. I look over my shoulder to see him smiling. "You have a beautiful ass, baby." He shrugs, walking out of the room. I walk into the closet smiling.

Chapter 10

Cash

"One more flight," I hear Lilly tell Jax as we board the small plane. I don't mind flying, but this day has been exhausting. We woke up at five this morning, got both the kids up and ready, then drove the forty minutes to the airport where we caught our first flight. That one took us from Tennessee to Seattle, and once in Seattle, we boarded another flight to Anchorage, Alaska. Once we arrived in Anchorage, we made our way quickly from the terminal to our gate in order to head outside and board another plane to the small town that her parents lived in.

"I want to sit with Daddy," Ashlyn says when we all file onto the plane. The seats are all two-by-two, so we have to split up into pairs.

"That's fine," Lilly says as she helps Jax buckle into the seat next to her across the aisle from Ashlyn and me.

"How much longer?" Ashlyn asks, and I can tell she's getting tired. Lucky for us, both kids are pretty well behaved, so we haven't had any real drama or breakdowns today, but it has been a long day and it's starting to wear on all of us.

"Forty-five minutes," Lilly answers. Once all the other passengers are on the plane and the door is closed, the sound of the engines fills the plane. It's so loud I look nervously over to Lilly who smiles. "They call these planes pond hoppers." Lilly laughs when she sees the look on my face. "Don't worry, we're up then back down on the ground before you know it," she says with a smile as Jax takes her hand. The plane starts to speed up, and I know we're off the ground when the plane shakes and the sound of the engine gets even louder than before. This has got to be the scariest flight I have ever been on; I feel like the plane is going to rattle apart. About twenty minutes into the flight, Ashlyn has curled up in her seat with her head against my ribs. I look over at Lilly and Jax, seeing that they are both asleep. Lilly's head is back against her headrest, and Jax is in much the same position as Ashlyn. The stewardess doesn't even come through the cabin for drink service; she just stays strapped into her seat. Before I know it, the captain makes an announcement that we will be landing soon. Once I feel the plane touch down, I reach across the small aisle and run my fingers down Lilly's cheek. Her eyes open and meet mine before looking down at Jax, who is now awake, then over at Ashlyn. We wait until most of the passengers are off the plane before we stand and get our carry-ons out of the bins; it's easier than trying to fight everyone to get off.

We step off the plane, and I have never been happier in my life to have my feet on solid ground. All I want to do is eat, shower, and sleep.

"Do you want me to take her?" Lilly asks, looking at Ashlyn, who is still asleep.

"No, baby, I got her," I say, grabbing her hand as we make our way into the terminal.

"Mommy…I mean…Lilly," Jax says, and I look over at Lilly, who is smiling down at Jax.

"Yeah, honey?" she says quietly, running her hand down the back of his head. My stomach drops as I watch the woman I love and plan on asking to marry me interact with my son, who has gotten so close to her that he slipped and called her Mom. I wish his mother was normal and sane and had a relationship with him, but she doesn't. I don't even think she cares one way or another what happens with Jax. The more time that goes by, I'm convinced that the only reason she is involved in Jax's life at all is to hold him over my head or fuck with me.

"Can we go fishing like Grandpa talked about?" Jax asks.

"Yes, I'm sure Grandpa will take you fishing, just not today."

"Okay," he sighs, grabbing Lilly's other hand. "Can we go look for beers?"

"Yes, honey, but not today." She laughs softly. I drop her hand so I can shift Ashlyn, and I feel Lilly's hand go into my back pocket.

"Can we go out on the boat and see otters, like Grandpa said?" Jax asks and I chuckle. He and Ashlyn have been having Skype sessions with Lilly's parents every few days since our first time a few months ago. Every time the kids talked to Lilly's parents, her dad told Jax about all the cool things that they were going to do when we came to visit.

"I'm sure we will go out on the boat at some point while we're here, honey."

"Can we go to McDonald's?"

"There is no McDonald's here." Lilly laughs when Jax's eyes get huge, and he looks around the airport—if you can even call it that; it's more like a large metal building with a check-in counter and two doors, one where you enter, and one where you go out onto the tarmac. Every plane that lands has to be boarded from outside.

"Oh, my babies!" is cried loudly and echoes through the metal building. Ashlyn startles in my arms, and Lilly and Jax are plowed into. Both of them are hugged and rocked back and forth.

"Hey, Mom," Lilly says, smiling and untangling herself and Jax from her mom. Once her mom steps back, she looks down at Jax. "This guy here that you just scared the crap out of is Jax," she says, putting her hand on Jax's shoulder, "and this is Cash." She slides her arm around my waist, looking up at me. And I don't know what it is about that exact moment, but the look on her face and her introducing us to her mom as a family makes me shift Ashlyn so that I can kiss her. When I take my mouth from hers, her eyes are soft and so full of emotion that my heart beat kicks up a notch.

"Uuuummm," I hear Lilly's mom clear her throat and I smile, my face still near Lil's. She grins before going back to flat-footed.

"They do that a lot," Jax says, and I pull completely away from Lil and meet her mom's eyes.

"Nice to meet you, Mrs. Donovan." I lean forward slightly, kissing her cheek and giving her a one-handed hug, trying not to wake Ashlyn. She shakes her head and rolls her eyes.

"Call me Mom. Obviously, you're not going anywhere." I chuckle and look at Lilly when I hear her laugh. She shakes her head before looking back at Mom.

"So where's Dad?" She looks around, and I do as well. I can't see her dad anywhere.

"Oh, well, he had to help Austin put his boat in the water," she says, and Lilly's posture changes slightly. I don't know why, but it starts to set off alarm bells. I want to ask who Austin is, but a loud buzz fills the room. I look over to the side to see bags being tossed in through a little hole in the wall.

"Our bags," Lilly says making her way to the conveyor belt.

"Here, baby, take Ashlyn and I'll get our bags." I make sure Ashlyn is settled before I go about collecting our bags. Once I've gotten them all, we make our way outside to a large SUV and load everything in before getting the kids settled. Ashlyn is still asleep, and Jax's little head has started to bob to the side.

"How was the flight?" Lilly's mom asks.

"Good, both the kids were well behaved, so we didn't really have any problems," Lil tells her. We talk on the way to her parents' house, Lil catching her mom up on the kids and telling her about what she hopes will be her new job at the school in town. She still hasn't told her parents about leaving the other school or what happened. I have tried to tell her that she should, but the damn woman is stubborn and won't listen. She only told her parents about living with me a few weeks ago. I wasn't around for that Skype session, but she said it went okay. My guess is they were not happy. But I honestly couldn't find it in myself to care. I had both my girls and my son under one roof; that's all that mattered to me. It takes about thirty minutes to get from the airport, which is in the middle of nowhere, to town. Well, if you can call it a town. We drive through it in about one minute. I swear,

242

if I would have blinked, I would have missed the whole thing. There is a bank, a few stores, and about three bars that I can spot. We turn off the main street, heading down to what I can tell is the water; the closer we get, the more boats and men in fishing gear I see.

"I want to stop by the pier and see if your dad wants to go out to dinner, or if he wants to cook at home," Mom says as we continue our drive, until we reach a dead end. Jax's head comes up, and when we stop, he looks around before yelling, "Yay, we're going fishing!"

"No, little dude, we're going to see Lil's dad before we go to the house."

"Oh." He slumps in his seat and I look to my other side when I feel Ashlyn grab my arm.

"Did you have a good nap, baby?" She nods then looks around, and I can tell exactly when she notices where we are by the smile that lights up her face.

"Memaw," Ashlyn says quietly, and I can see Lil's mom smile at her in the rearview mirror before hopping out of the truck and opening the back door on Ashlyn's side.

"How's my girl?" she asks Ashlyn, helping her out of her car seat. Once she's free, she's picked up and smothered in kisses.

"Stop, Memaw! Stop!" Ashlyn squeals, trying to get free.

"I need my sugar. I haven't had any in a long time, so I need to make up for lost time," Lil's mom says between kisses. Ashlyn finally squirms out of her arms and runs to stand behind Jax. "I guess your big brother is going to protect you," Mom says, laughing. "What do you say we go find Papa?" she asks, starting to walk towards a large boat with the name Wolf on the side in large black letters. I grab Lilly's hand, and we follow along behind her. Once we reach the boat that is tied to the dock, she steps onboard then leans over, grabbing Jax first and bringing him over before grabbing Ashlyn and pulling her on. I can see Jax's face is completely lit up with excitement as he looks around the deck of the boat.

"Papa!" Ashlyn yells. I follow her with my eyes just as Lilly's dad bends down to pick her up.

"Hey, angel girl," he says, hugging her and tucking her head into his chest before pulling her face away and looking her over.

"Look! My brother," Ashlyn says, pointing down at Jax.

"Hey, buddy," Mr. Donovan says, bending to set Ashlyn down before rubbing the top of Jax's head.

"Are we gonna go fishin'?" Jax asks, making Lil's dad laugh.

"Not today. But before you go back home, we will be going out on the boat to fish for halibut."

"Cool," Jax breathes, looking around again. Mr. Donovan stands back up, his eyes coming to us before Lilly lets go of my hand and takes off running into her dad's open arms.

"Hey, Dad," I can hear her say before she leans away, placing her hand on his cheek.

"How's my girl?" he asks her, pulling her back in for another hug.

"Really good," she says, and then looks over her shoulder at me. I step forward as he tucks Lil under his arm and sticks out his hand for me to take.

"Sir," I say, giving his hand a shake.

"Nice to have you here, son," he says, and a little bit of the knot that I didn't even notice before loosens.

"Nice to be here." I step back and look over Lil's dad's shoulder as a giant guy comes out of nowhere. He is tall, way taller than my 6'1. I would guess that he is closer to 6'6; his hair is blond and is overgrown, matching his beard. He is huge; his arms look as big as my thighs. His whole body is large, and I'm taken slightly aback. I start to step towards Lilly, wanting her near me while this guy is around, then I hear him speak and want her near me for a different reason.

"Lilly?" he says, and she turns around. Her face lights up and she runs to the guy, throwing her arms around his neck as his hands slide around her waist, pulling her in for a hug.

"Austin," she says low, but I still catch it and it sounds intimate, or maybe it's my own personal jealousy taking over. "How have you been?" she asks stepping back, but his hands are still on her hips and it's taking everything in me not to walk over to him, rip his hands off her, and toss his ass overboard.

"Good, better now I have seen your face," he says, and his eyes are soft while looking at her. My jaw clenches. Lilly steps back out of his touch, then turns to look at me.

"Cash, this is Austin. Austin, this is Cash." I take a few steps in their direction, putting my hand out to meet his.

"Nice to meet you," I say, but it sounds more like a growl. My hand slides around the back of Lilly's waist, pulling her tight against me. Jax comes up, grabbing Lilly's hand, and I wonder if my son senses the same threat I do.

"Cash. Cash?" Austin repeats, his eyes get big before narrowing. "You're Cash, as in Ashlyn's father, Cash?" he asks, his eyes going to Lil before coming back to me.

"It's a long story, Austin," Lilly says quickly, then pulls his attention back to her. "Maybe while were here, we can meet up for lunch and I can tell you everything."

"Or not," I say low enough for only Lilly to hear.

"Cash," she replies, her head swinging my way and her eyes narrowing.

"All right, well, we just wanted to stop by and see if you wanted to have dinner at home, or if you wanted to go out to dinner tonight," Lilly's mom says loudly, taking the attention away from what's going on.

"I think we should eat at home. I can grill up some of those elk steaks that I've got in the freezer," Lil's dad says, then looking at Austin, "You wanna come to dinner?"

"No, not tonight. I have to finish getting the boat ready to head out tomorrow." He looks around the boat. "Maybe when I get back we can set something up?" He looks at Lilly, who nods. We all turn around and head off the boat, the kids jumping onto the dock, followed by Lil's parents, then me. I put my arm around her shoulders, and lean my head to the side so I can speak to her without anyone hearing.

"Austin?" I ask, and her steps falter slightly.

"He's a friend."

"What kind of friend?"

"A good friend," she says, and I know I shouldn't, but I see red.

"A good friend," I repeat.

"Yess," she hisses, "he was a good friend. He was there for me when I needed him."

"How was he there?" I ask, wanting to take the words back as soon as I say them.

"You know, I can't believe you're going to act like a jealous ass when you were flipping married," she growls, and her elbow connects with my ribs, then she slides out from under my arm, walking up to where the kids are. I want to kick my own ass. I cannot believe I just did that. I look over my shoulder when I get the feeling someone is watching me. Austin is standing on the deck of his boat, his arms crossed and his legs spread apart. *Fucking great.* I shake my head. Lilly's dad looks back at me and I shrug, picking up my pace. By the time I get to the SUV, Lilly has both kids inside and is buckled in herself. She doesn't look at me when I pass by her to get into the back, and she doesn't say a word while we drive to her parents' house. But she doesn't have to say anything. I can feel the anger coming off her in waves. We drive for about twenty minutes and end up in front of a large, two-story log house with a large wraparound front porch. The kids both unbuckle themselves, and Lilly hops out before helping each of them down. I get out on the other side of the SUV and make my way around the back to get our bags. I watch as Lilly makes her way inside with Jax, Ashlyn, and her mom.

"You know, I wasn't happy about you two being back together." I turn my head to look at Lilly's dad when he speaks. I'm really not in the mood for any bullshit, but out of respect for Lil, I will let her dad say his piece. "But I trust my daughter, and I know she has always made smart decisions. Plus, your little speech about not caring what I thought about you marrying her may have earned you a few points in my book. It's hard not to respect a man who knows what he wants." He pats my back then squeezes down on my shoulder. "But you need to remember, son, she wasn't always yours. She had a life, just like you did, and the quicker you can learn to accept that, the better off you will both be."

"You're right." I take a breath. "I just never thought I would be seeing her life without me up close and personal."

"Not everything is what it seems." He smiles. "It's like that joke. A hound dog lays in the yard, and an old man in overalls sits on the porch. 'Excuse me, sir, but does your dog bite?' a jogger asks. The old man looks over his newspaper and replies, 'Nope.' As soon as the jogger enters the yard, the dog begins snarling and growling, and then attacks the jogger's legs. As the jogger flails around in the yard, he yells, 'I thought you said your dog doesn't bite!' The old man mutters, 'Aint my dog.'"

"What the hell does that even mean?" I question, wondering if Lil's dad has fallen off the deep end.

"Sometimes, we see what we want to see, and not what's really going on," he says low, his eyes going to the house. "It's not my place to talk about Austin's past, but him and Lilly were both dealing with the loss of people they cared about at the same time and were able to understand what the other was going though. Now trust me when I tell you that if I were to get Austin for a son-in-law, I would be a happy man. But I don't think that would have ever happened. I just think they each needed a friend during a difficult time, and that's all it ever was, a friendship. As for you, I knew when my daughter came home from Alabama with my granddaughter that she would never be the same. Not only because she was a single mom, but because she had felt like part of her soul had been ripped away from her.

"I know I fucked up." I shake my head. "I thought I was doing the right thing at the time. I mean, no, I didn't know about Lil being pregnant, but I thought I was protecting her at the time. I didn't want her to have to deal with what I was going through."

"I get that. But now think of it this way: Lilly says you have a big family, right?"

"I do."

"She has me and her mom." My gut tightens. I still hate myself for what I had unknowingly put her through. Okay, so I don't want to kill Austin anymore, but that doesn't mean that I want them alone together. "You're smart," Mr. Donovan says and smiles, reading the look on my face. "Now, go apologize; it works every time. It's best you learn that real quick-like." He pats my back again before reaching in to the SUV, grabbing two of our suitcases, and walking towards the house. I grab the other two bags out of the trunk before slamming the trunk, following behind him.

I find the kids and make sure they are okay before going in search of Lilly. I find her upstairs in a bedroom at the end of a hall, her back facing me. She is putting away the stuff from the bags her dad brought in, into a long dresser. "You need help?" I ask, walking farther into the room. Her body goes ridged, and I can hear her sigh.

"No. The kids are down the hall. Do you want to check on them?"

"The kids are fine; I just checked on them. I want to talk to you."

"I don't think I'm ready to talk to you," she says low, her head shaking back and forth in agitation.

"Lil."

"Don't 'Lil' me." Her eyes finally meet mine, and she points at me. "I have accepted your past since the beginning of our relationship. I accepted who you were the first time we were together, and I more than accepted you this time around. What did you think, Cash, that you were the only person I would ever be with?" she asks, and I can hear the anger in her words. Each one cutting through me.

"That's not what I was saying," I say, taking another step towards her.

"You know, you're right. You broke me. I couldn't be with anyone else. Austin is a great guy— sweet, considerate, loving, and handsome—but I couldn't be with him, no matter how many times I tried, no matter how much I liked him. He wasn't you. No one was ever you." As much as it kills to think of her trying to be with anyone, I understand. I see tears in her eyes, and I'm done with the space separating us. Walking towards her, I quickly pull her to me, not giving her a chance to argue.

"I'm sorry." I breathe her in, the smell of lavender comforting me. "It was a shit thing to ask you." I rub her back. "I love you, Lil. I just...shit...I just hate the idea of you with anyone else." I take a breath; I can still tell that she's crying. "Please don't cry because I'm an idiot," I say gently.

"You are an idiot," she says. I can feel her cheek move against my chest and I know she's smiling.

"As long as I'm your idiot, I couldn't care less." Her head tilts back, her glassy eyes meeting mine.

"You know, you make it really hard to be mad at you," she says, studying my face.

"I'm not going to complain about that. It seems to be working in my favor." She shakes her head before dropping her forehead to my chest.

"I hope you know that I will be meeting Austin when he comes back in from his fishing trip," she tells me and I take a breath, not wanting to say the wrong thing, but not wanting her to meet up with a man that she obviously cares about.

"Can I come with you when you meet up with him?"

"No." She shakes her head. "You have to trust me, Cash. Austin and I are friends, nothing more." Her arms wrap around my waist. "But that doesn't mean that feelings were not there, and Austin was hurt in the past and I want to make sure he's doing okay."

"I don't like it," I whisper into her hair before kissing the top of her head.

"I know, but it's something I have to do." She gives me a squeeze, trying to offer me comfort.

"I trust you," I say, and it's the truth.

"Thank you," she replies quietly, but I can hear in those two words how much I just gave to her. My hand goes to the back of her neck before traveling to her jaw so I can tilt her head back.

"I know what's in front of me, Lil. I know exactly what I have, so when I feel like it's being threatened, the first thing I want to do is lash out and kill anything that may come in and jeopardize it. I know what we had before, and I know what we have now. And I will always do everything within my power to protect it.

253

"Austin isn't a threat," she says, her hand coming up and traveling along my jaw.

"Lilly, your kind of sweet is hard to come by, so when you get even just a little taste of it, you want more. I'm saying that as a man who knows what bitter tastes like," I tell her gently. I don't know what happened with Austin and his past relationship, but I have a feeling he knows what bitter tastes like too. And he also knows the kind of woman Lilly is, and how hard that is to find.

"I think you're reading too much into this."

"I'm not, but that's okay as long as you know that you're mine. I will try to control the urge to throw you over my shoulder and carry you back to my lair," I tell her, making her laugh. She rubs her face against my chest before lifting her eyes to meet mine.

"We should go check on the kids and get them something to eat," she tells me before taking a step back. I pull her back to me, bend her back and put my mouth on hers. Once I feel her relax, I nibble on her bottom then top lip.

"Now, we can go get the kids," I tell her, my mouth still against hers.

"You have to let me go." She's right, but I don't want to.

"Are we good?" I don't like fighting with her.

"We're good."

"Good." I kiss her once more before righting her, turning her towards the door, and smacking her ass. She looks at me over her shoulder, and all I can do is shrug. "You have a nice ass."

"We're in my parents' house."

"Just because were in their house doesn't mean I'm going to stop touching you when I want to."

"My dad isn't going to like you smacking my ass," she says. I smile, pushing her out the door of the bedroom. "Cash, seriously, he won't like it." I ignore her, leading her down the hall with a hand in the small of her back to where the kids are. "I would hate to see my dad put his old Seal skills to use by making you disappear." I start laughing. "This isn't funny," she says loudly just as we walk around the corner into the rooms that the kids are playing in.

"What's not funny, Daddy?" Ashlyn asks, running up to us.

"Nothing, love bug." Lilly glares at me when I chuckle. "Are you guys hungry?" Lilly asks the kids.

"I'm starbing," Jax says, his head going back, his arms going straight out at his sides.

"Little dude, when are you not hungry?" I ask, and he looks at me. I can tell he is really thinking about what his answer is going to be.

"When I eat," he replies, making both of us laugh.

~~*

"Baby, seriously, are you sure you don't want me to take you?" I ask. I know I promised I would trust her with the whole Austin thing, but what the fuck? The idea of my woman going to meet another man for coffee seems ridiculous to me.

"Cash, we talked about this. I will only be gone for about an hour, if that, then I will be home," she repeats the same thing she told me five minutes ago.

"I know," I grumble. I'm sure I sound like Jax.

"An hour," she repeats, kissing me. She grabs her bag and a set of keys off the counter and heads out the door. I watch her go, wanting to drag her back inside, but I know she will kick my ass if I try. I look around the quiet house; Jax and Ashlyn are out with Lilly's dad. Her mom is sleeping, so it just me and my imagination. I need to keep busy.

"What the hell are you doing?" I spin around, coming face-to-face with Lilly's mom, who is looking at me like I'm crazy, and maybe I am. I got bored, so I started cleaning. I had just finished vacuuming the whole downstairs when she showed up.

"Vacuuming," I tell her, lifting the vacuum up.

"I know. I was trying to take a nap when I heard you down here. What the hell is wrong with you?" Her hands go to her waist and she looks a little scary. "Austin is just a friend to Lilly, so you need to relax, and if you don't want to relax and cleaning helps you decompress, or de-stress, or whatever the hell it is you're doing, then take the vacuum upstairs and finish what you started," she says, walking past me into the kitchen. I'm just finishing my vacuuming when Lilly comes into the room. She looks just the same as she did before—no happier, no sadder—so I guess that's good.

"You vacuumed?" she asks, looking around, then at the vacuum in my hand.

"Yes," I say defensively. "I know the kids are messy; I just wanted to help out."

"Oooo-kay." She rolls her eyes. "I brought you a coffee and a cinnamon roll; they are both downstairs."

"Thank you." Ha! She thought of me when she was out with Austin. She starts to walk away, but I snag her, bending her backwards and kissing her, possessing her mouth. When I right her, she looks at me and smiles before skipping away. The damn woman is going to make me lose my mind.

~~*

I'm dying. I take a deep breath; my lungs are on fire, along with the muscles in my legs. I'm pretty sure I'm dead already. I look ahead and see that Austin and Lil's dad are about a quarter of a mile ahead of me. We're hiking up the side of the mountain they said was great for hunting bears. Honestly, I don't even want to see a bear in the wild, let alone get close enough to shoot it. "Hurry up there, son," Lil's dad calls back over his shoulder. I shake my head in disgust; I thought I was in good shape.

"I'm coming," I grumble, and glare when I see Austin look over his shoulder with a smirk on his face. He isn't even sweating, which is strange considering he has as much hair on his body as a wild animal. After about twenty minutes, we get to the top of the mountain. The view is breathtaking. "This is amazing."

"This is where I asked Lilly's mom to marry me," Frank says, his eyes landing on me, his arms crossing over his chest.

"It's a good spot," I tell him, looking out over the valley below.

"When are you going to ask my daughter to marry you?" I look at him, then over at Austin. My hand goes to my pocket where I have kept her ring since picking it up at the jewelers. I run my fingers over the metal before pulling it out of my pocket.

"I actually wanted to ask you for permission." I hold the ring out in his direction. The ring has three diamonds. They represent our past, present, and future. They're wrapped in white gold, with the kids' birthstones set in-between.

"I can't believe she took you back," Austin says, looking at the ring, then me.

"I can't believe it either, but she's mine, and I will take out anyone who stands in the way of us having a future." I look directly at Austin; his eyes flare, but he doesn't say anything.

"You have my blessing," Frank says. I look at him to see him smiling.

"Thank you," I reply, putting the ring back in my pocket.

"Where's the box?" Austin asks.

"What?"

"The ring box, where is it?"

"In the garbage." I sigh. "I can't have the box in my pocket; it's too obvious," I say, running my fingers over the ring again. This is a new habit; touching it does something to calm me.

"How long have you had it?

"A little over a month," I say, shrugging. I like having it with me. I don't know when I'll ask; I just have a feeling that when the time comes, I will know.

"It aint burning a hole in your pocket?" Austin asks, looking at me curiously.

"Honestly," I shake my head, "yeah, but I want to make sure that she is ready before I ask her."

"I know a spot she loves," Austin says, looking thoughtful. I'm not sure I would want to ask her to marry me at any location they used to go to together. He must read my face when the next words come out of his mouth. "Childs Glacier. She loves it out there. And no, we never went there together," Austin says, and I remember her telling me about that place, saying there wasn't anywhere in the world more beautiful. I can even remember the pictures she had in her apartment when I first started dating her.

"I'm not sure when I'm going to ask her. I want it to be in the moment." I look at Austin and Frank, who both smile.

"Well, if you want her to say yes, then you should be in the moment at Childs Glacier."

"She will say yes," I say, not feeling so confident when I read the looks on their faces. "What?"

"When she was a little girl, she told me she wanted her future husband to ask her to marry her at her favorite spot, just like I asked her mom to marry me at *her* favorite place."

"I don't know. I just keep thinking I will know when I'm supposed to ask her." I sigh, pulling the hat off my head.

"Bud, just take her out to the glacier. If you don't get the feeling when you're there, then don't ask her," Austin says. I really don't want to like this guy, but he makes it hard not to.

"I'll think about it," I say, thinking over the idea.

"All right." Frank smiles and pats my back. "Enough of the women-talk, time to go find our bear."

"Shit," I groan. "How the hell did I end up in this situation?" I look at Austin, who laughs.

"You need to man-up," Austin says, smiling. "We need to make a man out of you. Hunting is like coffee; it puts hair on your chest."

"If that's the case, I think you need to quit drinking coffee and hunting." I look him over, shaking my head. He looks like a bear.

"Jealous?" he asks, pulling down the top of his shirt and showing off his chest hair.

"Fuck no."

"Chicks love it." He smiles, and I can't help but laugh.

"What the hell are you two gossiping about? Get it together; we're burning daylight," Frank yells. Austin looks at me and shrugs before taking off hiking again.

"You better be careful, Austin, you could easily be confused with a bear," I tell his back. His hand raises over his shoulder so he can flip me off. I start to jog so I'm not so far behind and pray we don't see a bear.

Chapter 11

Lilly

I look out the window of the truck into the side-view mirror. The dirt road we're driving on is creating a large dust cloud behind us. All along the side of the road is empty space with large mountains off in the distance. My mom and dad are keeping the kids for us for a few hours so that Cash and I can go out to Childs Glacier. There are two glaciers near where I grew up in Alaska: one is Childs, the other, Miles. Childs Glacier has been one of my favorite places to go and think since I was young. There is just something about looking at a natural wonder that has been around for thousands of years. Along with the beauty of it—the amazing glaring white and turquoise color that is woven throughout the ice, and the river running along the front of it—if you're lucky, you can watch a piece of ice fall off into the water; the sound of thunder that fills the air when it happens is awe inspiring.

"What's going on in that head of yours?" Cash asks, pulling my hand up to his mouth to kiss my fingers.

"Nothing." I smile, looking over at him.

"Are you sad that were leaving in a couple of days?"

"Yes and no." I squeeze his hand. "I miss my parents, but I also miss home," I tell him and see him smile.

"I miss home too, but I am gonna miss it here." He puts my hand on his thigh with his on top of mine, his thumb running across the top. "This is someplace I could see myself living," he says, and I laugh; he is only saying that because he has never gone through an Alaskan winter. "What's so funny?"

"Honey, in the winter, there are times it snows so badly that you can't even open the front door. A couple of years ago, the National Guard had to come in and dig people out because there were fifteen feet of snow in some areas." I watch as his eyes almost bug out of his head. "So, now do you want to move here?" I ask him.

"I think we will just have to find time to visit in the summer."

"I thought so." I smile.

"What the hell is that?" Cash asks. My eyes go from him to the road, and I see a giant black blur in the middle of the road ahead of us.

"I don't know," I mumble, squinting my eyes. The closer we get, the clearer the object in the middle of the road becomes.

"Is it an elk?" Cash asks, and I shake my head no. I haven't seen a wild moose up close for years, and this one is huge; the antlers alone look as big as the truck we're traveling in.

"Slow down," I say, trying to breathe.

'What?" Cash asks, and I can see the moose take notice of us. I know we're screwed unless we can get the truck turned around.

"Slow down!" I repeat, this time shouting the words. Cash slams the brakes, making the truck skid on the gravel road. The moose, who had been standing in the middle of the road, has now started running towards us. In Alaska, wild moose can be very aggressive, especially the males. "Turn the truck around!" I yell as I watch the moose running at us.

"Holy shit."

"Turn the truck around now!" I scream, seeing the moose running at full speed. Cash looks at me, then slams the truck in reverse. The truck backs off the road, the tail end hanging off the road, down into the ditch. I look out the side window, seeing that the moose is still coming towards us. He is now a lot closer, his head down, and his large antlers swinging back and forth. "Go, go, go!" I cry, listening to the tires as they try to catch the road, but by the sound, I can tell that all they're hitting is air.

"Baby, when I say, I need you to throw yourself back against the seat," Cash says calmly.

"What?"

"Just do it…on three," he says, his eyes on me. I nod, then he starts to count. The second he gets to three, I push myself backwards hard against the seat and feel the truck tip back. The tires hit the gravel, and the truck lunges forward. The only problem is now we're heading right for the moose. "What the hell are you doing?" I scream, my hands going to my face to cover it.

"Shit!" Cash yells. I feel the car jerk to the right, making me slide across my seat, we jerk to the left. And I wait to feel the impact from the moose running into us, but nothing comes. "We're good, babe," Cash says, and I remove my hands from my face. "Are you okay?" Cash asks, and I nod as his hand goes to the back of my neck where his fingers move in slow circles. A few minutes later, he pulls the car over, unbuckles my seatbelt, and then pulls me over into his lap. "Are you okay?" His hands and eyes run over my body.

"Yeah, I'm good." I wrap my arms around his shoulders, burying my face in his neck.

"We're not moving to Alaska."

"Agreed," I say, breathing him in.

"I thought I was afraid of seeing a bear; now I know I should have been afraid to see a damn moose." He chuckles, and I feel the rumble against my cheek. I don't know if it's the near death experience or what, but I want…no, I *need* him. I feel my clit pulse and my mouth opens up

266

on his neck. My tongue comes out, traveling up his neck to his ear, and I feel him grow hard under me. "Baby, what are you doing?" His voice is rough and goes right to my core, where I feel myself become wetter. His hand at my waist travels up my side so that his thumb is resting under my breast.

"Please, touch me." I move my mouth to his, where I bite his bottom lip, giving it a hard tug. "*Please*, touch me," I beg as I watch his eyes flash. Then his hand is in my hair at the back of my head.

"You want me to touch you?" he asks, pulling my face away from his. I nod and he tugs my hair again.

"Give me the words, Lil."

"Yes, I want you to touch me," I say barely above a whisper.

"My girl misses my touch?"

"Yes," I agree. Since we have been in Alaska, we haven't had sex. Being in my parents' house isn't really conducive. Their walls are like paper, and the kids have ended up in bed with us every night since we got here.

"Tell me what you want, baby." He pulls my head forward, and I can feel the slight sting of his fist in my hair.

"Anything," I say; I just need to feel his hands on me.

"Anything?" he asks, looking me over. His hand goes under the seat, and we slide back suddenly. "Don't forget that you just said anything." His hands go to my waist, where he turns me so that I'm straddling him. "Wait, take off your pants," he says, helping me move so I can get my shoes and pants off. Once I get them off, he pulls me back over on top of him. I'm so turned on that the feel of the denim of his jeans rubbing against my inner thighs has me moaning out loud. "Put your hands on the steering wheel behind you." My hands go behind me automatically, grabbing onto the steering wheel. This position causes my breasts to thrust out and my back to arch. I watch as Cash's hand comes up and wraps around my neck before traveling down, and I hear the distinct sound of the zipper of my hoodie being pulled down. Once he has it open, his hands come up, palming my breasts through the thin tank top I'm wearing. My eyes close and I feel him tug the tank top and my bra down until my breasts are free. "You have beautiful tits," he says, pulling on each nipple. "But you know I love your ass," he says, his hands going to my behind, squeezing and pulling me hard against him. I cry out against the friction. "You're really wet, baby." I can hear the hunger in his voice; my eyes open and he is looking down between my thighs. His fingers run over the center of the thin material covering me. My body jerks, and his eyes come up to meet mine. Then I feel his finger move the material aside, the tip of his finger sliding over my clit. "Jesus, baby, what the fuck?" he growls

268

before I'm flying through the air. I land on my back in the seat. I don't even have time to react before my legs are thrust open, my panties ripped to the side, and Cash's mouth is devouring me.

"Yes!" I cry, my hands going to his hair, holding him to me. My leg that is on the floorboard of the truck comes up to wrap around his shoulder. "Oh, God, don't stop." My head thrashes back and forth against the seat, and the minute I feel two fingers fill me, I come hard and fast. The force of it takes my breath away, and my hands in his hair fist and pull, trying to get him away from me. My eyes open when he stops; his eyes are on me as he wipes his mouth on the inside of my thigh. He sits up on his knees, still between my open legs, his hands go to the button of his jeans, and he unbuttons and unzips them quickly. His hard cock springs free when he pulls down his boxers, and his hands go back to my thighs, then under. He pulls me up, then leans his big body over me, filling me full in one long stroke.

"So fucking tight." His words are said against my mouth. I can taste myself on him, his hands at my ass pulling me up to meet each stroke. My hands go up the back of his shirt, my nails digging into his skin. My foot goes to the steering wheel, getting leverage. "Fuck me, baby," he rumbles, his body arching so he can bend his head to pull my nipple into his mouth.

"Yes," I hiss, my head going back to push my breast deeper into his mouth. His pace picks up, his hips slamming into me so hard that my head starts to bang against the door until he puts his hand at the top of my head to cushion it.

"I love this pussy," he groans, and I know he's close when I feel him get even bigger inside me.

"I'm close," I tell him, my mouth going to his shoulder and my legs tightening around him. His free hand comes between us, zeroing in on my clit. I thrust up against him and break apart, biting down hard. I feel myself convulse, and I know that my orgasm has caused his to set off. His hips jerk a few more times before his strokes slow and then stop. His forehead comes to rest on my shoulder. He is breathing heavily, the skin of his back wet with sweat.

"I missed being inside you."

"I missed you too," I breathe, my limbs squeezing him more tightly against me. His forehead comes off my shoulder. His eyes meet mine and he smiles.

"Are you okay?" His hand rubs the top of my head; it feels tender from being banged into the door of the truck.

"Yeah." I smile then start to laugh, shoving my face into his throat.

"What's so funny?" He chuckles, kissing the top of my head.

"Nothing." I smile, feeling happy.

"You ready to take me to the glacier now that you've had your way with me?" he asks.

"No, I think we should stay here for the rest of the day," I tell him, pulling my face out of his neck and my hand out from under his shirt so that I can run my fingers down his jaw.

"This is a good place to be." He smirks, rotating his hips and making me bite the inside of my cheek. "But we only have two more days in Alaska, and I really want to see this place that you have been telling me about since I met you." He gently touches his mouth to mine, and his hips pull away so he can slide out of me. He bends forward, kissing my belly, then helps me sit up. I watch, fascinated as his hips lift off the seat and he tucks himself back into his jeans. "Babe, seriously, get dressed." I nod and look away, picking my jeans up off the truck floor. I pull them on, then my socks and boots. Once I have straightened out my clothes and hair, I put my seatbelt back on and he puts the truck in drive. It takes twenty minutes to get out to the glacier. Once we reach the Million-Dollar Bridge, better known as 'The Bridge to Nowhere', I know we're close. "So you're telling me that that bridge goes to absolutely nowhere, and that the state of Alaska paid a million dollars to have it built just so they could get rid of the money so it wouldn't go back to the government?"

'That's what I'm telling you." I smile. "Well, that's what I have always been told about the bridge, anyway." I shrug. We pull off the road and get out of the truck so we can walk across the bridge. It is in much better shape than it used to be in. About fifteen years ago, you would have to walk or drive across wooden planks; now that it's refinished, you don't have to worry about plummeting to your death. We stand in the middle of the bridge. Cash's arms wrap around me from behind, and we look down at the water below and at the glacier off in the distance. I feel him kiss the back of my head. I always wanted to share this place with someone. It really is beautiful. I snuggle into his embrace, just enjoying the feeling of having him here with me. I miss the simple life of Alaska; everything is so different here. In the winter, you know every person in town since there are no tourists. And if something ever happens to one of the residents, everyone comes together to offer any support needed. I guess the town where I now live in Tennessee is similar. You just have to multiply the number of residents by a few thousand.

"You ready to show me the glacier?"

"Yeah." I smile, looking over my shoulder. He leans in and places a kiss on my forehead before taking my hand and leading me back to the truck. Once we're both buckled in, he drives the next few minutes to the bridge leading to the perfect spot to see the giant body of dense ice. We both get out and meet at the front of the truck. Cash takes my hand again, and I pull him down the long dirt path to the glacier and the viewing area. You can't see anything until you climb to the top, then you see nothing but a beach area, a giant river, and Childs Glacier sitting on the other side.

"Holy shit," Cash says, making me smile. I know it's one thing to talk about seeing a glacier, but it's another thing completely to see it for yourself. The air near the glacier is so much colder, but it is also so much cleaner.

"I told you it was awesome." I tug on his hand, dragging him behind me to the edge of the river. "You would think just by looking at it that it's close, but it's actually miles away," I tell him, looking across the river at the giant white wall of the glacier in front of us. The colors of turquoise and blue that run through it are so vibrant that the whole thing looks like a painting.

"It really is the perfect place," he says, standing behind me. One of his arms wraps around my waist, the other around my chest, his chin resting on the top of my head.

"I love coming out here." I put my hands on his arm at my chest. "This is the one place where you really are apart from all the stresses of normal life. I know, standing here, just how small I am in the giant scheme of things."

"You may be small in terms of the whole world, but to me and my kids, you make up our world," he says softly against my ear. My tummy flips over, and I can't help the tears I feel filling my eyes. I feel his hand leave my waist, and he reaches into his pocket. I think he is going to pull out his cell phone so he can take a picture, so when his hand comes around in front of me, it takes a second to realize what he is holding.

"Holy shit," I breathe, my nails digging into his arm. In between his fingers is the most beautiful ring I've ever seen.

"I have been carrying this thing around for a while now, waiting for the right time to ask you to marry me." My brain slowly registers the words. It starts screaming 'yes, yes, yes!' but I can't make anything come out except, "What?"

My eyes are glued to the ring; it's absolutely perfect. I feel myself being turned, but my eyes are locked on the design of the ring—three diamonds, and two smaller stones in-between. I don't really notice the change in position until Cash is kneeling in front of me.

"Lil, I need you to look at me." I shake my head before taking my eyes off the ring and meeting his. "I kept telling myself that when the time was right, I would know it, and this is the moment." I watch him take a breath, his hand grabbing mine. "This is the moment I have been waiting for. This is the moment we start our forever. This is the moment you tell me you will marry me and make me the luckiest fucking man on this planet."

"Yes." I cover my mouth and drop to my knees in front of him, burying my face in his chest. I start to cry immediately. If someone would have told me a year ago that I would be with Cash at my favorite place in the world, with him on his knee asking me to marry him, I would have laughed in their face. I never would have believed that this was a possibility for me.

"Baby, you're freaking me the fuck out right now." His arms are wrapped tightly around me, his mouth close to my ear.

"I…I'm…s-so…h-happy," I say on a sob, and laugh because I sound like an idiot.

"I would feel like you are telling me the truth if my shirt wasn't soaked with your tears, baby."

"Sorry." I take a deep breath and pull my face back so I can look at him. His hands go to the hair at the side of my head, pulling it away from my face.

"What do you say we see how the ring fits?" His eyes search my face and I smile, looking at his hand. He leans forward and places a light kiss on my lips before taking his right hand away from my face, pulling the ring off his finger, and pulling my hand towards him. I feel the cool metal slide along my finger and over my knuckle. The fit is just right.

"It's perfect." I put my hand against his chest, looking at the ring there.

"I had it made to represent our family, and all of us coming together as one."

"I love you," I say, looking up from the ring on my hand and into his handsome face.

"You are my world, baby. I never thought I would be this happy again. Now, having you back, and having Ashlyn and Jax, I have surpassed happiness." He smiles, showing off both dimples.

"I feel the same. I didn't think I would ever feel like this again." I wrap my arms around his waist, laying my head against his chest. We're turned to the side so that we can both look out at the glacier. "Thank you for giving this to me."

"There isn't anything I wouldn't do for you." His arms give me a squeeze. "There is no way for you to know what you have given me," he says softly, kissing the top of my head. I don't say anything, just hold him a little tighter. I know what I have given him, because he has given me the same thing.

"We're getting married," I blurt after a few minutes. I feel Cash shaking with laughter. I know it's dumb, but the realization that he just proposed to me and what that means hits me hard.

"Yeah, baby, that's usually what happens when someone asks someone else to marry them."

"Whatever." I roll my eyes, even though he can't see me do it. We stand there watching as a large piece of ice falls off the glacier, crashing into the water below, the sound echoing around us sounding like thunder.

"Where is everyone?" he asks, looking around. The whole area is completely empty.

"There are guided trips out here a couple times a week, but for the most part, the only people who come out here are residents." I shrug. "It's a long drive, and not too many people want to make the trip."

"I can see why you like it out here." His hand reaches around his back, grabbing mine and bringing it between us. "I like this." He smiles.

"I love it."

"No, I like knowing that people will see this and know that you're taken."

"You're an idiot." I laugh. "Will you wear a ring?" I ask. I know a lot of men don't; my dad doesn't, and he is more in love with my mom than the day they met.

"Yes," he says in a way that I know he really likes the idea.

"I wonder what the kids will say."

"They'll be happy. I thought about involving them in asking you, but I knew that the minute I told them, they wouldn't be able to keep the secret.

"This has been the best day ever."

"Even with the moose attack?" I laugh, shaking my head.

"Well, that was scary, but what happened afterwards made it well worth it."

"True." He smiles and kisses my forehead. "What do you say we go back to your parents and share the good news?"

"Yeah," I agree, and we walk back to the truck. The whole way home, we talk about our future, and when we get to my parents' house, we are greeted with two very excited kids, and my parents are beyond happy for us. It really is the best day ever. I am sad to be going back to Tennessee, but also excited to be starting a new chapter with Cash when we get there.

~~*

"It's a sign," Cash says, and I almost laugh, but I can tell he is being completely serious.

"It's not a sign; its bad weather and a lack of available hotels," I reply, looking out the window of our hotel room in Las Vegas. We were supposed to have a short layover in Vegas, but the weather changed, and tornados have been touching down all over the south. So they canceled all flights, leaving us to spend the day and night in Vegas.

"No, *that* is a sign," he says, pointing down at The Little Chapel of Love that is across the street from where were we're staying for the night.

"We're not getting married here." I laugh.

"Oh yes, we are. It's meant to be."

"You just asked me to marry you the day before yesterday. I haven't even gotten used to the idea that I'm your fiancée."

"Good, then it won't be difficult for you to get used to the idea of being my wife."

"You're crazy."

"No, I'm a genius."

"Cash."

"Lil, I love you. You love me. Our kids are here. It's perfect."

"I don't even have anything to wear," I tell him. I have no idea why I'm even considering this; I must be just as crazy as he is.

"You and Ashlyn go dress shopping while Jax and I go get our tuxes, and we will meet you across the street at five," he says, and the hive of honeybees that is always in my stomach when he's around starts to move even more rapidly.

"This is crazy," I whisper, looking at the small white chapel.

"This is perfect." His arms around my waist give me a squeeze. "What does it matter if we do it now or in a few months?"

"Um…my parents. Your parents," I remind him.

"They will be fine, and we can plan a party."

"You're really serious about this aren't you?"

"One-hundred percent serious."

"Okay, well then, let's do this." I smile, my belly flipping over.

"I thought I was going to have to try harder to convince you." I feel his body relax behind me, but his arms squeeze me a little more tightly.

"You're going to be the one to break the news to my parents," I tell him, not looking forward to that conversation.

"Works for me. Your dad loves me; he'll be cool," he says, sounding so sure that I can't help but to laugh.

"How did you win him over?" I ask. My dad really does love Cash. I know that if my dad had his way, we would be moving to Alaska, and Cash would be working with my dad on his boat and guiding people when they weren't out fishing. I was even surprised that Austin gave Cash his seal of approval. They had gotten close after Dad had taken Cash and Austin out on a hunting trip.

I guess they all bonded while killing poor defenseless creatures.

"I didn't have to win him over." He runs his nose along my ear before kissing me underneath it. "I love his daughter; that's all he needed," he says, his warm breath causing goose bumps to break out over my skin.

"That may have helped, but you did win him over," I tell him softly. I don't know how someone who is so strong can have doubt himself so often. "You're a good man and an amazing father. A great friend, a goo—"

"Shut up."

"What?" I turn my head to look at him.

"Stop talking, Lil," he says, and I can see so many emotions on his face that it makes it hard to breath.

"It's all true, Cash," I say lightly. His mouth goes into a flat line, and his eyes close.

"It is, and all of those are the reasons why I'm going to take Ashlyn, go and pick out dresses for us, meet you across the street in a few hours, and tie myself to you in a way that makes it hard for you to get rid of me." I run my fingers down his cheek.

"I want that." He shakes his head. "No, I need that." His eyes open, and all I can see is love. I can see so much love that I can feel it all the way to my soul. "I need you tied to me."

"Good, I need and want the same thing," I tell him. We stand for a few more minutes, his arms around me while we look out the window at the little chapel across the street.

"All right, babe, go get Ashlyn and go find a dress. Meet me across the street so I can make you mine."

"Okay." I smile and go get Ashlyn, who is sitting in the small sitting room watching cartoons. "Hey, love bug, I need your help," I tell her, then explain exactly what we're going to do, and all the while her smile gets bigger and bigger. My daughter is a girly-girl, and anything that involves dressing up and looking pretty she is always down for. The boys come in and tell us goodbye, and we leave shortly after them to head out in search of a dress boutique. I find a small shop in a huge casino and happen across the perfect ivory strapless gown. It hugs all my curves and fits me perfectly, and for Ashlyn, I let her pick out a very poufy pink dress and matching shoes. We head to a salon next, spending over an hour getting our hair done, along with manicures and pedicures before heading to the chapel. When we arrive, I don't know what to expect, but I never would have thought the place would be so beautiful inside. There are no crazy impersonators, or gaudy decorations; it was just a simple room with a large alter, and six pews along the sides with beautiful cream and white flowers running between them.

"It's so pretty," Ashlyn says. Her eyes are lit up, and then she sees her dad at the same exact moment as I do. She takes off in a run while I'm stuck in place. He looks so hot in his tux that it's going to take everything in me not to jump him. His eyes leave my face and travel down my body, then back up again. By the time his eyes meet mine, they are so dark and so hungry that I squeeze my thighs together, trying to release some of the ache which has settled there. "Daddy, me and Mommy had the best time eber! Look, I got a new dress," Ashlyn says excitedly, twirling around. His eyes leave me and he smiles, looking down at our daughter.

"You look like a princess," he tells her.

"I know!" she squeals, jumping up and down. I look to Cash's side to see Jax standing there, looking very handsome in his tux that matches his dad's. His hand is at his throat, trying to loosen his tie. His eyes are on his sister when he rolls them in annoyance. I smile because as much as she gets on his nerves, he really does love her. I take a step forward and squat in front of Jax. I want to make sure he is okay with us going through with this.

"You want my help?" I ask, moving my hands to his tie, where I loosen it up and undo his top button. "Are you okay with me and your dad getting married?" I ask him quietly. I know he and Ashlyn were both excited when we told them that we were engaged, but this is something different, and I need to know that he is okay with it.

"Will you be my mom?" he asks, and my eyes fly up to meet his. I take a breath; I don't even know how to answer that.

"Well I—"

"Ashlyn is my sister already."

"She is," I agree.

"So if you marry my dad that will make you my mom, right?"

"Um...I will be your stepmom," I tell him gently. I don't want him to think I'm trying to take his mom's place. He seems to consider this for a few seconds before replying, "So, can I call you Mom?"

Jeez, what the hell do I say to that? I would love for him to call me Mom, but I'm not sure how everyone else will feel about it. I watch his shoulders slump, and I make up my mind right then and there, *screw everyone*. Okay, not everyone, but I love this kid.

"I would be honored if you called me Mom, but I think it's something you should talk to your dad about."

"Dad, can I call Lilly, Mom?" Jax yells, making Cash swing his head towards us. *Oh no, he doesn't look happy. Crap, crap, crap.* I go to stand when Cash squats beside me.

284

"Is that what you want, little dude?"

"I know she's not my real mom," he says, looking at Cash, then me, "but can't I have two moms?" His little head drops, and I want to hold him so badly that I feel my skin prickle.

"Of course you can," I tell him, not caring for one second if it's the right thing or not. I love Jax as much as I love Ashlyn, and think of him as my son, so I'm happy he feels the same about me. Today really is the perfect day; not only am I marrying the man I love, but I'm also gaining a son.

Chapter 12

<u>Cash</u>

I look down at my little man, my chest feeling tight. I knew he loved Lilly, but after today, I know how deeply that love runs. The lady who runs the chapel has Lilly standing at the end of the aisle. The music begins, and Ashlyn starts down the aisle, dropping flower petals as she goes. My baby girl looks beautiful in her princess dress. When she makes it to me, her head turns to look over her shoulder, looking back at what she's done. When her eyes came back to me, her head tilts back in pride, and a smile lights up her face, letting me know she is happy with the results. "Stand where they told you, baby." I pointed to the spot. Once she is standing there, Lilly starts making her way towards me. The cut of her dress shows off her breasts, waist, and hips; I can't wait to get it off her. Lucky for me, a good friend of mine lives in Vegas with his wife and kids. He agreed to watch the kids for the night. Lilly doesn't know about my plan yet, but there is no way that I'm not going to spend our wedding night without being inside her. The music continues to play as Lilly comes down the aisle. Her hands are in front of her, holding a bouquet of pink flowers that match Ashlyn's dress. Once she makes it to me, she smiles, then laughs. "This is serious business, baby. Why are you laughing?" I reach out, grabbing her hand and dragging her to me.

"I don't know. I was just thinking this is nothing like what I pictured when I thought of a Vegas wedding." I chuckle and pull her even closer so I can whisper to her.

"Should we leave here and find Elvis so he can marry us?"

"No, this is perfect," she whispers back, her eyes soft as they search mine, the smile on her face telling me everything that I need to know. I thought that I may have been rushing her, and a part of me felt guilty about it, while the other part couldn't care less, so it's a relief to see her excitement and happiness.

"You ready to do this?" I ask quietly.

"Yes."

I lean forward to kiss her, but she leans back, away from me. "You can't kiss me yet."

"I can't?"

"Not until after we're married." She shakes her head.

"Well then, let's do this so I can kiss you." She steps back until she is standing next to Ashlyn, who grabs her hand. The man who is going to marry us takes it as his cue to begin the ceremony. I listened as he speaks, and repeat when necessary, but for the most part, I'm in awe looking at Lilly, wondering how the fuck I got so lucky. I had fucked up huge in the past with her, and now having her standing across from me, agreeing to be my wife, is something I would never have even considered as a possibility.

"Cash, would you please repeat after me."

"I have my own vows," I tell him. Lilly's eyes widen, then she giggles and shakes her head.

"Sure," the officiator says.

I clear my throat, feeling nervous all of the sudden. "I vow to love you unconditionally, without hesitation. I will encourage you, trust you, and respect you. As a family, we will create a home filled with learning, laughter, and compassion. I promise to be your biggest fan, your partner in crime, and the person you can always depend on. From the moment we met, you have owned me, and I will love you until I take my last breath. I will work every day to make now into always. With these words, and all the love in my heart, I marry you and bind your life to mine." I slide an infinity diamond ring up against her wedding ring, bring it to my mouth, and place a kiss on it.

"You're really good at this," she whispers. I can't help but laugh and kiss her forehead.

"Lilly, do you have vows?" the officiator asks.

"Um, no, but can I just make it up?"

"If that's what you would like." He smiles.

"Yes, please," she says, taking hold of my hands. "Today, standing here with our children watching, I choose you, Cash, to be my partner. I am proud to be your wife, and to join my life with yours. I promise to support you, push you, inspire you, and above all, love you, for better or worse, in sickness and health, for richer or poorer, as long as we both shall live." She is crying harder now, and I can feel tears fill my eyes as she speaks. She shocks me when she pulls her hand away, reaching down the front of her dress where she pulls out a ring. We both start laughing when she mouths the word 'storage' to me. Her hand comes back to mine, lifts them, and slides the ring on my finger, her finger running over it before looking back up at me. Then she reaches her hands forward, one going to either side of my face, pulling my head towards hers.

"Hey, no kissing until we're married," I tell her, laughing. I look over at the man and he grins, nodding his head.

"By the power invested in me and the great state of Nevada, I now pronounce you Husband and wife. You may now kiss the bride," he says. My hand goes into the back of Lilly's hair; I tilt her face back, and my mouth covers hers, my tongue sweeping in. The sound she makes urges me on. I can't wait to be inside her. There is nothing better than her thighs wrapped around my hips, her arms around my neck, and her wet heat strangling my cock. I reluctantly pull away from her, kissing her lips one more time. Both kids start yelling and running around in circles.

"We're married," she says with a smile.

"We are," I agree. After our short ceremony, we have a few pictures taken of us and the kids. We're almost done when Jax yells, "Flex!" at the top of his lungs and takes off running. "Yo, my man!" I yell when I see my buddy Flex walking in holding his wife's hand, their kids walking near them until they see Jax, then they take off, ready to play.

"Who is that?" Lilly asks. I'm not surprised that she looks nervous. Flex is a scary looking dude. He's not very tall at 5'8 but he is built like a bulldog, with tattoos and chocolate-colored skin—the total opposite of his very blonde, beach-bunny-looking wife.

"Flex, he is one of my best friends. We went to school together." I grab her hand and start heading towards the front of the chapel when Lilly trips and I have a nanosecond to catch her before her head hits the pew. "Even on our wedding day," I joke, helping to get her feet underneath her. Making sure she's steady, I give her another kiss.

"I can't help it; I have two left feet," she replies, trying to catch her breath.

"You are the clumsiest person I have ever met."

"So you've said," she mumbles.

"It's the truth, and it's even documented."

"My mom and her big fat mouth," she grumbles, looking adorable. Lilly's mom told me that Lilly would get hurt so much when she was little that CPS were called in to review her case. They didn't believe that it was the case of a clumsy child until she fell down, splitting her forehead open in the office of the caseworker. She still has a tiny scar to prove it.

"You have to admit it's pretty funny," I tell her.

"Maybe a little." She smiles. I stop when Ashlyn grabs my hand, and I pick her up and walk the few steps separating Flex and me.

"You really did it?" he asks, pulling me in for a hug. I pat his shoulder and lean back.

"Flex, Christy, this is my daughter, Ashlyn, and my beautiful wife Lilly. You both already know my little hellion, Jax."

"Jax, my man," he says, giving Jax a fist bump before he runs off to the other kids. Then Flex reaches over, touching Ashlyn's hair. "You look like your old man, pretty girl."

"No, I'm a girl; I look like my mommy." She

scrunches up her face, looking all kinds of cute.

"Is that so?" Flex laughs.

"Yes." Ashlyn smiles, then looks over at Jax talking to the other kids. "Can I go play with them?" she whispers to me. I nod, setting her down, and she runs right over to Jax's side. Flex and Christy's kids are beautiful, all caramel skin, curly golden hair, and big hazel eyes.

"Nice to meet you both," Lilly says, putting her hand out in Flex's direction, then she squeaks when he pulls her in for a hug, rocking her back-and-forth.

"Don't mind him, girl. He may look scary, but as you can see, he's a big teddy bear," Christy says, giving Lilly a hug. "Congratulations. You've got a good man," she tells Lilly, making her nod.

"Yeah, I kinda lucked out."

"Man, you should have told us to come earlier so we could watch," Flex says.

"Nah, I just wanted it to be us and the kids. But you guys should fly out for our reception in a few months," Cash tells him, slapping his shoulder.

"That would be good. I haven't seen your brothers in a while."

"So you're only in town for the night, and the

whole time you're here, you're gonna be locked up in your room at the hotel? You don't even want to come to the house and watch a game with me?"

"Did you not hear the part where I just got married to this beautiful woman?" I ask him. He looks at Lilly and smiles.

"Gotcha." He pulls Christy into his side, kissing her temple. "So you still want to meet up in the morning for us to drop off the kids and have brunch?" I feel Lilly tense at my side, so I soothed my hand over the smooth skin of her arm.

"Jax has known Flex, Christy, and their kids his whole life, and they are going to watch the kids overnight for us."

"Ashlyn?"

"She will be fine," Christy tells her. Lilly looks over to where Ashlyn is playing with the other kids. "If she isn't okay, we will call and bring her back to you," Christy says, and I realize I never even thought about the fact that Lilly has only been away from Ashlyn once, when my mom kept the kids for us. After we talk a few more minutes, we head over to the hotel to get some clothes for the kids. Ashlyn has taken right to Christy and the kids, making Lilly feel better about leaving her with them. Twenty minutes after we get to the hotel, I finally kick everyone out of the room, ready to start our honeymoon. I know one day we will have a real one, but I'm not sure when that will be, so I'm going to enjoy the fuck out of this night while we're here, and I'm going to make damn sure Lilly never forgets her wedding night.

I close the distance between us, loving the way she looks in her dress. She is so effortlessly beautiful. "Want to play a game?" I ask her, smiling when her eyes flare.

"What kind of game?" She bites her lip, and her breathing has sped up.

"Naked Hotel."

"Hmm...I don't know. Last time we played Naked House Day, you almost killed me."

"Death by cock." I chuckle, but my smile dies when I notice how hard her nipples are through the thin silky material of her dress. My hands slide up the curve of her waist, then up, cupping her breasts. Her head falls back and she moans. I pull my hands away and take a seat, spreading my legs wide. I rub my jaw. Part of me wants to rip the dress from her body, but the other part of me wants to watch her as she undresses slowly.

"What's wrong?" Her eyes dart around the room before coming back to me.

"I want you to undress for me," I tell her, palming my cock through the too-thick material of my tux. I want inside of her so badly I can feel my balls drawing up tight.

"Undress for you?" she repeats, looking around the room again.

"Look at me, baby." Her eyes meet mine, and this time, they are dark with lust. "Pull down the top of the dress and let me see your tits." She looks unsure, but her hands go to her top at the same time I start unbuttoning my dress shirt. Once I have my shirt unbuttoned, I sit back. "Pull down the top of your dress." She looks down at my lap, then back up, her hands running up her sides, over her breasts, before pulling down the top. Her breasts are firm and high, and her nipples dark pink and pebbled tight. I unbuckle my pants and pull down my zipper before pulling my cock free. Lilly's eyes flash and she licks her lips. "Tug them, baby. Touch yourself how you like me to touch you." She does, her back arching, eyes closing, and I palm myself, running my hand up and down the length in steady strokes. "Pull that dress the rest of the way off." My voice is rougher.

I watch as she shimmies the dress down, showing off inch after beautiful inch of skin. Once free of the dress and standing in only a sheer thong and heels, her hands cup her breasts. "Don't hide from me; give me what I want. Pull on those pretty little nipples for me." Her fingers pull at her nipples as her eyes watch what my hand is doing. She crosses her legs. I know she's wet; I can see her arousal. "Come here." I spread my legs wider so she has room to stand between them. She starts to kneel, but I stop her with a hand on her hip. "No, I want you to turn around and bend over." Her breath begins coming out in short pants. She searches my face before turning around. Her beautiful ass is toned and round, giving her body an hourglass shape. Her body curves over, the fullness of her pussy peeking out from between her legs, showing through the sheerness of the thin material covering her. Running my hands up the outside of her thighs, I feel her shiver under my palms. Once I have her hips in my hands, I pull her back to me, covering her with my mouth.

"Oh," she moans. I suck deep over the material before sliding it to the side and licking her again, this time harder. Her legs begin to shake, and placing my thumbs on the outer edges of her pussy, I spread her open wider, laving her with my tongue, loving the way she tastes. I start working two fingers in and out of her, feeling her begin to clamp down around my fingers. She whines as I pull my mouth away.

"Easy, baby. I need inside you." I sit forward, tugging my pants over my hips before ripping her thong from her body. Without warning, I lean forward, pulling her down onto my lap. I run the head of my cock over her opening and her hips start to grind against me. I lift my hips, sinking inside her slowly until I'm balls-deep.

"Cash," she whimpers. I hold her in place, enjoying the feeling of being wrapped tight inside her.

"I got you, baby." My hands roam her body before one captures a breast, the other zeroing in on her clit. I pull on her nipple at the same time I roll her clit between my fingers. I pull her back against me, rocking my hips in tandem with hers. I know she's close when I feel her heat start to strangle me. "That's it, baby. Come for me." I bite into her shoulder, pushing her over the edge. She calls out my name, her pussy contracting around me before her body falls limp against me. I hold her close, enjoying the feeling. My cock is throbbing; I need to come, but I want to see her face when I lose it inside her. I pick her up off my cock, sliding free. "I need you to stand up, baby." She does, her legs unstable, so I make sure to hold onto her hips. Once she's good, I pull off my clothes and pick her up, heading to the bedroom. I lay her on the bed, and looking around, I see that the hotel did as I asked. The bed is covered in rose petals—that may be overkill, but there is also a bottle of champagne and chocolate covered strawberries. I look at Lilly and her face is flushed, her eyes dark with lust. I climb onto the bed with her, dragging her higher up the bed with me. Leaning forward, I suck one nipple into my mouth, then the other.

"I need you in me," she cries, her body writhing beneath me. Her leg wraps around my hip, and her fingers run through my hair. My gaze travels up her body from my marks on her breasts to her beautiful face.

"I love you, Lil," I say, sliding into her. Her eyes stay locked on mine, my mouth lowering to hers.

"I love you too," she says against my lips. I slide deeper, her nails going to my ass and I know what she wants. I sit up on my knees, wrapping her legs around my thighs, my arms going straight into the bed so I can pound into her harder.

"I wanted to give you sweet," I grunt, leaning forward and pulling a nipple into my mouth, sucking hard before biting down.

"I don't want sweet!" she cries, her nails digging into my skin. My balls pull up and I thrust harder, each time grinding my pelvis against hers. Her body starts to pull me deeper. I feel the tingle in my spine and my balls draw up tight. I close my mouth over hers, sucking her tongue into my mouth at the same time she tightens and cries out. I lose myself inside her. My weight sinks down on top of her, my body molding to hers and I thrust more gently. My hands go to the sides of her face, I pull her hair away, and I lean forward to kiss her forehead, nose, and then her mouth.

"How you feeling?" I ask, whispering against her mouth, enjoying the feeling of having her under me, and still buried inside of her.

"I can't believe we're really married." She smiles, one which lights up her whole face. The smile that made me fall in love with her. The smile that she gives my kids, and the smile that I will be blessed with looking at for the rest of my life.

"Believe it, baby. You're my wife." I smile back.

"And you're my husband," she says, running her fingers down my jaw.

"I am," I slide out of her, "and as your husband, I'm going to give you a bath and order some food, that way you have enough energy to make it through Naked Hotel Day." She giggles, rolling away. I stand at the side of the bed and start laughing when I notice that she is covered with rose petals.

"What's so funny?" she asks. I pull her out of the bed, sliding a petal off her nipple. "Oh." She looks down at the bed, then between the two of us before cracking up. I don't have time to think before she runs off. I don't know what she's doing until she grabs her phone and I hear the sound of the camera clicking.

"What are you doing?"

"I want a picture of you covered in rose petals. I figure if I ever need to get my way, I can use this to blackmail you." She laughs as I lunge after her, and when I catch her, I toss her over my shoulder, slapping her ass one time before heading towards the bathroom.

"You're gonna pay for that," I tell her.

"What are you gonna do, spank me?" she asks, and I can hear the need in her voice.

"No, you like that too much. I say you're going to

get punishment-by-cock." I bite the inside of my cheek to keep from smiling. Her eyes narrow, then widen as I slide her down my body before turning, pressing her into the wall. "Are you ready for your punishment?" I press my hips into hers.

"Yes," she moans as I fill her, giving her the first part of her punishment, then again in the bathroom on the floor, then pressed against the glass windows where we decided to get married this morning, overlooking the little white chapel, and then in bed, where I fall asleep with my wife in my arms.

~~*

"I can't believe you!" Jules yells, running out of her apartment. I knew it was coming, I just didn't know when. I shake my head and roll up the window of the truck. I didn't want Jax to hear this conversation. We have been home for a week from our trip to Alaska and layover in Vegas, and today was the first time Jules has called and asked to see Jax. I hate taking him to her, but I can't deny him his own mother. I never want him to look at me and see the person who kept him from her.

"Hey, dude." He's looking out the window at his mom when I call his name. His eyes meet mine in the mirror. "I need to talk to your mom for a second, so stay buckled in." He nods, his eyes going back to Jules. I know he is conflicted about her. Shit, *I'm* conflicted about her. I fucking hate her guts, but there is nothing I can do because she is the mother of my son, so I'm forced to get along with her. I get out of the truck, shutting the door. I hold up my hand, holding her off until I can get her to the back of the truck. "Don't start your shit and let my son hear," I growl.

"Don't start my shit?" She puts her hands on her hips and I know she is itching to fight. She is always ready to fight. "You got married, and you don't want me to start my shit?" she asks, glaring.

"Me getting married has absolutely nothing to do with you," I tell her firmly. Marrying Lilly was the smartest thing I have ever done, for myself and my kids.

"My son lives with you."

"He does," I nod in agreement, "because that's where the courts put him."

"I think he should come live with me." My fists clench. I have never hit a woman in my life, and never would, but there have been times that I could see myself strangling her for how fucking selfish she is.

"You see him *maybe* every couple of weeks, only when the mood strikes you, and you want him to move in with you? He doesn't even know you. He can't even be left alone with you without crying and freaking out."

"That's your fault! You have always babied him."

"He is a fucking baby." I pull off my ball cap, running my hand through my hair. "I don't have time for this shit today," I growl, my eyes meeting hers.

"Oh, I'm sure you need to get back to the wife. Good to know she is more important than your son."

"First of all, unlike you, I don't place people in my life on different levels of importance. Lilly, Jax, and Ashlyn have all of me, one not more than the other."

"Lucky them, I never got shit from you," she says with a hurt look, but I have been down this road with her a million times.

"You're right. You never had my heart, but you had me. I was there; you were just so caught up in yourself and what you could get that you didn't give a fuck about me or your son, so don't try to feed me some sob-story bullshit."

"You're such a fucking dick."

"Do you want to take Jax to the park, or are you gonna hang out with him here?" I'm done with

302

her drama. We will never see eye-to-eye on any of this.

"I don't have time to take him to the park. I have to be somewhere." She doesn't even look disappointed about missing out on time with her son.

"Why the fuck did you ask me to bring him if you don't have time to visit?"

"I thought I would have time, but I got a call right before you got here, and now I don't have time."

"Whatever." I shake my head in disgust. I knew coming here was going to be a waste of time. I keep giving her chance after chance, hoping and praying that she will change for Jax, or at lease show some interest, but she never does. It's always the same bullshit. "Do you at least want to say goodbye to him?"

"Um, sure." She shrugs her shoulders like it's all the same to her. Then she walks over to the back door of my truck, opening it up. I walk to the front of the truck, opening the door and climbing inside. I listen as Jules tells Jax that she will see him another time. He sits there quietly, not responding. She doesn't touch him like a normal mother would touch her child after a long period of not seeing them. She doesn't even talk gently to him like a mother would; her whole demeanor is exactly like it is when she talks to me or one of her friends. "All right, talk to you both soon," Jules says as she closes the door of the truck. I wonder if she even notices that Jax didn't say one word to her the whole time.

"You okay, little dude?" I look over my shoulder to talk to him; his tiny jaw is clenched, and I know that he is trying not to cry. He nods his head, and then looks out the window again.

"Can Mom make cookies when we get home?" My heart aches, and I take a deep breath to try to control my own emotions. Ever since the wedding, he has called Lilly, Mom. I love that he is able to get the kind of motherly love he needs from Lilly, but I fucking hate that he is suffering so badly because of his real mother.

"I'm not sure, but you can ask her when we get there." He nods again, resting his forehead against the window. I turn on some music, filling the silence. Once we get back to the house, he is ready to go as soon as I open his door, and before his door is even shut, he is running towards the house yelling, "Mom!" at the top of his lungs. Lilly comes to the front door. She is wearing a pair of jeans and a t-shirt, her hair is pulled back from her face with a small clip, and her face is completely makeup-free, showing off her naturally creamy complexion and rosy cheeks. She looks beautiful.

"What is it, honey?" she asks as Jax plows into her, his arms going around her thighs. Her hand goes to the top of his head, the other to the back of his neck. He holds on to her for a second and she looks at me; I shake my head, and she nods before looking back down at Jax.

"Can we make cookies?" he asks, leaning his head back.

"Well, your sister and I were trying to make cinnamon rolls. Do you want to come help us?" He nods, unwrapping his arms. "Well, go in and wash your hands. I will be there in just a second." She runs her hand over his hair as he walks into the house.

"Are you okay?"

"No, but coming home knowing you're here goes a long way to making it okay." I pull her towards me by the waist, kissing her lips, then resting my mouth against her forehead.

"Please, don't let her stress you out," she says, her fingers running along my jaw, her touch calming me down.

"I'm fine, baby. Let's go inside; I need to make a phone call, and you need to make me cinnamon rolls."

"I'm sorry," she shakes her head, "I didn't know I was making *you* cinnamon rolls; the memo must have gotten lost along the way."

"You would deny your husband?"

"I guess I would." She smiles, getting the look she

always gets when she looks at me, lighting up her face.

"You know what happens when you deny me, right?" I ask, crowding her.

"What?" she asks. I hear her breath hitch and I smile.

"Never mind, please, don't make me cinnamon rolls. It's been awhile since my palm has felt your ass, and you know how I love your ass, baby." I lean in, kissing her nose, and then I turn her around, giving her a gentle push inside before tapping her on the ass.

"Cash." She looks at me over her shoulder.

"Got stuff to do, babe." I walk away smiling, knowing that the minute I can get her alone later tonight is the minute she will go wild for me. The anticipation is going to be making her squirm all day. I walk into my office and set about getting things ordered for the jobsite that we're starting on next week. Once that's done, I pay some bills. I need to call Nico, but I know that he has been busy lately. I'm not sure what's going on with him, but Lil thinks he's hooked up with someone, and that would make sense. My brother was always around; even with him working for Kenton, he still finds time to come and see us regularly. Nowadays though, we're lucky if we see him once a week. I pick up my phone and dial his number; he answers on the second ring.

"What's up, bro?" he answers, sounding like he was sleeping.

"Yo, you asleep? It's two in the afternoon," I say, looking at the clock.

"Yeah, I was up late," he says, and then I hear a female in the background calling his name. "Just a second, baby, my brother's on the phone," he replies to her, sounding so gentle that I pull the phone away from my ear, making sure I have my brother on the line and not some other Nico. "I'm going to get some water, if that's okay?" I hear her say. I can tell he has pulled the phone away from his ear to talk to her. "I'll get you some. Go lay back down, baby. I'll be right there," he tells her. I hear the sound of a kiss, and then he's back.

"You still there?"

"Who are you, and what the fuck have you done with my brother?" I ask him. I have never heard him use that tone with anyone—not the kids, not our parents, and definitely not a female.

"I found her," he whispers.

"What?"

"I found my boom. I had no fucking clue that returning a lost phone would lead me to her, but I fucking found her."

"Holy shit. Wait, returning a lost phone?"

"Looong story, bro, but I found her, and she is beautiful, and sweet, and so fucking perfect that I worry about touching her and dirtying her up. But I can't walk away; it's impossible.

"Jesus, Lil was right."

"What?"

"Lil said that you haven't been coming around because you got hooked up with someone." I hear his laugh, and I can imagine him rubbing his head.

"It's a lot more than a hook up, but yeah."

"I get that." I sit back in my chair and look up at the ceiling. I never thought that our lives would be like this. I knew at one point we would all grow up and find women to share our lives with, but seeing each of my brothers happy, and now having my own family has strengthened my belief that nothing happens before its time. "So when do we get to meet her?" I ask him.

"Soon. She's just starting to accept that she's mine." He laughs when I hear her say something to him. "You are. Do you need me to prove it again?" he asks her, and that's my cue to get off the phone.

"Well, I'm gonna let you go," I tell him.

"Sure, man. I'll call you soon."

"Talk to you then." I hang up, smiling down at the phone. I'm happy that my brother is happy.

"Why are you smiling?" I looked up; Lilly's standing in the doorway holding a small plate with a cinnamon roll on it.

"Is that for me?"

"It depends on who put that smile on your face," she says, coming towards me.

"Actually, I don't know what her name is," I tell her, pulling the plate from her hand, setting it on the desk before dragging her around it so I can pull her into my lap.

"You don't know her name?" Her hand comes up to rest on my jaw, her beautiful eyes soft.

"No, Nico didn't tell me her name."

"I was right?" Her face lights up and I shake my head. So fucking cute.

"You were, and he seems like he is already lost to her."

"That's a good thing, right?" she ask quietly, searching my face.

"If she is the one for him, then yes, a very good thing." I palm the back of her head and pull her closer to me. "So you brought me a cinnamon roll?" I change the subject.

"No, I brought it in here to eat it while you watch."

"Really?"

"Yes." She smiles, looking sexy.

"I have a better idea."

"What's that?" Her tongue comes out, licking across her lower lip.

"Save it for later when then kids are in bed and I get you alone."

"Why?" she asks breathlessly.

"You said you brought it in here to eat in front of me, right?"

"Yes."

"Well, you're going to eat it in front of me later wearing nothing, and anything you drop I'm going to eat using no hands.

"Oh," she moans as I lick into her mouth, tasting cinnamon and sugar. And much later that night, I taste cinnamon and sugar from other parts of her body.

Chapter 13

Lilly

"Mommy, this is so heavy!" Ashlyn says. She's carrying one bag of groceries while I carry ten so I can avoid a second trip out to the car.

"Just a second, love bug, let me get the door unlocked." I finagle the bags so I can get my hand up high enough to shove the key into the lock. Once the door is open, Ashlyn walks ahead of me and starts dragging the bag she's carrying across the floor into the kitchen. I laugh as I watch everything that was once in the bag fall out as it tears open from being dragged as she walks.

"Where is Daddy?"

"He took Jax to see his mommy," I tell her.

"Oh," she says unhappily as I heft the bags up onto the counter. Once I've gotten free of the bags I'm carrying, I shake out my arms, trying to get the blood to flow again. "When is Papa Bear going to get here?"

"We have talked about this ten times today." I smile. "Remember, I told you he and Grandma will be here in three weeks?"

"Oh yeah." She shrugs and starts walking out of the kitchen, leaving the mess of cans she dropped along the way on the floor. "Hey, go pick up all the stuff you dropped please," I tell her. She goes, but I can hear the slight stomp of her feet. She has had a long day and is tired and cranky. I'm feeling tired and cranky myself. Jules had called early this morning. She told Cash that she had to see Jax today because she was going out of town and wouldn't be able to see him for a week or so. All I could think was good riddance, our lives were better without her in them. I start putting everything away when I hear the doorbell ring; I don't know who it could be. No one would show up without calling first. I look through the side window, seeing Officer Dan is on the other side of the door. Once I finally get the door open, I can tell by the look on his face that this isn't going to be a pleasant visit.

"Hi, can I help you?" I ask, looking behind him when I see another officer walking up the sidewalk.

"I'm sorry to do this to you, Lilly, but I'm going to need you to come with me," he says, and he does look sorry, but that does absolutely nothing to make me feel better.

"What is this about?" I ask.

"There has been more evidence brought forward in the case against you."

"Am I being arrested?" I question.

"Yes," he says, and my stomach drops, and I know I'm going to be sick. I look down when I feel Ashlyn's hand in mine. I really hate that she is here to see this.

"Can you go get Mommy's phone?" I ask her. She looks up at Officer Dan before nodding and walking into the house.

"Cash isn't here right now, and I can't leave until I have someone here to take care of Ashlyn," I explain, rubbing my hands together.

"That's understandable, Lilly. We can wait here until you find someone to come watch her. I also called James on my way over and told him what's going on. I suppose he is going to be showing up soon," he says, looking concerned.

"Can you please not handcuff me in front of my daughter? I really don't want her to get upset. I promise that I will fully cooperate." I wrap my arms around my waist.

"We won't cuff you until it's absolutely necessary."

"Thank you," I whisper.

"Here, Mommy," Ashlyn says, handing me my phone. I pull up Cash's number; it rings once before he answers.

"Hey, babe, we just got to the park. What's up?"

"Officer Dan is here at the house," I say, hoping he understands that I need him to come home. I really do not want to have a conversation about this with Ashlyn standing right here.

"Why is he there at the house?"

"He needs me to go with him," I say closing my eyes. "I need you to come get Ashlyn."

"Okay, baby, everything is going to be all right. I'm on my way home. I'm going to call my dad."

"Okay," I reply. I want to cry, but I know I can't in front of Ashlyn. I really do not want her to get upset.

"Love you, baby, hang in there. I'm on my way now," he says before hanging up. I pull the phone away from my ear.

"He is on his way." I take a step back, opening the door more fully. "Would you like to wait inside?"

"Yeah, honey. Why don't you g—"

"Dan, you know that's not allowed," the office behind him says, and Dan turns to look at him.

"Officer Mitchel, I suggest you stand down," Dan replies, stepping into the house. He doesn't wait for the other officer to come in before he shuts the door. I walk into the kitchen, looking around at all the groceries that still need to be put away. My eyes land of Ashlyn, who looks worried, and I hate seeing that look on my baby's face.

"Come here, love bug." Ashlyn comes to me and I pick her up, wrapping myself around her and breathing in her smell. I hate the idea of being away from her, Jax, or Cash for any length of time. Ashlyn doesn't fight me; she must know something is going on. After a few minutes, I hear a car outside. I stand in the living room watching the front door. As soon as it opens, my stomach drops. It's not Cash, but his dad.

"Hey, honey," he says, and I hold Ashlyn a little tighter. I really don't want to leave until I'm at least able to see Cash, but I wonder if I will be allowed to wait until he gets here.

"Hi," I say.

"Grandpa!" Ashlyn says and starts to wiggle, trying to get down, and as much as I don't want to, I set her down and watch as she runs to James.

"Hey, pretty girl," he says, swinging her up into his arms. Dan looks at me, and I know he is silently trying to tell me that we need to go.

"I'm sorry, James, but I need to take Lilly with me."

"I know. Can you wait until my boy gets here?" James asks.

"I really shouldn't have let her stay as long as I have, but I knew she needed to wait until someone got here to stay with her daughter," Dan says, looking upset. "I didn't want to bring the girl with us and get CPS involved." I feel nauseated by his last words; the thought of Ashlyn being put into the system, even for a short period of time, makes me feel grateful to Dan.

"I understand," James says. He looks at me, and I can tell he's worried. I know that Dan said he called James before this, so I wonder if he knows about what's going on.

"I'm very sorry, Lilly, but we're going to have to go," Dan says. I walk over to James and Ashlyn; her head is laying against his chest. I want to pull her away from him, but I just can't do it. I know that I need to put on a brave face for my girl.

"I'm going with Dan. Can you be a good girl for Daddy until I get back?"

"Why do you have to go?" she asks, and I take a breath before answering.

"He just needs to ask me some questions." I look at Dan, and he looks at Ashlyn and nods. "Can I get some love before I go?" She looks unsure before leaning away from James so I can grab her. Once I get her in my arms, I whisper into her ear, "Love you, love bug. Be good, okay?" She nods and I feel tears start to fill my eyes. I know I need to leave before she has the chance to see me upset. I hand her back to James, who leans close so he can whisper to me that everything will be okay. I grab my bag off the counter and follow Dan out of the house. Once we're at his squad car, I'm read my rights and placed in the backseat just as Cash pulls up with Jax. I lower my head. I really don't want Jax to see me like this. I know that my mascara has started to run down my face, and I try as best as I can to wipe the tears away before Jax can see them. Cash comes to my door and squats down in front of me.

"Baby," he says, his fingers tilting my face up. "It's going to be okay. I called the lawyer on the way over here and he said he would meet you there."

"Okay," I tell him, trying to be brave. Something in my gut tells me this isn't going to be so easily fixed.

"I love you."

"I love you too," I reply, and I can hear Jax begin to shout from off in the distance.

"We need to go," Officer Mitchel says, standing behind Cash with his hand on the door. I can tell he is becoming impatient.

"Just give me a minute," Cash growls, standing to his full height. "Dad, let Jax come here for a second," Cash yells, and I hear the pounding of Jax's feet on the gravel, then he is there, wrapping his arms around my neck.

"Hey, honey." I try to smile, but I feel it wobble.

"Why are the police taking you away?" he asks. I pull him away from me so I can see his face.

"Office Dan needs some help with something and has some questions for me."

"When are you coming home? We were supposed to make pizza."

"We can make pizza another night."

"But..."

I run my hand over his head, trying my best not to cry. "I have to go." I see his eyes get wet and my heart breaks. "I want you to take care of your sister until I get back, okay?" He nods, biting the inside of his cheek. I pull him into me and kiss the top of his hair before helping him down from the car.

"Go wait with Grandpa, little dude. I'll be there in a second," Cash tells Jax, who reluctantly walks back up to the front porch where Cash's dad and Ashlyn are standing with Dan. He resumes his place, crouching down inside the door, his fingers running down the side of my face. I close my eyes. "I will see you in a couple hours, okay?" I nod, but the lump in my throat won't let me talk. "I love you, baby." I nod again.

"We need to go," Office Mitchel says. I take my eyes off Cash to look at Officer Mitchel. When Cash's hand slides to the back of my neck, his fingers tangling into my hair, my eyes return to his. "I love you."

"Love you too," I finally speak.

"Don't worry, baby. Things will be okay." He pulls my upper body forward, and as soon as I'm close enough, his mouth opens over mine, and he kisses me so thoroughly I forget where I am. "I'll see you soon, baby," he tells me one last time, pressing his forehead against mine.

"See you soon," I agree, untangling my hands from his hair. He kisses my forehead before standing. He hesitates before shutting the door. His hand goes to the glass, and mine does the same. He turns to say something to Officer Mitchel before his eyes come back to me. I hate the worried look on his face. He steps away from the squad car and goes over to where his dad is standing. Ashlyn puts her arms out in his direction, and the second he has her, she wraps herself around him, his face going near her ear. I can see his mouth moving, and I watch her nod. Jax has his head back listening to what his dad is saying to his sister. I know he's upset when his eyes come to me and I see tears in them. I'm so lost in watching my family that I jump when I hear the car door slam closed.

"You know it's going to be your ass on the line if someone asks about what happened today," Officer Mitchel says to Dan.

"You gonna say something?" Dan questions.

"N-nu...No," Officer Mitchel stutters.

"So how the fuck is anyone going to know that we didn't follow procedure?" Dan growls, backing out of the driveway.

"I don't know, just...what if they wonder why it took so long, or why she's not cuffed?" he asks, sounding contrite.

"So you wanted me to handcuff her in front of her daughter, even though she was fully cooperating with us?"

"I didn't say that."

"Then what the fuck are you saying?"

"That we shouldn't show favoritism."

"Look, I have known James for the last twenty years. He is a good man, and from what I know, his boys are good solid men too. Yes, Lilly has been accused of a crime, but until she is found guilty, she is innocent. No, I didn't cuff her. She also has no history of violence and has cooperated since the beginning of this investigation."

"All right, you made your point," Officer Mitchel says, looking out the window. We drive the thirty minutes in silence, and once we pull up outside of the precinct, Officer Mitchel gets out, opening my door. His hand goes to his back, and I hear the distinct sound of metal and know what's coming. My stomach rolls, and I swallow against the nausea.

"I'm sorry about this," Officer Mitchel says, and I can hear his sincerity. Once I'm cuffed, the weight of the metal on my wrist feels like a thousand pounds. I'm lead inside the police station by Dan with a hand wrapped around my elbow. He directs me to a small room that has a long metal table and a large mirror across from where I'm seated.

"We will be back in a few minutes, darlin'," Dan says, and I nod looking at myself. I wonder how the hell this kind of thing keeps happening to me. It takes about twenty minutes for Dan and Officer Mitchel to come back into the room. Dan un-cuffs my hands but places a cuff around my ankle so that I'm attached to the chair.

"Thanks," I say softly, rubbing my wrist. I can still feel the cold weight of the cuffs even now that they are gone.

"All right, let's get started," Dan says, pulling out a large envelope. I watch as he opens it and starts pulling out papers. I can see my name and copies of checks; my breathing picks up and I start to feel lightheaded. Even knowing I didn't do what I'm being accused of, I still feel guilty that my name is involved. "Now, as you know, the last time that we brought you in we didn't have enough evidence against you to charge you with a crime," Dan says and I watch him take a deep breath before his eyes come back to me. "Unfortunately, that has changed."

"No," I whisper, looking at myself in the mirror. This all feels like I'm living a bad dream.

<u>Cash</u>

"How much fucking longer are they going to keep her in there?" I roar; the rage inside of me is burning so brightly I could explode.

"Son, you need to calm down."

"Calm down? Fuck that! Dad, she has been in jail for a week now!" I shout. It's killing me having her away from me and the kids, and worse, knowing that she's in jail, when she of all people should never even know what the inside of a jail cell looks like.

"Son, you going off half-cocked isn't going to help anyone, and it especially will not help Lilly right now."

"Dad, you and I both know that Lilly is not built to be in a place like that with real criminals," I tell him, something he already knows. Yesterday when I went to see her, I could see it in her face that she was exhausted. I knew my dad was doing everything in his power to keep her away from the general population, but he could only do so much, and his friends could only do so much without making it look like favoritism, risking all of their jobs.

"Cash, I promise you I'm doing everything in my power to get her out of there."

"I know." I sit down in one of my parents' lawn chairs. "Did they get the video from the check cashing place?" I ask him.

"It's being reviewed now," he tells me, sitting down across from me.

"When will they know something?" I ask, dropping my head forward. I hate this.

"I'm not sure, son," my dad says quietly. I lift my head to look at him.

"I need her, Dad. I feel like I can't breathe." I scrub my hands over my face. "I feel like I'm dying inside." I look at my wedding band, rubbing my thumb over the shiny piece of jewelry. "Her parents are going to be here today. I have to take the kids with me to go pick them up. Her mom and dad are going to have a lot of questions—questions I don't have answers for."

"I will come with you. The kids can stay with your mom. You and I will go to the airport and pick them up."

"Thanks," I say, not looking up at him. I have already failed Lilly as her husband. *What kind of man lets his woman go to jail? I don't deserve her.* "I have never deserved her."

"Hey, none of that feeling sorry for yourself bullshit," my dad says, and I realize I must have spoken out loud.

"It's the truth," I tell him.

"You're probably right. You probably don't deserve her, but she's yours, and I raised you to be a good man, a strong man, and a man worthy of a good woman's love." He stands and pats my shoulder. "You need to be strong for her and those two little ones." I know he's right, and I won't let my kids be touched by what's going on, but it doesn't make it any easier to look at myself in the mirror. The worst part is that Jules is claiming me to be an unfit parent, and at this point, the judge is considering joint custody due to her claims about my wife—though Jules has been *gracious* enough to tell me that if I left Lil, she would be willing to let things be. I let her know where to shove that idea. There were no forces on this Earth strong enough to tear me away from Lilly. Just because I wasn't good enough for her doesn't mean I would ever give her up.

"I got it," Nico says the second he steps through the sliding glass doors.

"Please tell me that it's good," I say and stand up.

"We need to talk," he says.

"What the fuck are you talking about? I want to see what's on the tape," I say, sliding open the door he just came through.

"Wait, we need to talk for a second before I put this in," Nico says, grabbing my elbow.

"What? You have a tape that proves that Lil is innocent and you want me to wait?"

"No, I want to make sure that you know that no matter what's on this tape, we've got your back."

"Jesus, you still don't trust her," I whisper in disgust. I haven't even thought once that she may not be innocent. I know that she didn't do what she is being accused of.

"Did I say that I didn't believe her?" Nico asks, shaking his head. "Dude, I know she didn't fucking do it. The thing I want you to prepare yourself for is *what else* is on this tape."

"What does that mean?"

"You will see, but know that we've all got your back." I lift my chin, wondering what the fuck is on the tape, feeling like I don't even want to know at this point. We walk into my parents' house where the kids and I have been staying since she got placed in jail. I don't want to be home without her, and I know that with us staying at my parents' they seem to have fewer questions about where she is. That doesn't mean that when bedtime, bath time or any time that they normally spend with her during the day comes along they don't cry for her or look around waiting for her. That's the part that kills me. I hate seeing that lost look on my kids' faces. It has been bad enough dealing with the look on Jax's face over the past couple years when his mother doesn't show up. But now it's worse knowing that if Lil had it her way, she would be with them. This isn't something that she is choosing to do. "You ready for this?"

"Put it in," I tell him. He sets up the video and my dad comes into the room, taking a seat in his old recliner. I sit on the couch and wait for the blank screen to light up.

"All right, now, the first part of the tape is all garbage, just normal people cashing their checks. Then around two, something interesting happens," Nico says, and I watch the screen go black.

"What the fuck did you do to the tape?" I stand up.

"I didn't do anything." He shrugs like it's all the same to him, and then stands as well. "So I'm guessing that you didn't catch it, huh?"

"Catch what?" I growl. "I'm not in the mood for your fucking games."

"I'm going to play it again; calm your tits." He smiles. "This time, pay close attention to what happens right before the screen goes black. He presses play again, and this time I stare at the screen so hard that I feel like my eyes are going to dry out, but right before the screen goes black, I catch it.

"You have got to be fucking with me." I take a breath and then another, trying to squelch the urge to find a gun and put a bullet in someone's brain.

"I guess you caught it that time," Nico says smiling.

"I'm going to fucking kill her," I say, my hands fisting at my sides.

"Now, son," Dad says, and I hear him, but I couldn't fucking care less right now.

"I'm going to fucking kill the bitch," I repeat.

"Cash, son, I need you to calm down and think about this."

"She has done it again. She has fucked with my life again." I close my eyes, images of Lilly when I first met her flashing in my mind—how the love we had for each other back then could have grown, and how lucky I am to have it now. Images of Ashlyn come next, everything I missed with her, all the moments I will never get back. Then Jax, and how my son has suffered having her as a mother. How until Lilly, he never knew what it was like to have a mother who loved him completely. Yes, I'm going to kill the bitch. "Where the fuck is she?" I ask, looking at Nico. Now he has Sophie, he should know the anguish I'm feeling.

"Jules doesn't know I have this tape," Nico says. "I say we call the lawyer and have him get this tape admitted into evidence, then Lilly can finally get her chance in front of the judge. Hopefully, he will look at this and realize he has the wrong person and let her go.

"Yeah, but that's not a lot of evidence proving her innocence," I realize and speak out loud.

"They took writing samples from Lilly that say that she is not the one who wrote those checks. The evidence against her is not solid, so maybe with the tape and the other evidence we can get her home. All the rest can be worked out after that."

"Jules needs to go down for this shit."

"And she will, but first, let's get Lilly home." He squeezes my shoulder. "Look, you go with Dad to pick up her parents, and I will get this to the lawyer."

"Thanks, man," I say to Nico.

"You would do the same for me," he says before leaving. I sit back down, scrubbing my hands over my face.

"You want me to go get her parents?" my dad asks.

"Nah, I need to get out of the house." I stand, and after we say goodbye to the kids, we head out to my dad's truck.

After we pick up Lilly's parents from the airport, the lawyer calls and tells me Lilly has seen the judge, and he is releasing her on bail. The tension that had been weighing heavily in the car since we picked up her parents disappears with that one call. I have never felt such a sense of relief in my life. Now I just pray Nico finds a way to clear her name completely. I also want Jules to go down for what she did.

I drop Lilly's parents off at the house. Yes, I know they want to see their daughter, and the kids want to see her too, but I don't give a fuck. I need her to myself for at least a little while.

Chapter 14

<u>Lilly</u>

I look down at the sudsy water I'm washing dishes in, enjoying doing something so normal. I missed being home the last week. Jail is scary and lonely, and I never want to go back to that place. The second I was free, I ran to Cash and cried into his chest. I missed his smell and the way I felt when he held me. I missed our kids too, and couldn't wait to be home with them. On the way home, Cash explained to me about Jules and what happened with her. No one has been able to find her yet, but I hope they catch her soon. I need to know why she did it. I look up from the soapy water and out the window. The kids had been playing in the tree house, but have now disappeared. I don't think much about it until twenty minutes later when I realize I haven't heard anything from them for a while. Since I got home, they have been coming in to check if I'm still here every ten minutes or so. I step out the backdoor into the yard. It's completely quiet out here, not even the sound of leaves moving with the wind.

I walk around the side of the house to see if maybe the kids are there playing...but nothing. I get a bad feeling in the pit of my stomach, and that's when I take off running. I look everywhere and I can't find them. I run back towards the house, trying to catch my breath. "Where are the kids?" I run into the house screaming. "I can't find the kids anywhere! They were out back playing in the tree house. I had been watching them through the window above the kitchen sink. Then they disappeared. I thought that they had decided to play along the side of the house, but I wanted to check on them to make sure they were okay when I didn't hear anything for a few minutes." I know I'm rambling, but I feel sick, and I know I'm going to have a break down.

"They're outside honey," my mom says, and I start shaking my head, clutching at my throat, trying to rip the words out but I can't speak.

"Breathe, baby," Cash says, concerned. His arms are around me, but I push him away; he needs to go look for the kids.

"Th-they're not there!" I take a huge gulp of air. "I can't find them anywhere!" My dad is the first to move. He is up off the couch and heading out the backdoor. Cash looks me over before handing me off to my mom, and then he follows my dad.

"It's going to be okay. They're kids, honey. I used to lose you all the time," Mom tells me, trying to lighten the mood. Any other time I would have laughed, but not now. I get up and head towards the bedrooms, checking each one, but they are nowhere to be found. A few minutes later, I hear police sirens and my stomach drops. My worst nightmare is becoming a reality. When I get outside, Cash and my dad are talking to James. A few minutes pass and the whole yard is full of people. My mom holds me next to her as we listen to the guys plan out a search party. No one knows where they are, so they all split up.

Jax

I always wanted a little brother, but got stuck with a little sister. We are playing hide-and-seek, and when I'm getting ready to find her like I always do, I see someone pulling her into a truck. I'm scared, but my dad always says that it's my job to keep her safe because I'm her big brother. So I climb into the back of it and lay down, hiding under a tarp.

~~*

Cash

This cannot be fucking happening. Someone is going to die. I'm not saying that as a threat—I mean it all the way to my soul. As soon as I find out who has done this, I'm going to kill them.

"All right, man, I want you to hear me out, okay?" Nico says. I lift my chin in response. I'm too angry to answer him right now. We have searched everywhere for the kids, and come up with nothing. They wouldn't have wondered off. Someone has to have taken them, I just don't know who.

"Who do you think would do this?" he asks.

"I don't know." I rack my brain, trying to come up with someone who would do this. I can't think over the pain in my chest. My kids are missing; someone has them and I have no idea who it is.

"I want you to think for a second. Who would do this?" I pause, coming up with nothing, then for some reason a name comes out of my mouth without thinking.

"Jules."

"Jules," he nods, "you know she has been missing. Kenton is running her cards to see if he can latch onto her."

"She's not *that* crazy," I say, knowing it's a lie.

"She *is* that crazy." He pauses, looking like he is weighing his words. "Look, I know you feel bad for her, and I understand that she is Jax's mother, but the bitch is fucking crazy and needs some major help—and not the kind that she can receive from a therapist."

"You're right."

"All right, now I need you to tell me anything you know about her and her family," he says, and for the next thirty minutes, I tell him everything that I know. When I'm done, I realize how very little there was. "We're gonna find the kids; don't worry." He pats my back, walking away and putting the phone to his ear. My phone buzzes in my pocket, and I answer right away.

"Yo?"

"We're still looking," Trevor says; he and Asher took off not long after my dad did. "Any idea of which way we should head?"

"Look for Jules," I tell him.

"What?"

"I talked to Nico and I think he may be right; we need to be looking for Jules."

"You're fucking shitting me."

"Dude, I don't know what the fuck to think right now, but something in my gut is saying Nico is right and that Jules is behind this."

"All right, we will look for her. Keep us up-to-date if you find out anything," Trevor says, and I can hear the anger in his words.

"Will do," I say and then hang up. I head back into the house. Lilly and her mom are inside waiting to see if the kids will show back up. As soon as I walk inside, Lilly is in my arms, her eyes red from crying.

"Did they find them?"

"No, baby." She starts to cry again, and my heart is breaking. "I will find them and bring them home. You stay here with your mom in case they show back up."

"Okay, but maybe I should be out looking too."

"No, I want you to stay here in case they come back."

"But—"

"No buts. Stay here with your mom. Keep your phone on you and I will call you."

"Okay, just bring them home." I can hear the strain in her words as she wraps her arms around my waist, burying her face in my chest. I want to comfort her, but I need to be out looking. I pull her away from me, kissing her once before turning and heading out the door. I see Nico still on his phone, so I motion him towards the truck and climb inside. Once he's in, I take off. I have no destination in mind, but I do know Jules had been sleeping with a guy in town, so that's my first stop. When we arrive at his place, there is an old truck in the driveway. The yard is littered with garbage. We get out and head up to the front porch; the dogs behind the door go crazy when I knock. I hear rustling, then the door opens and a guy my age is standing there rubbing his face, the smell of alcohol wafting off him.

"What do you want?"

"Have you seen Jules?" I ask, and his eyes narrow. He looks between Nico and me then smirks.

"I know you," he says when his eyes come back to me.

"Yeah?" I ask him, crossing my arms over my chest.

"Yeah, you're Jules's ex. She's always talking about you."

"Is that so?"

"Yeah," he slurs, and until that point, I didn't even notice that he is drunk. "She was always carrying on about you and how she was never important to you, and that you only wanted her because of the kid."

"She told you that?"

"She told me everything. The bitch never shut the fuck up." He runs a hand through his hair. "You know, she is hot as fuck, and not bad in bed, but she is nuts—and I mean *really* fucking nuts."

"Why do you say that?" Nico asks, leaning on the side of the house. His stance is casual, but I can tell that he is up to something.

"The last time she was here I thought I was going to get some, but she carried on about your daughter and wife—who, by the way, is a hot piece." I want to punch him in the face, but don't let it show.

"She is hot, right?" Nico asks, and I swing my head to him. *What the fuck?*

"Fuck yeah, she is. I mean, Jules is good looking, but that bitch is smoking."

"I agree," Nico says, and the guy smiles at him. "So what else did Jules want?"

"I don't know. I wasn't really listening; I was trying to get laid, you know?" Nico nods and he shifts, his head going back like he's thinking. "All I remember is her saying that the girl was a mistake on her part, and that she should have been smarter—whatever the fuck that means." He digs his hand into his front pocket, pulling out a pack of smokes, offering one to Nico, then to me. We both shake our heads no. He puts one in his mouth, lighting it and taking a drag. "I really don't remember anything else." He shrugs, taking another drag before tossing the still-lit cigarette into the yard. My brain is in overdrive; she told him Ashlyn was a mistake on her part. I know deep down she is the reason Lilly got pregnant, but there is no way to prove it. I know that if confronted, she would deny it.

"Do you know where she might be?" Nico asks him.

"Jules?" he asks, and Nico nods. "I don't know, at her house? Or with her fucked up aunt maybe?"

"Why are you here?" he finally asks the question he should have asked a long time ago.

"My son and daughter are missing," I tell him honestly. He looks between Nico and me, then backs up.

"Hey, I have nothing to do with that."

"We didn't say you did, but we need to know if you have any idea where Jules might be," Nico says, and the guy looks nervous.

"You think that Jules has something to do with it?" he asks.

"We're not sure right now; the only thing we know for sure is that Jules has disappeared, and so have my kids."

"Dude, that's fucked up." He shakes his head. My phone rings and I pull it out of my pocket, looking at the caller ID. I have no clue who it is.

"Hello?"

"Hello, sir," an older woman says.

"Can I help you?" I ask impatiently. I don't have time for this shit right now.

"Yes, I'm calling you because a little boy showed up on my property about five minutes ago. He says that his sister was taken by his mom, and that I needed to call his dad." My hand that's not holding the phone goes to my chest where my necklace lays. I put pressure on it, the metal against my skin reminding me that my family will be back together soon.

"Where are you?" I ask, jumping off the porch and heading to my truck. I get in and slam my door at the same time as Nico. She quickly rattles off her address. "Let me talk to my son, please."

"Dad!" Jax cries. "Mom took Ashlyn. I had to go with her to keep her safe, but she took her into a house, and there was a lot of shouting, Dad. So I ran as fast as I could until I found somewhere to call you."

"You did good, dude. I'm so proud of you. But I need you to be brave for a little while longer, okay?"

"Okay, Dad." I hear him sniffle, and I fight not to crack my phone.

"I love you, Jax, and I will be there soon," I tell him, clenching my teeth. A drive that would normally take forty-five minutes takes twenty. My dad gets ahead of us on the highway in his squad car, leading a long line of cars and trucks. The old lady Jax is with explains that he had ran through a cornfield that is on the back of her property, and that no one else lives close enough to her that would know we are on their trail. When we arrive at the location where Jax is, we all get out of our vehicles just as Jax comes flying out of the house, right into my arms.

"I got you," I tell him, picking him up. He wraps himself around me, his body shaking. "You're safe, bud, but I need you to tell me where your sister is." He nods into my shoulder then starts talking, his body shaking so hard that I have to sit down with him. He tells me that he and Ashlyn were playing hide-and-seek and that he knew where she was hiding because she always hides in the same place. He says he went around the side of the house, seeing someone dressed in black carrying Ashlyn away. He was going to go into the house to get me, but they were almost to the truck by the time he thought about it. Then he says when the person placed Ashlyn in the truck, he climbed into the back and laid down to hide. When the truck finally stopped, he peeked over the edge, seeing his mom carrying Ashlyn into a house. He didn't know what to do when he heard yelling coming from the house, so he ran to try to find someone to call me. I hold him close, rocking him back-and-forth the same way I used to when he was a baby. My dad, brothers, and a couple other officers listen. It only takes him a couple of minutes to tell us what had happened, but I know that it's a couple minutes too long. "Listen, little dude, you're going to stay here and I'm going to go with Grandpa so that I can get your sister and we can go home," I tell him. I stand and carry him over to my truck. Asher takes him from me, talking gently to him as I head over to my dad.

"Look, I shouldn't even let you come with us, but I know that I won't be able to stop you, and Ashlyn is going to need you when we get her out of there." My jaw clenches, but I hold my tongue. Right now, he isn't my dad, he is a cop, and I know the difference. "We're going to head across the field the same way Jax came. When we get there, I need you to stay out of sight with Nico until I give you the go-ahead."

"Got it," I tell him. All of us head across the cornfield. Once we reach the other side, there is an old, rundown, two-story white house; the place looks like it's ready to fall apart, but parked outside is Jules's old car, along with a small pickup. My dad waves me back and tells me to stay put as he and three other officers' head towards the house. I fight myself, wanting to go in and get my girl, but I know my dad will handle it. Two of the officers head around each side of the house. My dad and the other policeman walk up the front porch. My dad knocks with his gun trained on the door. He yells out it's the police, and when the door is opened, a man with a gun holstered on his shoulder answers the door. The guy nods to my dad, they talk for a second, and the guy pulls a shiny badge out from under his shirt. They talk a second more, and my dad waves Nico and me in. When I get to the porch, the guy looks me over, introduces himself as Jim, and then heads inside. The house is a mess, the living room right off the front entrance has the ceiling falling in. We walk down a narrow hall into what used to be a kitchen. That's where I see Jules handcuffed and sitting in a chair, along with another man. "Where the fuck is my daughter?" I ask, and her eyes widen in surprise.

"I did this for us," Jules says in a whisper, and if I had a gun right then I would have put a bullet in her.

"Whatever the fuck you did, you did it for yourself," I growl. "Now where the fuck is she?"

"Come on, man, your daughter is in here," Jim says. He takes me into a pantry off the kitchen. When he opens the door, he shines a flashlight into the small space, and there is my baby girl asleep on the floor. I rush over, picking her up. She is out cold, her body completely limp.

"What's wrong with her?" I ask in a panic, lifting her higher up on my chest.

"They roofied her. I checked her over already. All of her vitals are okay; she is just asleep," he tells me. I swear I can feel my body expand with rage.

"I'm going to fucking kill her."

"You're going to have to wait in line. Where she is going, they don't take too kindly to people hurting kids, and I'm telling you that everyone in the prison will know what she did. I will make it my personal goal to let everyone she has contact with know her history." His face is devoid of any emotion, and I don't give a fuck what they do to her. I don't care if that makes me an insensitive prick, but I hope she gets what's coming to her.

"What exactly was her plan?" I ask him, looking down at the sweet face of my baby girl.

"She was going to sell her to me."

"What?"

"We have been working this case for a while. The man in the other room is part of a child trafficking network. I have been undercover for a while now. He told me he had a piece of property for me to pick up and to meet him here. I did, and when I got here, the woman and child were here with him.

"You're fucking with me."

"No, man. I wish I was, but this shit is a lot more common than you think, and the sad thing is that normally the kids don't have people out looking for them," he says, and I hear sirens off in the distance. I say a prayer for all the kids who don't have anyone searching for them. I would be lost without my kids.

"Thank you," I tell him, my voice gruff with emotion. He pats my shoulder before giving it a squeeze. We walk back out to the kitchen; my ex and the guy with her are still sitting at the table. I don't even look at them. My dad is there with a couple of his officers, but I walk past them all, heading outside. Once I clear the door, I see there are three black SUVs filling the driveway. Jim, who comes outside as well, goes to talk to some of the men exiting the vehicles. I sit on the steps of the porch holding Ashlyn. I don't know what I would have done if something had happened to her, or if I had lost her permanently. I would be devastated. I look up to see Nico holding out a phone to me, and when I put it to my ear, I know exactly who is on the line. "Baby, I got our baby girl. She's okay," I tell her.

"Jax?" she questions.

"He is with Asher and Trevor." I can hear a loud thud and I know that she has fallen. Tears start to fill my eyes. I hold Ashlyn a little tighter, closing my eyes.

"Please bring them home soon," she cries. I can hear her mom talking to her, and I know that she is comforting her, which makes this a little easier.

"I will. Love you, baby," I tell her. An officer comes over, telling me that an ambulance is coming and that we should wait in one of the SUVs. I look through the front window of the SUV, seeing that Nico is standing with our dad on the front porch. His phone is to his ear, and I hope that he called Trevor and Asher. I need my son, but I don't want him to see what's going on. I watch as they escort Jules and the man out of the house and into the back of one of the vehicles. The vehicles carrying them takes off and an ambulance pulls up, along with Asher's truck. I hop out, taking Ashlyn to the ambulance. When I get her inside, they start looking her over. All of her vitals are fine, her O2 level normal. They hook her up on fluids and get her comfortable. I get out and take Jax from Trevor, who tells me that he had fallen asleep crying.

"You gonna take him with you in the ambulance to the hospital?" Trevor asks.

"Yeah. Can you call Lil's dad and ask him to bring the girls to meet us at the hospital?"

"You got it. Do you want one of us to ride with you?"

"Nah," I tell them, walking away. I get back into the ambulance holding my son and looking at my daughter. They are both so small and defenseless. When we get to the hospital, there is a blur of activity. We're escorted into a room, and the doctors run more tests on Ashlyn, who still hasn't woken up.

"Cash!" I hear yelled, and I stand with Jax still in my arms. He still hasn't woken up either. I had the doctor look him over and they said that he is fine, probably just crashed from having an adrenalin rush. When I clear the doorway, Lilly is running towards me still yelling out my name. When she sees Jax and me, her eyes close and she stops in the middle of the hall. I go to her, needing to touch her.

"Baby, they are both okay," I tell her, holding her with one arm. Her arms wrap around Jax and me, and we stand there for a few minutes before I kiss her forehead and grab her hand, leading her to Ashlyn. Once in the room, she goes right to her bedside, looking down at our daughter who looks so fragile.

"Why isn't she awake?" she asks.

"They don't know, but they said she is fine. Her vitals are all normal and she doesn't have any injuries; it just looks like she doesn't want to wake up yet. Neither of them wants to wake up yet." We wait for what seems like forever in silence for Ashlyn to wake up, and when she does, she doesn't even know what happened to her. She has no recollection of Jules at all. The police and everyone believe she was drugged while in the yard. My brave son, who had the courage to follow his sister, woke up not long after her. I can tell he's still upset about what happened, but he's happy to have his sister back, and us all together. That night, when we finally get home, and after getting everyone tucked into our bed, I thank God for keeping my family safe and together. None of us are going to be out of each other's sight for a while. I think Lil and I both need to be able to see the kids at all times for about the next six months.

Ironically, that happens to be around the time that Jules gets sentenced to twenty years in jail without the possibility of parole. The crimes against her are numerous, and she is proven guilty with each and every one of them. I sit down on the couch, and Lilly cuddles into my side while Jax and Ashlyn argue over which movie we are going to watch. I don't care what I do with my family; as long as we are together, I'm a happy man.

"Thank you for giving me this," I whisper into Lilly's ear. Her head turns towards me, her eyes searching my face.

"You know that you give us everything, right? You are the like the moon to our family ocean. You're magnetic; we will always follow you and try to give you back what you give to us." She leans up and kisses me before laying her head back against my chest. I don't know what I did to deserve her or my children, but I will always do everything within my power to keep them safe and happy.

Epilogue

Lilly

 "Mom, Dad, can you guys stop being so gross? No one wants to see their parents making out," Ashlyn says walking into the living room.

"Yeah that's some sick shit," Jax says, following behind his sister and ruffling her hair. She punches him in the arm in response.

"Hey, mouth," I scold.

"Sorry, but really, why don't you guys try acting like normal parents?" Jax complains flopping down onto the couch.

"If you don't like it, you got a room," Cash says and Jax rolls his eyes shaking his head.

"I had to come in here, I need some extra money. I'm taking Becky to homecoming." Jax says, his eyes lighting up and I inwardly growl. I hate that Jax is grown up. I was putting is his laundry away the other day and found a half a box of condoms. Condoms, I didn't even want to think about him having a penis let alone him using it on anyone.

"Chris asked me to go with him," Ashlyn says jumping up making Cash's eyes narrow. I know exactly what's coming so I sit back on the couch.

"You are not going," Cash says.

"Good luck with that, sis," Jax laughs, getting off the couch and leaving the room.

"Dad, if Jax can date, then I should be allowed to date too," Ashlyn says, her eyes narrowing on her father. I try not to laugh, but it's funny watching Cash try to come up with an excuse for why his sixteen-year-old son can date, but his sixteen-year-old daughter can't. His eyes meet mine and narrow. I give him my best 'I'm innocent' smile, making his jaw tic. After everything that happened, we agreed to not have any more kids. We both just wanted to enjoy Ashlyn and Jax without adding another baby to the bunch. Besides, everyone had gone baby-crazy, and there were plenty of Mayson children to occupy everyone.

"I have told you before that you're a girl."

"I know I'm a girl, Dad, but I really wanted to go to homecoming with Chris. It's not fair that Jax gets to go and I don't."

"You want to help me out here?" He looks at me, and I shake my head no. He mouths the word 'spanking' and I tighten my thighs in response. I don't know how it is for other married couples, but for us, our sex life has only improved with time. He knows exactly how and where to touch me, or what to say to have me craving him all day, so that when we finally connect, I jump him. I think it's why he does what he does.

"Dad, this is not fair," she whines, then looks at me. "Mom, tell him that it's not fair." She stomps her foot.

"Cash, this is not fair," I tell him, trying not to smile.

"See, Dad? Mom agrees that it's not fair." Cash looks at me over her head, and I know that whatever punishment I get tonight is going to be good.

"Honey, you have to agree that it's not fair for Jax to go when she can't," I tell him honestly. I try not to get involved with things like this, but it's ridiculous that he lets Jax do whatever he wants, while Ashlyn is supposed to be locked away in her room.

"She is younger than him. They are only the same age for a few months, so I do think it's fair," he growls at me, and I hold up my hands.

"I never get to do anything!" she cries, and that is a total crock. She gets her way, just like now. The only thing she has to do is wait it out, and her Dad will crack and agree to let her go.

"I'll think about it," Cash says, and just like that, Ashlyn won another round and she knows it. She makes it obvious by throwing herself at Cash.

"You're the best dad ever!" she cries. He wraps his arms around her, kissing her forehead, and then she's gone, bouncing to her room.

"You know that your daughter is a fucking handful," he grumbles, his hand coming down on either side of me.

"She is your daughter too," I tell him.

"She is all you, baby, so sweet when she needs to be, but a dog with a bone when the time calls for it."

"I think those are your traits."

"You know that you're getting punished for going against me in front of her, right?"

"Cash."

"No, don't you Cash me, baby. You earned this shit." I don't know why he always says it like a threat, when in reality, it's a reward and makes me want to be bad and go against him all the time.

"Did you talk to Jax about the condoms?" I ask him.

"I had the bird and the bees talk with him. And I know that you don't like it, and you still think of him as your baby, but he is growing up; he will be seventeen soon." I do still think of him as my baby, because he is. Jules has been in jail since she kidnapped Ashlyn. I was afraid at first, but my boy is so strong that he pushed through everything and ended up shining even brighter because of it. Jules is still in jail and has never once tried to contact him or Cash, or if she did, I don't know about it. Cash nuzzling my neck brings me back to reality.

"Hey, what are you doing?" I try pushing him away. "And what the hell do you mean that he's all grown up? I still buy his underwear, so until I stop doing that and he starts doing it for himself, he is not grown up." Cash starts laughing, his whole body shaking mine, and his face goes into my neck. I roll my eyes, running my hands through his hair.

"I love you, baby," he says once he gets control of himself. He lifts his head, looking at me. He still looks at me like I'm the most important thing in his life. Yes, he feels the same way about his kids, but each of us gets a different look from him.

"I love you, too," I whisper, looking into his handsome face. He was even more handsome than he was a few years ago. Age has made him even sexier, and I think having a happy home life makes his soul happy enough to shine through.

*   *   *

Cash

"Drop the towel and get on the bed," I tell Lilly as soon as I walk into the room. She doesn't even hesitate; her eyes darken and she walks right to

353

the bed, lying down. "Good girl, now spread," I command her, and she does as I say, her breath increasing. "You know, I should spank you for not agreeing with me about Ashlyn this morning, but since I know that you like that shit so much, I'm just going to give you a different kind of punishment," I tell her, stripping off my clothes. I walk to the edge of the bed, my hand on my dick working myself in smooth strokes. Her eyes are watching, and I know she loves to see me touch myself. She always thinks she can get away with everything, and most of the time that is the truth, but not this time. This time she is going to pay. I'm not ready for my daughter to date, and I need Lil onboard with me. I get up off the bed, kneeling near her head. "Open," I tell her, and she does what I say, her mouth opening eagerly. I feed her my cock inch-by-inch; her eyes light up when my hand goes to her breast and I pull on one nipple, then the other, getting them hard. Her body is writhing, wanting more contact. I move my hips, fucking her mouth. "Fuck, yes, just like that," I encourage her. "Now lift your hips so I can play with your pussy, baby." She does, and my fingers make contact with her clit before sliding two inside. "You're soaked," I growl and she nods, grinding her pussy against my hand. I play with her some more, then pull away when I feel her body tell me she's close. She whines, but she doesn't stop sucking me off. I pull her nipples again before going back to her pussy. She is in a frenzy; I can see it in her eyes. I pull my dick out of her mouth and position my head between her legs, propping her feet on my shoulders. My mouth latches onto her; my whole face is soaked with her arousal. I add a finger, and when I know she's close, I sit up. I want so badly to fuck her, but not yet; she needs to learn.

"Cash!" she cries.

"You gonna side with Ashlyn again?"

"What?" Her whole face is flushed, her lips swollen. Jesus, she is beautiful.

"You sided with Ashlyn. You gonna do that shit again?"

"If I say no, will you make me orgasm?" she snaps.

"Only if you say it and mean it, Lil."

"Fine, I will only side with you." And that's all I need to bury my face in her pussy. My arm wraps around her thigh and I slide two fingers inside her. She comes, and her orgasm is so powerful I'm surprised she doesn't buck me off her and the bed. Once she's settled, I flip her to her stomach, lift her ass, and slide home. I pound hard, her ass moving with every stroke.

"Lift your ass, Lil," I growl, my cock balls deep inside her. I love her ass; I love the way it moves when I fuck her from behind, and I definitely love this position. "Higher." I slap her ass hard, watching my handprint appear on her creamy skin. I still love when she wears my mark. I don't think she has gone one day without a hickey or some other mark from me somewhere on her body since we got back together.

"I can't, Cash. I'm going to come," she cries, shoving her face into the pillow.

"I know, baby. I feel you starting to squeeze the fuck out of my cock." I ram her harder, beginning to feel my balls pull up, and the tingling in my spine intensifies. Her hips start thrusting back against me harder. I wrap a hand around her waist, running it down her stomach and over her clit. She cries out again, her wetness and the silkiness of her walls closing tightly around me from her orgasm, making me come hard inside her. I slow my strokes, drawing out each of our climaxes before falling to the side and bringing her with me. She turns around, crawling on top of my chest. I run my fingers through her now-blonde hair, trying to get my breathing to calm.

"You know you can punish me anytime, right?" she jokes, making me smile.

"Yeah, I know." I give her a squeeze. "But I'm serious, Lil, against the kids, we are a unit. If you think I'm doing something wrong, we talk that shit out in private. I know that you and Ashlyn both think I'm not fair between her and Jax, and a lot of times I'm not, but I have my reasons. She is a girl, and she's vulnerable in ways that Jax isn't."

"Okay," she agrees, and I pull her hair so that she is forced to lift her head.

"Okay?" I ask.

"Yeah, since you put it like that, okay." She shrugs and lays her head back down. "Love you," she says, kissing my chest then snuggling closer.

"Love you too, baby," I whisper, closing my eyes and following her off to sleep.

Stay tuned for Until Nico coming June 2014

Until Nico

Sophie

I jump when the desk phone starts going off, it never rings so I'm caught off guard by the shrill sound inside the quiet library.

"Middle school Library, Ms. Grates speaking, how can I help you?" I answer on the second ring.

"I found a phone and this is the number that came on the screen when I turn it on." A deep male voice answers. His smooth southern draw making the hairs on my arms stand on end. I pull my handbag out from under my desk and dig through it looking for my phone. "Hello, did you hear me?" The guy on the phone says more impatiently. I forgot that he was even on the line during my search.

"Yes I'm here, sorry it's my phone." I tell him holding the phone between my shoulder and ear.

"Look, I gotta get out of town and I won't be back for a week so can you meet me somewhere?"

'Um I'm not sure that's a good idea." I tell him worrying my bottom lip.

"Do you want your phone or not?"

"Yes of course I want my phone." I say becoming annoyed. What kind of stupid question was that?

"Then you need to meet me so that I can give it to you."

"I don't get off work for another hour so can you meet me after that?" I crossed my fingers hoping he could. I didn't know what I would do without my phone for a week. Not that I wanted to call or text anyone but I was kicking ass in candy crush and wanted to beat my last score.

"Jesus, where the fuck do you wanna meet?" He grumbled and I smiled. I don't know why but it kind of made me happy that I was annoying this person on the phone.

"Can you meet me out front of Jacks bar-b-q in an hour and a half?"

'Sure, fine." I can tell by his tone that he is completely annoyed and I smile bigger.

"Thanks a lot."

"What are you wearing?" He asks

"What the hell does that mater?"

"Look," He huffs out. "I have your phone, which means you don't have a phone right?"

"Right." I repeat like an idiot.

"So that means that I can't call you and tell you when I get there, so I need to know what you're wearing so I can spot you on the street, right?" I can hear the smile in his voice now.

"Oh... I guess that makes since." I say and I can hear him laugh and the deepness of his laugh makes my belly flutter.

"So what are you wearing?"

"Oh." I look down at myself feeling stupid about what I'm going to say to him. "Um.. A grey skirt, a white silk blouse oh! And I have brown hair." I add the end part; I don't know how many women may be wearing the same kind of thing as I am.

"Alright sweetheart I'll see you in an hour and a half." He says and the phone goes dead. I hang it up and toss my bag back under the desk and start putting back all the books that have been checked out by students away.

I started working at the school library a year ago when I moved to Nashville from Seattle. I work here three days a week, the rest of the time I work from home as a medical insurance specialist. I like working here, it's quiet and the pay is good. I finish out my day making sure to update the computer system and locking up. When I leave the building most of the staff has left for the day. The parking lot is mostly empty except for my red Audi. I get in my car and turn it on, flip the button for the top, it takes a second for the top to go back and lock in place. The sound of Addicted to love by Florence and the machines starts playing as I head out to down town. When I reach the area that I'm supposed to meet this guy I find parking about a block away. This part of town is always crazy around this time of day; by the time that I reach Jakes I'm about ten minutes later than I planned of being. I look around wondering what this guy might look like. There are so many people walking around that I feel like an idiot that I didn't ask him what he was wearing. I stand next to the building with my arms crossed over my chest. I want to sit down so bad my feet are killing me.

I have a sick love for heels and the ones I wore today are paying me back for wearing them for more than a few hours. I see a guy looking at me he's about my age not much taller than my 5'5, he's cute and wearing a suit and tie. I start to wave to see if it's that the guy, then a guy about 6'3 and huge I don't just mean in height, his body looks like it's chiseled from stone. He's wearing washed-out blue jeans and a white t-shirt; every piece of skin exposed is covered with tattoos. He is beautiful in a way that is unusual but no less gorgeous. His ears have those gauges in them. His hair is cut low on the sides, the top in a fohawk. His jaw is strong with a few days of stubble. His eyes are blue that almost looks like contacts. His eyes come to me before looking away quickly then the next second they come back to me doing a head to toe sweep. I gulp at the look on his face. I look past him to the other guy or try to. When Mr. Tattoo starts towards me blocking my view. I want to take a step back but I can't go anywhere. Then I see my phone in his hand.

"This yours?" He asks. I nod like an idiot. He shakes his head running his free hand down his face. Then his eyes sweep me again. "You have got to be fucking kidding me." He says looking upset. I look down at myself wondering how I could have offended him. I look normal or my working out of the house normal. When I'm at home working I wear baggie sweats, some I cut off into shorts just hanging off me, with tank tops or t-shirts. But the few days a week that I get out of the house I like to dress up or at least wear heels. "This cannot be fucking happening." He says and I wonder if he is completely crazy.

"What?" I ask, finally finding my voice. I have to look way back even in my four inch heels he is still towering over me.

"You."

"Me what?" I ask confused.

"Never mind, who's this?" He presses the button on my phone, the screen lights up and a picture of Jamie Dornan wearing nothing but a pair of jeans takes up the screen.

"Um... That's Jamie." I say wondering why he is asking but too afraid to ask, the look on his face isn't very open for conversation.

"He your man?"

"I wish." I mumble and I hear him growl. My head flies back and I search his face, his jaw is ticking and his hand holding my phone has his knuckles turning white.

"What does that mean?" he ask

"That's Jamie Dornan he's playing fifty I don't know him." I feel my cheeks heat up and I look down at my feet what the hell's wrong with me? Why am I not afraid right now? I have been scared my whole life and now when I should be running for cover I'm not scared at all.

"I don't have time for this." He says and I don't know what he is talking about but I really want my phone. When I look up and see that he is walking away my eyes come together and I wonder what he is doing. Then I realize that he still has my phone.

"Hey you can't steal my phone." I cry grabbing onto his arm. He looks down at me then stops short I'm completely caught off guard when he wraps an arm around my waist pulling me flush against him. His free hand goes into my hair pulling my head back and kisses me, no, not kisses, he consumes me. My body starts to buzz like someone just plugged me into an electrical outlet. I start to feel light headed when he pulls his mouth from mine. I gasped, my fingers going to my mouth. "What was that?" I whispered looking into his eyes.

"What's your name?" He asks.

"Sophie." I tell him my words spoken against my fingers. His body is hard as a rock against mine I can feel every muscle, every contour.

"Sophie." He repeats, stands up to his full height pulling me with him. This is the first time in my life that I have ever felt small. I look around wondering if time stopped for anyone else. "My name is Nico."

"Of course it is." I say thinking that a guy that looks like him would have a name like that. Cool and hot something that rolls easy off your tongue but is hard to forget.

"I'll see you when I get back into town Sophie."
He says making sure I'm steady on my feet.

"What?" I ask looking around again.

"Here's your phone." He hands me my phone and
I'm still a little light headed. He starts to walk off
again I watch in a daze then he turns around to
face me from about twelve feet away. "Sophie."

"Yeah?"

"Change the picture on your phone." He says
before he turns and disappears into the crowd. I
stand there for a few minutes wondering what
just happened. Eventually I pull myself together
enough to make it to my car. When I get there I
realize that I hadn't even put the top up. I turn
quickly looking in my back seat. Thank god my
bag is still there.

I start my car and head home. I live in a
small two-bedroom house, I bought the place
cash when I moved, and it's not much but its
home. I pull into my garage and hop out. I drag
my bag with me. I need a beer or a shot of
something. I unlock my door and kick my shoes
off; they fly down the hall towards my room.
Dropping my bag by the door and the infamous
phone on the table I head to my kitchen open my
freezer, pull out the bottle of vodka I keep there
in case of emergency. I pull a coffee cup down
from the cupboard fill it half full and shoot it
back. Coughing up a lung and trying to catch my
breath, I fill the glass up again. I shakily take

another shot holding my breath as the burn fills my chest but this time I'm prepared for it. I put the stuff away feeling more relaxed already. I head to my room stripping off my clothes I put on a t-shirt. It's early so I head to the living room grabbing my phone along the way. I plop down on my couch, put my feet up on the coffee table and turn the TV on and start up the DVR and press play on the big bang theory. I sit there for a few minutes in a daze. I look at my phone in my hand, clicking on the screen and look at the picture of Jamie. I don't know why but I can't help but to smile. Nico was hot slightly scary but defiantly interesting.

Nico

I was happy to be home. I had been gone four days chasing a Skip. I thought it would take me a little longer to catch up with the guy but lucky for me he was half moron. I pull up in front of my town house shutting off my car and my phone rings. I look at the caller id, I know it's not going to be sweet Sophie but that doesn't mean I don't want it to be. Kenton's number flashes on the screen, I'm sure he has another case for me but right now that's not happening. I'm going to have a beer go to bed then tomorrow I'm going over to the local Middle school.

"Yeah." I answer, I pull my bag out of the backseat.

"Didn't take you long to catch Johnson.'

"That's because he is a moron." I tell him. "He hid out at his mom's house. You would think that he would have learned his lesson the last two times I went after him. Most of the time I was gone was spent on the road getting there then getting home. When are you going to get a private jet so I don't have to put miles on my car?"

"Stop bitching, you made fifteen hundred dollars in two days." He wasn't wrong. I had a nice little nest egg going between selling my part of the construction business back to my brothers and chasing after skips, I was sitting on a nice stack of cash.

"So why are you calling?"

"What! I can't call and see how my cousin is doing?"

"Do I sound stupid to you?"

"Alright, alright. The thing is that I need you to help me out with something.

"What?"

"Look a friend of mine from Vegas called. He has a girl that needs a place to crash for a little while."

"And what does that have to do with me?"

"Can she stay with you until Cassie gets the rest of her shit out of my house?"

"Hell no!" I say as I shove my keys into the door. The second the door is open daisy starts going wild. I scoop her up in one hand as she begins licking my chin or any piece of me she can get to. "You still have that dog?" He laughs.

"Yes." I growl. All the fuckers in my life think it's funny that I own a little fur ball for a dog. I rescued daisy from a flophouse. She was so small at the time that she could fit in the palm of my hand. I was going to give her to one of my family members but I couldn't do it. After a week of having her with me I grew attached to her.

"Look man I just need your help this one time."

"No, you should have put that bitches shit out months ago."

"Don't make it seem like I haven't wanted to. She swore that she was coming this weekend to get all of her stuff but until then I don't have room for this chick that's coming."

"Who is it that's coming?" I ask curiously.

"A friend of mine works in Vegas as a bouncer at a strip club. This girl saw some shit go down. He called and asked me to keep an eye out for her until the right people can be contacted."

"Wow your own personal stripper living with you."

367

"She could live with you first." He says.

"I'm seeing someone. So your gonna have to find something else to do with the chick or toss your ex's shit outside or burn it behind your house for all I care."

"You're seeing someone?" I can hear the disbelief in his voice. I'm not surprised, I don't date, I hook up and go home.

"I just got home I don't have time for this right now. Call your ex tell her that she needs to come get her stuff tomorrow or you're burning it. And honestly if she doesn't show up I say burn that shit."

"Look, you and I both know that she is not going to come get her shit she thinks if it's here that she has a reason to come back."

"So put it in your car and take it to her house and put it on her lawn."

"I would have done that but I need a truck and I haven't had time."

"She has been out for almost a year, how the hell haven't you had time?"

"Okay I've had time I just haven't wanted to deal with all the crying that comes along with seeing her."

"Aw you cry when you see her." I laugh.

"Tears of joy that she's out of my life fucker." I laugh along with him as I set Daisy on the ground and grab a beer out of the fridge popping the top and taking a swig.

"If she doesn't come by this weekend to get her stuff let me know and I will go with you to take it to her we can borrow Cash's truck."

"Sound's good. So who's this chick you're seeing? Is it the red head from the bar the other night?"

"No, and you don't know her." Shit I don't even know her. All I know about her is that she smells like apples and cinnamon. Has the softest brown hair that I have ever seen or felt. Her brown eyes darken to almost black when she's kissed and her skin is the color of milk and turns pink when she's nervous or embarrassed.

"Did you hear me?"

"What?"

"I asked if you were up for another job this week."

"I'm not sure right now."

"Alright let me know."

"Yeah, sure later."

"Later." I clicked off the phone while tossing it onto the counter. Daisy is sitting at my feet looking up at me. I open up her treat jar, her eyes following my every move. I hold it up and she dances around before I drop it to her.

I wonder from the kitchen into my room pulling off my shirt. Tossing it onto the floor followed by my jeans and boxers. Going into the bathroom I start up the shower letting the glass stall steam up before stepping inside. I let the hot water run over me, my head goes back thinking about Sophie and her big brown eyes looking up at me with nervousness and hunger, something that I have never seen on a woman's face before but something that will forever be etched into my brain. I knew the minute that I saw her that she was it. How I knew? I don't know but it was like my soul lit up, cheesy as fuck but also true. I don't really have time for her right now and she is not someone that looks like she would ever be interested in someone like me but that doesn't mean I'm not going to try. She has a look of innocents about her. I guess that could be a front but something tells me that it's not. I feel my self-getting hard thinking about those fucking heels that she had on, they should be illegal. She looked like any man's dirty librarian fantasy or maybe a naughty secretary. I palm my self-moving in long steady strokes. I wouldn't mind seeing her on her knees in front of me, her skirt up around her waist legs spread showing off her pussy, her top open, breasts hang over the top of her bra, her nipples hard and dark pink from being sucked, licked and bitten. I would stand in front of her feeding her my dick. My hands in her hair, dictating her pace, I feel my balls draw up my strokes moving faster. Her hand would cup my balls gently, her other hand moving with her mouth as I fucked her mouth. "Shit" I groan into the empty shower. Long jets of cum hitting the wall in front of me, I haven't jacked off to the thought of a woman since I was thirteen and Margret Jenkins showed me her tits in the boy's bathroom on a dare. I catch my breath before I wash up and head to bed. Tomorrow is going to be a busy day.

When I walk into the middle school I'm not surprised when the security guard ask who I am, and what I'm doing here. I tell him that I'm looking for a librarian by the name of Sophie. He doesn't know who she is so he sends me to the principal's office for someone there to help me out. I'm used to being judged for my appearance. I'm covered in tattoos, have a fohawk, and gadgets. I basically look like a person you should run from. When I get to the office I look around.

"Can I help you?" I look down at an older woman with lite purple hair.

"I'm looking for Sophie."

"Sophie that works in the library?" She questions with a smile.

"Yes, can you point me in her directions?"

"Oh! She's not here today."

"Why are you looking for Sophie?" A male voice asks and I turn my head over my shoulder.

"She's a friend." I tell him turning back around.

"Sophie doesn't have friends." He says in a way that makes it sound like he has tried to be her friend but she wasn't interested. I turn to face him looking him over. He's dressed like he works here most likely a teacher. His khaki pants and button down shirt give him away.

"She has me." I tell him. His eyes look me over before speaking again.

"I find that hard to believe."

"Is that so?" a raise a brow.

"Honey she will be here tomorrow." The lady says and I look at her and smile. She smiles back.

"Thanks." I tell her tapping on the top of her desk before walking past the guy, out the door down the hall and out to my car. I have to wait another day but that's okay.

       The next day when I get to the school I go directly to the office.

"You came back." The same lady as the day before greets me." I'm Sue by the way. Then leans forward like she is going to tell me a secret. "Mr. Rasmussen was not happy yesterday." She wags her finger then smiles like the cat that got the canary before sitting back in her chair and claps once. "So I guess you need directions to the Library.

"That would be helpful." I smile.

"You sure are pretty." She laughs. "If I was a few years younger I would have been a jaguar for you."

"A Jaguar?" I chuckle

"You know an older lady with a younger man?"

"A cougar."

"Sure whatever you say honey all I know is that I would have given Ms. Grates a run for her money."

"Sue if you want me you got me." I tell her leaning in."

"Oh no honey I wouldn't even know what to do with you." She smiles, her eyes sparkling. I shrug and she laughs. "Alright Mr. Go to the library. Take a right out the door walk until you get to the end of the hall and take a left it's the last door on the left.

"Thanks doll." I say smiling as I walk out of the office. I have to say that's the first time I have ever been hit on by a woman my grandmother's age. When I get to the library doors I look through the small window I spot Sophie right away. She is on her tippy toes putting away books. Today she is wearing navy blue slacks that have a wide leg and a high waist that ends under her breast that are covered in a bright red short sleeve button down top that matches her heels. Jesus her in heels looking like she does was going to be the death of me. I open the door and I'm bombarded by the smell of books. She turns her head to look at me and her eyes go wide her mouth opens and closes a couple of times.

"What are you doing here?" She finally asks before looking around like she is waiting for someone to jump out at her.

"I told you that I would see you when I got back to town. I'm back in town." I state the obvious.

"Um... Okay but what are you doing here?" She repeats pointing to the ground.

"I don't have your number. I wanted to take you out to dinner."

"Dinner?"

"Yes, a meal that you eat at the end of the day."

"I know what dinner is. I just don't do that." She mumbles.

"You don't eat dinner?" I ask confused.

"No I don't do dinner with other people."

"You don't do dinner with other people?"

"Like date, I don't date." She says crossing her arms over her chest accentuating it. My eyes are drawn there and she immediately lowers her arms.

"It's not a date its dinner."

"I know, you said that."

"So what would you like to eat at our not date dinner?" I ask taking a step closer to her. The smell of apples and cinnamon getting stronger the closer I get.

"Nothing we're not having dinner together."

"What time do you get off work?"

"Six. I mean I don't know." She chews her lower lip, her cheeks turning a pretty shade of pink.

"Alright so no dinner then." I shrug. "Can I get your number?" She shakes her head no, her cheeks getting even darker. Fuck me she's cute.

"Sorry." She whispers looking away. For some reason alarm bells start going off in my head.

"It's all good." I beat back the urge to hold her. My mind warring with my body, I watch her for a second then come up with a plan.

"I have to get back to work." She tells me looking at the floor.

"Alright sweet Sophie I'll see you around."

"Bye Nico." She says softly I turn giving her a chin lift, my chest feeling tight at my name leaving her mouth. I leave the school knowing that this wasn't over not by a long shot.

Acknowledgements

First, I want to thank God.

Second, I need to thank my fans. You are all amazing! I couldn't ask for any better; I love you all. Your messages, comments, and love of the Mayson boys has been mind-blowing! Thank you so much.

Next, I need to thank my husband for being my biggest fan and supporter. Your love and encouragement and daily inspiration means the world to me, and without you, I would not have followed my heart and started writing.

To my all of my friends and family I love you all and couldn't be more grateful to you.

To my mom, I love you thank you for being such a great mom and fan.

To Mommy and Daddy, I'm grateful to god every day for giving you to me as inspiration on what love really is.

I need to give a special thanks to all my adoptive family your support means so much. I also need to thank Hot Tree Editing. You have been amazing to work with.

A GIANT, over-the-top, crazy-huge Thank You to Kayla Robichaux also known as the amazing Kayla the Bibliophile. You are crazy-awesome. (Sometimes just plain crazy but I wouldn't have it any other way.) Thank you for not only being an amazing editor but an awesome friend.

To each and every blog, reader, and reviewer this wouldn't be anything without you. Thank you for taking a chance on an unknown author. I wish I could name all of you but this would go on forever just know that I love you guys.

To Love between the Sheets, Thank you for working so hard. Last, but not least, to my Beta Readers Jessica, Carrie, Marta, Laura, Jenny, Rochelle and Midian, Natasha, Lesley. I love you ladies. I know I have the best betas in the world. Thank you, girls, for telling me what I need to hear, not what I want to. And thank YOU for loving the men who live in my head as much as I do.

And a special thanks to the ladies of S- IRACG you know who you are. You have all become amazing friends I'm so happy to share this journey with you all.

XOXOXOXOXO,

Aurora Rose Reynolds

Something else you might like

PUSH THE ENVELOPE

ROCHELLE PAIGE

PROLOGUE

Flowers…check.

Chocolates…check.

Champagne chilled and ready to go…check.

Noise-canceling headphones so I didn't have to listen to whatever noises were going to float up from the rear cabin…check.

This was so totally not the normal pilot's checklist. When I talked to Dad over the summer about offering Mile High Club charter flights so we had some extra money coming in to cover my room and board at college, I had no idea how the idea would take off. I'd figured I would take a couple flights out each month so Dad wouldn't have to scrimp on anything so that I could live on campus. He really wanted me to get the whole college experience, especially since I had chosen to stay in town for school.

Who knew there were so many middle-aged housewives looking to spice up their marriages? I usually had three to four flights booked each week now. At a cool grand per booking, we made enough to cover my room and board and maintenance on the planes, and we even had money left over to pay off my student loans and to cover my tuition for my next two years. I guess they're right when the say sex sells!

Since the flights were offered in the evening, they didn't interfere with my classes. Dad wanted as little to do with this venture as possible. He had told me that this was my idea, and he expected me to run with it. Talking about anything connected to sex with his daughter wasn't really high on his list of things to do. I figured I was lucky that he was willing to let me use the Cherokee for the flights. I just had to make sure I booked them when I was able to be in the pilot's seat. The last thing i wanted to do was screw my grade point average over because I was skipping too many classes to pilot the flights I was only offering so I could pay for school in the first place.

Today's flight was due to depart in about thirty minutes, so the lucky couple should be here any minute now. I needed to get my butt in gear so I would be ready when they arrived. The plane was set up for their romantic rendezvous. I was dressed in my charter pilot gear of loose khaki pants and a Hewett Charters polo shirt. I'd pulled my long brown hair back in a low ponytail. This appearance seemed to help the wives feel more comfortable with the idea that their pilot was a twenty year-old girl. Add into the equation that I am passably attractive and I could have a problem on my hands with my paying customers. So I did what I could to make sure I presented myself as a capable pilot and nothing else.

I know it's crazy for some people to picture me piloting a plane, but I started flying with my dad before I ever got behind the wheel of a car. He lived to fly and taught me to love it as well. I had my permit when I was sixteen, earned my private license when I was seventeen, and got my professional license when I turned eighteen. Some days it felt like I spent more time during my life up in the air than I did on the ground.

Yet another reason Dad wanted me to live on campus this year—so I could hang out with girls and act my age. Dad and I had been two peas in a pod forever, and now he worried that I needed to have a normal life with girlfriends, parties, and boys. I admit that my upbringing wasn't exactly orthodox, but I was happy with the way things were. I just wished Dad would understand that.

Damn, it sounded to me like my housewife of the day had gone all out for this trip based on the click of her stilettos hitting the tarmac. I didn't understand how women could walk on shoes that looked like skyscrapers to me. Guess that was just the tomboy in me, much to my best friend's dismay. Time to get my head in the game so I didn't scare off the paying customers.

"Welcome to Hewett Charters," I greeted the middle-aged couple as they made their way towards me. "You must be Mr. and Mrs. Williams?"

"Yes, that's us," tittered the platinum-blond woman as her husband looked at me quizzically. I guessed that she hadn't used their real name in the hope that they could keep their trip private. She needn't have had that concern since I offered complete confidentiality.

"Thank you for booking your flight with us today," I said. "Everything is all set, and we can be in flight as soon as you are ready to go. Did you have any questions before we board?"

"Ummmm, are you our pilot?" asked Mr. Williams.

"Yes, I'm Alexa Hewett. Don't worry. You're safe with me. I've been doing private sightseeing tours for a couple years and have had my pilot's license for almost three years. I might be a little young, but I grew up with my dad in the cockpit of a plane. I can assure you that I am fully qualified to take you up," I answered.

"And how does this work exactly?" he questioned.

I couldn't help but smile at the question. It seemed that the wives always booked these flights, and the husbands always seemed uncertain once they got here. I even had flights where the husband had no idea that his wife had booked the tour with the sole purpose of getting it on mid-flight. The expressions on their faces when they saw the bed in the cabin were priceless. It kind of cracked me up since I always figured guys were less shy about sex. Which may still prove to be true since I hadn't seen a single guy yet turn down the opportunity offered by my special charter flights.

"If you will follow me this way, you can see how we've set the Cherokee up so that you will have plenty of room in the rear cabin. Once we are in flight, I will draw the privacy curtain and wear noise-canceling headphones during the flight. I will be able to communicate with the tower but won't be able to hear anything from the cabin. Any of your activities while on board will be as private as possible." They both nodded and looked at each other while blushing.

I walked the couple towards the plane, showed them the bed area we had fashioned by removing four of the seats, and asked them to sit in the rear-facing seats during takeoff for their safety. If the hot looks they were flashing each other as they buckled up were any indication, they were ready to go.

"Enjoy the refreshments, and I will let you know when it is safe to move about the cabin," I said as I got settled into the cockpit.

As I prepared for takeoff, I couldn't help but chuckle to myself about the irony of me helping couples to spice up their sex lives. I wasn't exactly qualified to do so except for piloting the plane. I couldn't really be described as very experienced in the bedroom. Yet, I have turned my beloved Cherokee into the equivalent of a by-the-hour hotel room.

Axel by Harper Sloan

Prologue

God... please let him be late. Traffic? Boss needed help? Hell, at this point I would even pray for his shoe being untied.

ANYTHING to give me just five extra minutes.

Taking a frustrated breath, I remember... I gave up pleading to the heavens years ago. Ten years to be exact. The day he walked out of my life. The day the sun stopped shining and my world turned gray. The day that my dreams turned into nightmares. I miss my dreams, the sun, and I miss him. So fucking much, even though I know I shouldn't. After all, what good does it do to miss a ghost?

Come on... come on.... I silently beg the light to change. Why is it that the only time I'm running late, every single light catches me? "Fuck! Just fucking change!" I just know if I am not home in the next ten minutes all hell will break loose. Finally, as soon as the light turns green I slam on the gas. All I need to do is hurry and everything will be fine.

Right?

I roll into the driveway at 5:45, throw the car in park and rush into the house. Thankfully I had enough foresight when I left earlier to start the slow cooker. "Okay, Okay..." I mutter to myself, while rushing around the kitchen island to the table. If I didn't hurry... nope, I can't go there. There would cause me to lock up in fear, and cutting it this close, I can't lock up.

"Deep breath, Iz... just breathe." I remind myself, setting the bowls of chili down. As quickly as I can manage I set the table, make sure the glasses are spot free and the silverware is perfectly aligned. I was not going to make those mistakes again. Rushing back to the kitchen, I make sure I've washed and dried all the cookware, and signs of my slow cooker use. I have just enough time to make sure that my 'face', as he so lovingly calls it, doesn't look like I just rushed my duties.

At 6:05, on the dot, I hear the garage door rolling up. Breathe. A few moments later, he walks in. Of course, he would never be running late. God forbid he would make it home a minute past his normal scheduled time. The world might end, sky might fall, and pigs might start flying.

No, not my husband; he is never off his game.

"Good evening, Isabelle. How was your day?" He asks, while unloading his arms of his coat, briefcase, and keys. He makes sure his coat is hung perfectly; wrinkles wouldn't dare mess with him. Even they know not to poke the bear. After he disposes of his cell, wallet, and other pocket shit, he finally looks up at me with his cold, dead eyes.

Permission to speak has silently been granted.

"Good evening, Brandon. Things were normal as always today. Did some laundry, ran the errands you asked me to do, and got home around three. I know you said your parents are thinking of coming this weekend, so I wanted to make sure I had enough time to get the spare room situated before I started dinner."

Lies, all lies … just enough to hopefully make him think I wasn't out.

"Hmmm," he states, while rolling his sleeves up. "So," he looks up with his evil smirk and those dead eyes. "That wasn't you I just saw speeding down Oak Street like the bats of hell were on your bumper, Isabelle?"

Fuck. Me.

"Brandon, I swear it's not what you think." I squeak out. Shit, this is going to be bad. "Dee stopped by, she's in town and just wanted to say hi, catch up a little. I haven't seen her in six months- -"

His smile stops me cold, immediately I start backing away. Oh shit, I know that look.

"Now, now... Isabelle. What have I told you about Denise? Hmm? If I remember correctly, it was something along the lines of you are not to talk, call or take calls from her, and you are definitely not to FUCKING SEE HER!"

He's starting to step closer now. Frantically I look around for an escape, but he's blocking my only exit. "You have been told, and I would have thought you learned this lesson six months ago. Isn't that how long you said it's been? What do I need to do for you to get it through your dumb fucking head? Jesus Christ, you're a stupid fucking bitch." His eyes are so cold as he steps right into my space. "What part of you being mine, and only mine, did you not understand the last time I was forced to explain this to you. I will not share you with fucking anyone. Do you hear me, Isabelle?" He sneers my name like its very presence on his tongue disgusts him. I've hit panic mode now, he has me backed into the wall, no escape in sight. "No fucking person in this goddamn world is allowed you. Only. Fucking. Me!" He continues, his eyes bugging out and his spit hitting me in the face. "You're nothing but a stupid fucking slut! Isn't that right, Isabelle? I should have walked the other way that night at Fire. I should have known a bar slut from a mile away. But, no! It's all your fault my dick wouldn't walk the other way." He rears back and slaps me hard across my cheek. I squeeze my hands into fists, digging my nails into my palms to keep from screaming out. I can feel the blood running down my neck from the cut his ring must have caused on my jaw. I might be stuck, but I'll be damned if I will let him break me.

"What did I fucking say, Isabelle? NO DENISE! No afternoons chatting like little fucking bitches. You're to be here, cleaning my fucking house, cooking my fucking dinner, and spreading your fat fucking thighs for my dick!" He reaches out and grabs a bowl of chili, throwing it with all his strength against the wall. I watch chunks of meat, beans and sauce run down my happy yellow walls. "And what in the fuck is this shit? I told you, you fucking bitch, I wanted lasagna. Does that look like lasagna?" I should have seen it coming, but my attention was still focused on my happy yellow walls and the globs of dinner still rolling down. I was just turning back to him when his fist hit my temple, momentarily making my vision blur. At least that seems to have knocked some sense into my sluggish brain. I dart to the right, quickly trying to escape the second fist I know will soon be following. Too late, always too late, I catch the second one in the ribs, knocking the breath right out of my lungs. Brandon grabs my thick hair and with a twist of his wrist, I'm right back at his mercy.

Mercy I know he doesn't have.

Throwing me into the hallway, with what feels like the strength of ten men, he's quick to follow with a kick to my stomach. "You stupid bitch. You just can't listen. I own you, all of you. No one else. No one else touches what is MINE. Especially not fucking DENISE! I warned you what would happen. No, I promised your dumb ass what would happen if you went near her again." Kick... slap... punch... kick. "You're never going to learn are you?" He's panting with exertion and it's taking everything I have not to let the blackness overcome me. Even if I know numbness would be following quickly.

I lost track of how long he stood over me, screaming and beating, alternating between his feet and his fist.

Freedom, that's all I crave now.

I close my eyes and pass out.

~~*

When I wake up, the house is dark. Every bone, muscle, and hair on my head hurt. I can't take a deep breath without wanting to die. I can feel wetness on various parts of my head and body. Fuck. It's never been this bad. I can't hear anything out of my left ear, what the hell happened to my ear? Fuck, I need to move.

Clutching my arm around my middle, I slowly climb to my feet. I take a look around, out of my very swollen eyes, and see that dinner is still sitting on the table. The broken bowl, chili dried to the wall, and even the spotless cups are sitting there mocking me. With a slow and silent step I glance into the living room. No sign of Brandon. Shuffling, more like dragging myself to the kitchen, I see his keys are gone. Holy shit! He's not here. Never, not once in six years has he left me alone in the house after a 'lesson'.

I walk along the wall, holding on for support until I reach my purse, unzipping the side zipper; I reach in and take out my phone. The phone Brandon doesn't know I have. I'm not allowed to have a phone, and he disconnects the house phone and takes it with him when he leaves. I can barely see enough to turn the phone on. I slide my finger across the screen and unlock it. Finally, after a few wrong buttons, I place the call.

"Hello? Hello, Iz? Iz, are you there? Is everything okay? IZ??" I can hear her, she's practically screaming. But I can't get the words out. She knows I wouldn't be calling this late. Hell, she knows I wouldn't call at all.

I take a shallow breath, and rasp out the only word I need to bring my salvation.

"Help..."

Then the blackness pulls me under.

Chapter 1

(Izzy)

I haven't always been this weak person... this broken woman. I used to dream, and when I did, I dreamt big. I had plans, plans of a future so bright it would blind you. I can still remember the day those dreams, those grand plans, and that future as bright as the sun went poof.

I just didn't know it at the time.

At the time I thought everything would be okay. After all, what seventeen-year-old girl doesn't think she's invincible?

That, coincidently, was the same day I decided fate hated me. No, she didn't hate me... she loathed me. People say karma is a bitch, but I have news for you, karma doesn't have anything on fate when she is after blood. Not a single thing.

I wish I knew what it was that set fate on the path of my doom. Maybe it was just being born? I like to think I was at least okay there. My parents loved me, they prayed for me, and I was everything to them. So, no, I don't think that was the day.

Or it could have been the day I stole Maggie Jones' pudding cup. But Maggie was a bully, never nice and always stuffing her face, so I like to think I did her a favor.

I once stole a chocolate bar from the grocery store, but seriously? Fate would have been after every little teenage shit if that was the case. Point fingers all you want, but where I come from it's like a rite of passage.

No, I think fate decided she hated me the day I walked into Dale High School freshman year and my path collided with Axel's. It would make sense that the reason she hated me was the reason for all my pain.

The reason I'm convinced fate will never shine in my favor again. Why would she? She took it all away. Wiped out every single thing I had ever loved in one swift kick.

One day I might figure it out, the reason fate hated me, Isabelle West. But, until that day I damn sure will be careful with my dreams and my plans; my heart and my soul.

Fate might hate me, but that doesn't stop me from hoping one day she forgets about her favorite chew toy. When that day comes, I hope karma has some fun with that bitch, fate.

Made in the USA
San Bernardino, CA
10 June 2014